A Certain Dilemma

*This book is the third instalment to:
Deceitful.
Beyond Any Doubt.*

Nicholas Ralph Morgan

iUniverse, Inc.
Bloomington

A Certain Dilemma

Copyright © 2011 by Nicholas Ralph Morgan

All rights reserved. No part of this book may be used or reproduced by any means, graphic, electronic, or mechanical, including photocopying, recording, taping or by any information storage retrieval system without the written permission of the publisher except in the case of brief quotations embodied in critical articles and reviews.

This is a work of fiction. All of the characters, names, incidents, organizations, and dialogue in this novel are either the products of the author's imagination or are used fictitiously.

iUniverse books may be ordered through booksellers or by contacting:

iUniverse
1663 Liberty Drive
Bloomington, IN 47403
www.iuniverse.com
1-800-Authors (1-800-288-4677)

Because of the dynamic nature of the Internet, any Web addresses or links contained in this book may have changed since publication and may no longer be valid. The views expressed in this work are solely those of the author and do not necessarily reflect the views of the publisher, and the publisher hereby disclaims any responsibility for them.

Any people depicted in stock imagery provided by Thinkstock are models, and such images are being used for illustrative purposes only.

Certain stock imagery © Thinkstock.

ISBN: 978-1-4502-7726-6 (sc)
ISBN: 978-1-4502-7727-3 (ebook)
ISBN: 978-1-4502-7728-0 (dj)

Printed in the United States of America

iUniverse rev. date: 1/10/2011

Contents

Chapter 1	The Return	1
Chapter 2	The Beach Party	23
Chapter 3	Conspiracy	42
Chapter 4	Incriminations	60
Chapter 5	The Ransom	80
Chapter 6	The Witness	100
Chapter 7	Apprehension	116
Chapter 8	Deliverance	136
Chapter 9	Suspicions	154
Chapter 10	Egypt	170
Chapter 11	Sorrow	188
Chapter 12	Disaster	211
Chapter 13	Merry Christmas Gavin	227
Chapter 14	A Raging Furnace	249

The Mango Tree Nursery Rhyme

I acknowledge my good friend Emma Wilkinson who computerised this manuscript and provided the base accompaniment.

List of Characters

Gavin Harrison
Gregori Harrison
Tobias Torluba
Karl Stevens
Sebastian
Ursula Chambers
Kirsti Løvik
Fr Vincent
Sister Jamima
Truls Haugvik

Veronique Torluba
Loretta Torluba
Rebecca Chambers
Detective Martinez
Dominic
Godwin Chambers
Chester Hargreaves
Marcel
Rosie Hezmuller
Per Jørstad

The Prologue

Deceitful

Gavin Harrison emigrated from England twenty years ago with his parents and brother Greg. The family invested in a sugarcane plantation on the Caribbean island of Martinique. This enterprise became very profitable. Since their parents' death Gavin and Greg inherited a small fortune and became millionaires. With this wealth Gavin bought Snøby, a ski resort in Norway. Greg focused his riches in Calypso Tavern, a casino and cabaret complex. Gavin lives in a five-bedroom Mediterranean house. Loretta and Tobias Torluba live adjacent in the cabana. They are indigenous to the Caribbean and Loretta enjoys fussing over Gavin and Greg. Their daughter Veronique is a nurse and has yearned for Gavin's affection for many years. However, her romantic dreams are unfulfilled as Gavin loves Susannah. Susannah Crawford is a singer from England, and employs her English snobbery to perfection. Veronique is extremely jealous, and Susannah enjoys taunting her.

    Susannah has a secret. She wants revenge on Gavin as she blames him for her husband's death in a cable car crash at his ski resort. Susannah only pretends to be Gavin's girlfriend. She was the star attraction at Calypso Tavern until her faked death. But Gavin's grief was not enough. She knew then she had to kill him. The family suspect Gavin has been killed in a plane crash. However, his true absence is due to Susannah. She has plotted to kidnap him and slowly torture him to death. No one is aware of Susannah's sinister quest for revenge. She does not act alone. Jarvis, Chad and Nils also lost loved ones in the cable car crash so they help her kidnap Gavin. Jensen was also a victim. He and Gavin manage to escape the mountainous prison killing Jarvis, Chad and Nils in the process. Gavin and Jensen are lost in the frozen wilderness. Sadly Jensen dies. When Gavin is finally rescued he relates this bizarre encounter. No one believes him. Everyone assumes he is the sole survivor of the plane crash and is suffering from post traumatic stress disorder.

Karl Stevens is Gavin's best mate and is a senior ski instructor at the ski resort. They have known each other since primary school in England. Karl has an affair with Kirsti Løvik who is a Norwegian businesswoman. She owns a perfumery business and easily dominates this male world. However, Karl suspects her to be dealing in drugs under the guise of her business. Therefore he breaks off their relationship.

Angelo was head barman at Calypso Tavern but is caught up in Susannah's revenge. He has a wonderful night with Jarvis but this blissful passion turns to anger and Angelo is murdered. Rebecca Chambers works as a dancer at Calypso Tavern. She is a native Texan whose family were exiled from Martinique during the slavery period. Returning to the Caribbean rights history's wrong doing. Rebecca is also Greg's girlfriend. Their wedding was just a week away. However, Rebecca's happiness is destroyed when Susannah reappears to exact her revenge and shoots Greg. Susannah is about to turn the gun on Gavin when Loretta attacks her with a harpoon.

<>

Beyond Any Doubt

Susannah survives the harpoon attack. She uses her acting ability to escape imprisonment and pretends to be mentally ill. To a degree she is successful and is sent to a sanatorium. Gavin and co are furious and seek to kill Susannah. They are afraid she will escape justice. Rebecca goes undercover as Cassandra and visits Susannah in the sanatorium, pertaining to be her closest friend. Rebecca arranges a weekend leave. This is a ploy to kill Susannah. Susannah realises that she will be arrested the moment she is discharged so sees the weekend leave as her chance to escape the sanatorium and imprisonment. But Susannah is no match for Rebecca, Veronique and Gavin. They force tablets down Susannah's throat and leave her for dead. However, Detective Martinez comes to Susannah's rescue. Susannah pleads that the overdose was a suicide attempt. This emotional confession suits her fictitious deranged act. Susannah is returned to the sanatorium.

Romance begins to blossom for Gavin and Veronique. They get engaged and plan their wedding. But life is never trouble free. Susannah escapes the sanatorium and is eager to seek revenge. She decides to kill Rebecca but murders Jeswana by mistake. Susannah relents and agrees to leave Martinique. She manages to con $500,000 out of Gavin and starts a new life in Paris with a new identity as Chantelle Duveton. This new lifestyle gives her confidence. She takes the lead role as Eva Peron in the musical Evita. Yet Susannah cannot resist returning to Martinique to scupper Gavin and Veronique's wedding. During the reception she holds the family at gunpoint, but her murderous intent is thwarted by Detective Martinez.

Susannah is arrested. During the trial it transpires that Kirsti Løvik is Susannah's sister-in-law. The jury find Susannah guilty and she is sent to prison for thirty years. Susannah hates prison. Della is the Top Dog and also a lesbian. Susannah is desperate to escape, but Della refuses to help her unless they have sex. Susannah does not agree. She is confident she will find her own way to escape. One despicable night Della rapes Susannah.

Eight months later Susannah manages to escape from prison. Gavin and Veronique flee to Norway for safety. Susannah is in pursuit and traps Veronique and Gavin on the cable car at the ski resort. She almost kills them but Karl intervenes. They fight. Karl overpowers her by using a fire extinguisher and a ski stick. He stabs her to death. The local coroner, Tor Hegland appears on the scene and removes Susannah's body. Air rescue arrive to save Gavin and Veronique from the doomed cable car which is about to drop into the mountainous valley.

Now that Susannah is dead life can return to normal for the Harrison household. However, two years later Tor Hegland is brutally murdered. So who killed him?

Chapter One

The Return

Our marriage is a ménage a trois and I deplore it.

The sixth anniversary of Greg's death brought with it the usual solemnity for Gavin. He spent part of the day in deep reflection at his brother's graveside. The heat of the July sun bore down on him as he sat on the ground. A vibrant hibiscus shrub grew decoratively behind the tombstone. Its tropical foliage embraced the masonry plaque. The shrub had been planted to commemorate Greg's life. Ironically, Greg had hated gardening. His low boredom threshold had prevented him from cultivating nature's pleasant bounty. He may have admired his tropical surroundings, but that was as far as his interest had reached.

It had become a regular custom for Gavin to spend time talking to his departed brother. Even after six years he had not learnt how to separate Greg from his daily life. His younger sibling was buried in the grounds of Gavin's Hispanic dwelling. The white walls and rustic roof embellished the west side of the estate along with the cabana. The tropical garden and acres of sugarcane plantation fields stretched east and northwards.

Greg's tombstone faced the family home. This of course made it easy for Gavin to visit. He would openly speak at Greg's grave about recent events. They had grown up together and had shared their lives as one. Although Veronique was Gavin's devoted wife and completely supportive in any consequential matter, Gavin still felt the need to involve Greg. Death could not detach this kindred spirit.

That evening Gavin went to Calypso Tavern, his late brother's entrepreneurial establishment. The three-in-one complex of a casino lounge, cocktail bar and cabaret diner was a popular attraction. Greg would be well pleased with how Rebecca had harnessed his business and had continued his passion for nightlife entertainment. Rebecca was eager to take the helm. She had stood over Greg's grave during his funeral on the day they should have wed. By a hidden strength she had used Greg's business as a comforting sanctuary. It was now the only way she could be close to him. Fate had denied their marriage, but she had at least married his business.

Calypso Tavern was well attended with a mixture of tourists and local inhabitants. Gavin entered and approached the cocktail bar. The chrome edged décor sparkled under the coloured lights. A tranquil rendition of Gershwin's Summertime enhanced the relaxed atmosphere. People sat at the bar or lounged on the softer seats that neatly scattered the floor. Adjacent to the cocktail bar came the casino lounge. The gambling antics enticed many to participate. Hordes of folk gathered around the roulette table. A huge ornate crystal chandelier glistened above them.

To the left of the cocktail bar customers sat in the cabaret diner, enjoying their meal. The resident seven-piece orchestra played romantically. The customers now waited for tonight's entertainment to commence.

Gavin stood at the bar and ordered his usual whisky and soda. Marcus, the head barman, served him.

"I know what day it is," commented Marcus as he prepared Gavin's drink. "Have this one on me, for Greg, Angelo and Jeswana." Marcus had been a staff member for many years. He had a fondness for his employer Greg. Working for a millionaire had its bonuses. Though emanating from different backgrounds he and Greg had a similar personality, a happy go lucky approach to life, and the sort to play practical jokes on folk. Of course Marcus had also known Angelo and Jeswana, as they were his work colleagues. And being of Mexican origin Marcus and Angelo had shared a close friendship. Unlike Angelo, Marcus was not gay. He had a wife named Sinita and a three-year-old daughter named Belano. Marcus, along with all the other staff carried a tinge of sadness for their departed colleagues.

"Thank you," replied Gavin, accepting Marcus' generosity. Marcus always reminded Gavin of Angelo. It was inevitable, being the same race and having similar features. However, his friendship with Marcus had not grown as deep as the connection Gavin had experienced with Angelo. Today Gavin's heart wallowed with sadness and guilt for Greg and the departed Mexican, all because Susannah wanted revenge for her husband's accidental death. What pain and suffering she had caused. Surely after the amount of grief Susannah had inflicted with the murders of Greg, Angelo and Jeswana, had she not reaped more than enough revenge than she first intended. Her initial plan was to kidnap and torment Gavin. Well her actions since have far surpassed that intention. The love Gavin had for Susannah had turned to hate, once her true colours had flourished. But she had now encased his heart in guilt for bringing her into the lives of those he loved. The only comforting thought for Gavin was the fact that Susannah was dead. She no longer was able to reap any further havoc or murder. But this did not lessen Gavin's guilt. Perhaps that is why he and Veronique had become an item and had married, for she knew this guilt existed in Gavin's heart and was able to pour love into his life. Veronique had managed to break through the emotional barrier that would otherwise have prevented Gavin being intimate with anyone else.

"It will soon be your wedding anniversary won't it?" said Marcus, trying to steer the conversation in a positive direction.

"Yes," replied Gavin. "And no thanks to Susannah who almost killed us. Had Detective Martinez not arrived when he did she would have succeeded."

"At least she got what she deserved," added Marcus.

"Give the bitch credit she was a good raconteur. The lies she told during her trial were an attempt to fool the jury, to appear meek and mild, the unequivocal victim. She had a nerve and total disrespect for human life and the judicial system. Thankfully, the jury saw through her charade. I am glad she is dead. A thirty-year prison sentence was not punishment enough. I would be forever wondering if she would escape again," stated Gavin.

"Yes, it was a miracle you survived the cable car attack."

"If it had not been for Karl's intervention and killing Susannah, the outcome would have been different. That was now three years ago. At least we can all live in peace."

How Gavin's life had been transformed from being an inconspicuous teenager in England, to a wealthy forty-one-year-old tycoon in the Caribbean. It was never his ambition to lead an entrepreneurial existence, but with his parents' untimely death he had been forced to hold the reins and make his father's sugarcane plantation business a success. Harrison S.C.P limited had secured Gavin's future. Further more he had wisely invested his inheritance in a ski resort in Norway, which he named Snøby. Never in a million years would Gavin have believed he would own two companies on opposite sides of the planet. Yet his fortune did not end there, for after his brother's murder he inherited Calypso Tavern, thus increasing his independent wealth.

Gavin's lifestyle and location may have changed for the better, but his feelings were still the same. Fortune had not robbed him of his sensitivity, and regardless of all the riches he now experienced he would forsake it all to have Greg back. No amount of money could replace his brother, nor compensate the guilt Gavin endured daily. A guilt that had encapsulated his heart and would shadow the rest of his life.

Between serving customers, Gavin and Marcus exchanged conversation. Gavin sat on a barstool and drank his whisky and soda, somewhat oblivious to those around him. When he finished his drink he ordered another. Perhaps one would accuse Gavin of being engrossed in self-pity. He was consumed with grief and memories of Greg as he drowned his sorrows. How else could he be? He had to remember his brother, set aside a certain amount of time to reflect on their lives together. This day was Greg's anniversary; a day which Gavin felt compelled to dedicate to his departed brother. Gavin's day-to-day life became suspended as he detached himself from the world. It was an act that he felt unable to dismiss. Let anyone or everyone criticise him, he was impervious to such comments. Despite the sadness, it made him feel closer to Greg, at least for twenty-four hours. There was no power on earth that would deny him this sentimental solitude.

After consuming a third whisky and soda, Gavin decided to circulate the complex. He left the busy cocktail bar and wandered into the cabaret diner. It was a hive of activity with people enjoying their meal and the chatter was at a moderate level. The night's entertainment was due to start. Pale blue curtains draped the side of the stage. A gold glittering backcloth enriched the visual effect. The venue was packed. The audience sat around the dozen circular tables, each table able to seat ten. The smaller tables for those romantic couples edged the side of the diner. The interior fabric of the chairs and tablecloths was pale blue to match the stage curtain. Those that were not fortunate to have a seat stood at the back, waiting for the show to commence. Gavin's attention was drawn to the seven-piece orchestra that jubilantly began to play. Gavin equated the similarity to previous occasions when he had frequented Calypso Tavern. This was during the time he had dated Susannah all those ill-fated years ago. He recognised the music the orchestra now played. It was L'accordéoniste, one of Edith Piaf's songs. The band ceased the introduction as Dillon, (the evening compare), graced the stage. Whilst Dillon quelled the noise of the audience, Gavin shunned the negative thoughts on hearing the brief Edith Piaf rendition. Edith Piaf's music, as great and classical as it was, would always stir unwanted memories. The last time he had listened to her music was on his return from Norway over six years ago. That was before he knew Susannah for the evil, vindictive woman she was. He had played her infamous song, Padam, Padam, enjoying fond memories of Susannah, when all the time she was looking down on him from his integral balcony, intent on shooting him. Susannah had even used Edith Piaf's name to sign the wedding card she had sent them. This clearly portrayed Susannah's twisted and clandestine nature. One could not blame Gavin for never wanting to listen to Edith Piaf's music again.

Dillon addressed the audience that had crowded into the cabaret diner. All the seats had been taken, leaving the surplus guests to stand wherever they could. Amongst them was Gavin. Dillon displayed his confident and comic demeanour as he introduced the following act.

"She's magnificent, vocal perfection beyond reproach, and very pleasing to the eye. Please welcome tonight's entertainer, the lovely, the adorable, the amazing Kelly Kristal." Dillon left the stage as the audience applauded with anticipation. All except Gavin applauded. The orchestral reprise of L'accordéoniste perturbed him. Of all the days he had to be reminded of Susannah, why today? This was Greg's day, a time when Gavin only wanted to remember his brother. He certainly did not want memories of Susannah plaguing his thoughts. That woman had already consumed too much of his life.

The resounding orchestral introduction abated, but not before Kelly Kristal had delivered her entrance. Her white skin glistened from the glitter gel that covered her arms and legs. The silky black slinky number she wore accentuated her slender figure. She stood centre stage with her back to the audience; a stance Susannah had used many times. Kelly Kristal's similarity to the woman who had blighted Gavin's life was uncanny. Even down to her auburn hairstyle that cradled a shimmering tiara.

"She looks exactly like Susannah," muttered Gavin. He stood as if in a trance and stared at Kelly Kristal, anxious for her to turn and face the audience. All he needed was to see her face to allay his fears, but then he knew it could not be Susannah, after all, she is dead, though what an extraordinary resemblance.

The female artiste transfixed Gavin. He eagerly watched as the orchestra struck up the preceding chord to L'accordéoniste. Flaunting her femininity, Kelly Kristal slowly manoeuvred her body. She dragged her hands up the side of her torso before stretching them outwards to each side. She raised her left shoulder and turned her head. Her side profile was now revealed to the audience. Kelly Kristal looked over her shoulder. For several seconds she retained this coy stance. Although Gavin could only see the side of her face he stared in horror. Was it Susannah? Was it not the same profile and cheekbones of that nefarious woman? Kelly Kristal began to sing. Gavin's inner fright did not subside. His heartbeat increased. There was no mistake in her voice. It was definitely Susannah.

His mind must be playing tricks. To prove otherwise Gavin pushed his way through the crowd of onlookers. He needed to get a closer look at her, if only to quell his agitated mind. Logic was telling him it could not be Susannah, but his fears were stronger and overshadowed any reasonable judgement. He moved closer to the stage and stood as if in awe, watching intently. But standing in front of a table where others were seated and blocking their view caused a certain amount of irritation.

"Move out of the way," came a voice.

"Do you have to stand there," said another.

Gavin took no notice, unable to look away from the woman before him. Not unlike the first time he had seen Susannah at Calypso Tavern, performing Padam, Padam, all those years ago. He could not look away then, nor could he now. Susannah had caught his attention by displaying her charm and charisma, the same qualities that Kelly Kristal now delivered. *Yet Kelly Kritsal could not be Susannah for Susannah is dead.* That was the constant message running through Gavin's mind. Kelly Kristal just has a striking resemblance to her. There is no need to be alarmed, thought Gavin.

Kelly Kristal employed an emphatic gesture and turned on the spot to face the audience head on. The reality was incredulous. Gavin's heart thumped louder. His body perspired. Either Kelly Kristal was Susannah's twin sister, or Susannah was not dead.

Those near to Gavin must have heard his gasp as he stared directly at the woman calling herself Kelly Kristal. Gavin knew he was looking at Susannah. Out of fear he continued to stare, hoping to be mistaken. For several moments Gavin tried to convince himself otherwise.

"It can't be Susannah," he muttered. "I've had too much to drink."

Gavin struggled to accept the reality and was compelled to watch. Gavin's initial desire was to confront her, probably kill her. He slowly edged his way forward towards the stage, still trying to accept whom he saw. Gavin maintained a certain amount of obscurity amidst the crowd. He was temporarily hidden from sight as Susannah, alias Kelly Kristal, viewed the audience. Finally, Gavin accepted that Susannah was not only alive, but had the audacity to return and perform at Calypso Tavern. Gavin knew he had to kill her. The means and method seemed irrelevant. The desire to kill Susannah overwhelmed him. Despite everyone watching, Gavin was prepared to kill her now.

The orchestra continued playing L'accordéoniste. Gavin slowly edged his way towards the stage. Susannah performed the song exquisitely as on many previous occasions. Her contralto voice produced such a rich sound. Keeping with her traditional style of performance she descended the stage, using a portable step-block already in place. She had always enjoyed mingling with the public. Neither Susannah nor Gavin had made eye contact, but they intuitively drew closer to each other. Gavin was now only a few feet away from the woman he hated so much. She turned and looked at him. She was not in the least bit perturbed. Susannah's beaming face stared back at Gavin as she manoeuvred towards him. They were now inches apart. Gavin was enticed by her insolent and intrepid attitude. He was ready to strike Susannah and take her to her grave. What else could he do? Surely he is blameless for wanting her dead? Gavin raised his hands ready to strangle her. Suddenly Susannah gave him an evil look. Her pleasant façade had vanished. One could see the hatred in her eyes. She stopped singing, leaving the orchestra to play on without her. Abruptly Susannah raised her right arm. It was at that moment Gavin caught sight of the dagger clenched in her fist. Without a moment's hesitation she plunged the offending weapon into Gavin's chest, not once but several times. Gavin seemed defenceless to stop her. The pain was excruciating. He screamed out in agony as he sat upright in bed.

"Gavin, Gavin, it's ok, calm down, it's just another nightmare," consoled Veronique, putting her arms around him. "Was it the same dream of Susannah killing you," she added. Gavin panted, the sweat falling from his brow.

"It seemed so real," he gasped.

"They always do," mentioned Veronique. The cries of baby Gregori filled their bedroom. Veronique got out of bed and walked over to his cot. She picked Gregori up. "There, there, has Daddy made too much noise and woken you up," she said, comforting their two-year-old son. She held him against her shoulder and gently patted him on the back. Gavin sighed heavily.

"I'm sorry for waking you both," he stated.

"It's getting to be an annual occurrence," remarked Veronique. "I understand but I don't think Gregori enjoys hearing the screams of his father."

"It will be six years tomorrow since she killed Greg," mentioned Gavin. He paused before continuing, "Maybe you're right, I aught to take sleeping tablets around his anniversary. It might help to quell the nightmares and put my mind at rest, and from waking you up."

"I am used to it. At least I am not working tomorrow morning, being part-time, so a sleepless night is not such a problem," replied Veronique as she mildly bounced Gregori in her arms. "It's the distress it causes you and our little one here that worries me." Speaking to their restless child she added, "We don't want to be miserable for the new nanny, now do we. We want the nanny to like you. Yes we do," she stated in a baby-mother's voice.

"Are you nervous about the interviews tomorrow?"

"A little but I shall stick to what we discussed already. I'm glad I've got the day off work to concentrate on what to say," replied Veronique. "I'd have thought we would have had a better response though."

"We only need one nanny, let's hope one of the three applicants so far meet our expectations."

"Well in a few hours time we shall find out," stated Veronique.

"Are you sure you don't want me with you?" questioned Gavin, his anxiety level reducing from the nightmare.

"Me and Mama will be fine. Call it feminine intuition but we will know which applicant is the right nanny for us, won't we my little sunshine," replied Veronique, aiming the latter comment at Gregori. His distressed cries had abated to a mere grisly chuckle.

A hot refreshing drink was in order. Gavin applied his fatherly role and took charge of Gregori whilst Veronique went downstairs to the kitchen to boil the kettle. Gavin held the dependant infant in his arms. He spoke reassuringly, making various comments about his deceased uncle and how Gregori's baby features had a certain resemblance of Greg. Although only two years between Gavin and Greg, he still had memories of his departed brother as a baby. Gavin picked up Marmajuke, (Gregori's toy monkey), and gave it to his son who immediately clenched it.

"Shall we go down and see Mummy in the kitchen," said Gavin to his son.

"Yes," agreed Gregori. Gavin descended the stairs carrying Gregori in his arms.

"He is wide awake," mentioned Gavin as he entered the kitchen.

"You need to have counselling," replied Veronique sternly. "This has gone on for far too long. You need to deal with your guilt." Gavin noticed she seemed irritable.

"I will take sleeping medication, that will do it."

"If only taking a tablet would solve the problem," returned Veronique curtly.

"What is that supposed to mean?" retorted Gavin. Veronique glanced at him. She was happy to see Gregori in his arms so refrained from arguing. Yet she had to air her thoughts.

"You endangered us all by bringing Susannah into our lives. And you think taking a tablet is going to make amends," voiced Veronique. Her irritability showed as she made the coffee.

"I am sorry," uttered Gavin. He hated seeing Veronique annoyed with him. Gregori clutched Marmajuke, oblivious to the strained atmosphere.

"So you keep saying," replied Veronique. "I tell myself one day this will end, this constant reminder of Susannah. But it won't end will it. She will always be a part of us. How many more times do I forgive you? How many more times will I be reminded of Susannah? Our marriage is a ménage a trois and I deplore it. At times I even feel second to Susannah." Veronique placed the mugs down abruptly on the kitchen work surface.

"No one has regrets more than me," remarked Gavin. "Don't give me a hard time."

"Well maybe I have grown tired of being the supportive wife," stated Veronique. The kettle boiled and she poured the water into the mugs.

"That is a hurtful thing to say."

"Do you ever stop to consider me in all of this? Four years we have been married and I still feel as though Susannah lives here," argued Veronique. She saw Gregori looking at her. She turned away and continued. "How can we ever be happy, truly happy with this hanging over us all the time?"

"You should have said something sooner, not bottle things up. How long have you felt like this?"

"There are times when I just want to scream. I feel so angry with you, our situation. I know I'm a romantic fool, see life through rose-tinted glasses, but this is not how married life should be." Veronique paused for breath. She had refrained from arguing before, and had willingly overlooked all the turmoil she had previously felt. It did not matter; she loved

Gavin and was glad to be with him. But she was feeling to perplexed to remain silent.

"Do you regret getting married?" questioned Gavin.

"No, of course not," replied Veronique. "I want to be married to you, but not Susannah." She looked at Gavin holding their son. She saw the hurt in Gavin's face and suddenly became remorseful. "I am sorry Gavin, I should not have said anything. I guess being tired has made me irritable. I love you and I will always support you. I just feel at times you don't support me." Gavin moved over to her. He saw her watery eyes as she looked at him. Her ebony face was very pretty and yearned for reassurance.

"After everything you have tolerated I do support you. Perhaps I don't show it as much as I should." Gavin put his arm around Veronique. She inclined her head to rest on his shoulder. He kissed her on the forehead.

"At times I cannot see a way forward. I hate us being strangled by the past," commented Veronique. "It is so frustrating."

"We cannot change the past, but we can stop the past from changing our future. From now on, at this time of year we will have a holiday, a complete change of scenery. I have drowned myself in self-pity for too long. I thought it was the right thing to do, but it is far from the best way. Instead, we will celebrate life. How does that sound?" comforted Gavin.

"I see no objection," stated Veronique. She broke from the embrace. Gregori looked across at her. Veronique picked up the two mugs of coffee. They returned to the bedroom to drink the hot beverage. Gavin placed Gregori in his cot. The little child lay still, sucking his thumb and tightly holding Marmajuke. Gregori had his own bed in the nursery but as of yet he did not settle in sleeping alone. He much preferred the presence of his parents, like most infant children. Gavin and Veronique sat up in bed as they drank their coffee.

"Why are we drinking coffee?" asked Gavin. "It will keep us awake."

"I meant to do us a milky Horlicks," confessed Veronique. They looked at each other and laughed.

<>

11am saw the arrival of the first applicant for the post of nanny. Loretta applied her homely charm as she showed the lady in. The hopeful nanny was in her mid forties and indigenous to Martinique. Loretta proudly introduced her daughter. Veronique sat elegantly posed on the armchair in a typical lady of the manor stance. She viewed the applicant as she entered the room. Her name was Mrs Hezmuller. Although casually dressed, her taste in clothes seemed fresh and modern. Mrs Hezmuller smiled, displaying a warm and welcoming expression. From her résumé Veronique knew she had worked previously as a nanny. Mrs Hezmuller had stated she prefers to take charge of infants rather than destructive children who had already lapsed into bad ways, largely as a result of bad parenting. Veronique broke from her initial pose to greet the first applicant.

"Please take a seat," remarked Veronique, gesticulating to the sofa.

"Thank you," she replied.

A nest of tables was positioned within arms reach. Loretta poured out three cups of coffee. The ceramic coffee pot, cups, plates and nibbles were pre-arranged.

"From your application letter I can see you live on the Southside of Martinique, Mrs Hezmuller," stated Veronique, holding her résumé in her hand.

"That is correct but please call me Rosie, let's not be so formal. I'm married but unfortunately I am unable to have any children of my own. That's why I'm a nanny for it fulfils my maternal instincts. And I keep in touch with all my children as they grow older." Rosie delved into her shoulder bag and retrieved a handful of snapshots. "Here are some photos of them. This is Kyle as a baby, and this is him now as a teenager." Veronique took interest in the snapshots and felt very relaxed in Rosie's presence.

"You seem to be well-experienced," commented Loretta as she viewed the various photographs that Rosie handed out. "How many children have you looked after?"

"Six in total, from three different families," replied Rosie.

"And all from a baby?" enquired Veronique.

"Yes, I think it is important for a baby to grow up with the same nanny. You hear of so many instances of child rebellion, and it doesn't help if they have been pushed from one nanny to another. Parents don't seem to realise how disruptive that is for a child. It inbreeds instability which manifests in later life in all sorts of problems," proclaimed Rosie, who spoke with authority. "That is why I insist in keeping in touch with all my babies, if you pardon the expression."

"One can clearly see how dedicated you are to the job," stated Veronique.

"It is a bond that develops which remains intact throughout one's life," explained Rosie. "Take Kyle for example, why only the other day he rang me to help him with his homework. He's at high school now of course. It is comforting to know that I am there for him, someone he can turn to, even if chemical fusion is not my strongest subject. He hopes to become a doctor," she added proudly.

"I'm a nurse at Fort General," said Veronique. "I know all about chemical fusion."

"Oh well in that case I'll tell him to give you a call," joked Rosie, causing a mild wave of humour. "I take it that's the little fellow in question," assumed Rosie, looking across the room and seeing Gregori playing happily in his playpen.

"Yes," confirmed Veronique. "His name is Gregori. We named him after his uncle Greg."

"Isn't he a beauty," returned Rosie. "May I go over and say hello?"

"Of course," replied Veronique. Rosie got up and walked over to Gregori. Veronique and Loretta followed her. The playpen was relatively large and contained several of Gregori's toys. He held a teddy bear in his hands. This prompted Rosie to ask:

"Does your teddy bear have a name?"

"Yes," replied Gregori, looking up at her.

"This is Rosie, Gregori. She's come to see you," said Veronique. Gregori gazed happily as he stared at her.

"What is your teddy bear's name?" asked Rosie.

"Teddy," said an excited Gregori.

"Oh isn't he adorable," commented Rosie, turning to face Veronique and Loretta.

"He is a well behaved child," mentioned Loretta. "Everyone who sees him gloats in admiration."

"I can well believe it," agreed Rosie. "Has he had a nanny before?"

"No, he has not. Between Mama and myself we look after him but it gets increasingly difficult with my shifts at the hospital. I can't always guarantee being here," said Veronique.

"I understand," replied Rosie. "What hours would you like me to work?"

"Between 11am and 2pm. I should be home by 2pm," responded Veronique.

"I work afternoons at the craft shop in town so I can only mind him in mornings," said Loretta.

"Are you working at the moment?" Veronique asked Rosie.

"No, I have been a lady of leisure for the past six months. A few hours work a day seems perfect," remarked Rosie.

A Certain Dilemma

Veronique enjoyed interviewing Rosie. Her presence extinguished any prior apprehension. Conversation flowed effortlessly, and Veronique could imagine Rosie being Gregori's nanny. Almost an hour later the arrival of the next applicant brought Rosie's interview to an abrupt end. However, both the following two applicants failed to make a better impression than Rosie. To some extent this would make Veronique and Loretta's choice easier, but neither were able to draw any conclusion. Rosie had remained the likeliest candidate due to her experience, relaxed personality, and the rapport she had engaged. However, Veronique became indecisive, a trait she does not normally have. She could not bring herself to choose Rosie for the nanny. Perhaps she was not ready to surrender her child to the arms of a stranger. Veronique had a powerful maternal instinct, which made her now realise she would not be enamoured with hiring a nanny. She felt jealous that a stranger would be sharing her baby, watching him grow up and taking those moments that should be a mother's.

Veronique lifted Gregori out of the playpen. He had fallen asleep and did not appreciate being woken up. Consequently he began to cry.

"What are we to do with you?" remarked Veronique in a comforting manner. "Crying like that you'll frighten any nanny away." Veronique returned to the sofa carrying Gregori in her arms. "It is no wonder he fell asleep, he was awake last night. Gavin had another nightmare," said Veronique.

"Did he. I noticed you both seemed a little frail this morning," remarked Loretta.

"We also argued. I couldn't help myself, but things are ok now. We have decided to take a holiday at Greg's anniversary to hopefully lift our spirits."

"That seems sensible," replied Loretta.

"Still, what do I do about a nanny?"

"I don't think we need to make a decision right now," suggested Loretta. "Besides, with the two of us working part-time we shall have to ensure we stagger our shifts so one of us is always here."

"My shifts often run over though, that's the problem," replied Veronique. "After going to such trouble in advertising and interviewing the applicants, how can I refuse to hire one? Have I wasted my time as well as theirs? The truth is I now feel reluctant to have a nanny. I just don't like the thought of a stranger watching him grow up."

"You give him to me," said Loretta, reaching for him. Then turning her attention to Gregori she continued, "You wanna come to your grandma, yes you do, yes you do," added Loretta, putting on a baby style voice. She held out her arms. Gregori's crocodile tears had ceased. He now chuckled at his humorous grandma as Veronique passed him to her.

"I'll go and make some more coffee," said Veronique. "Gavin should be home soon," she added before disappearing into the kitchen.

Loretta took delight in her grandson, just like a grandparent should. She sat him on her lap. His chubby face looked up at her. Loretta gently bounced Gregori on her knee, causing him to emit spasmodic bursts of laughter. Several times she recited a well-known nursery rhyme.

Sit beneath a mango tree.
Gazing at the sunny sea.
See an egret soaring high.
Soon my boy you'll touch the sky.
Soon my boy you'll touch the sky.

Flying high just like a bird.
Flap your wings just coo and chirp.
See below that mango tree.
Sitting there is you and me.
Sitting there is you and me.

On repeating the last line Loretta lifted Gregori up into the air, as if like a bird he had taken to flight. Naturally, in the nursery rhyme one would replace the word boy with girl to suit the child's gender.

"I remember you singing that to me Mama," said Veronique, returning with a fresh pot of coffee.

"So do I Honey, so do I. My Ma used to sing the nursery rhyme to me," recalled Loretta. At that moment the telephone rang. Veronique put down the coffee pot before answering it.

"Hi, Veronique speaking."

"Veronique it's Karl."

"Hello Karl, nice to hear from you. How are things in Norway?"

"Norway is fine, the long summer days make us all feel relaxed. Snøby is quite busy with tourists enjoying the midnight sun and twenty-four hours of constant daylight," replied Karl.

"I would love to see that too. It defies logic to see the sun at midnight. We must pay a visit again soon," responded Veronique.

"Yes you must. Listen, I have been in two minds whether to call you or not, but now I realise I should," began Karl.

"This sounds serious, is everything ok with the ski resort?" questioned Veronique.

"Yes, yes, Snøby is fine, that is not the reason I'm calling. For months I thought the name was familiar but I couldn't fathom out why. Now I fail to understand why the penny didn't drop sooner."

"You've completely lost me now."

"Does the name Tor Hegland mean anything to you?" questioned Karl.

"Tor Hegland did you say?" repeated Veronique. "No I can't say I know that name."

"He is the medic that dealt with Susannah's body after I had killed her," informed Karl.

"Is he, well I never actually met him. If you remember I was unconscious at the time, thanks to Susannah drugging me."

"Nor will you meet him," returned Karl. "He has been murdered. His body was mutilated beyond recognition. The police have had to use DNA to identify him."

"Oh my God, how gruesome," stated Veronique. "So how does this concern us?"

"Don't you think it is too much of a coincidence, him dealing with Susannah's body? What I'm trying to say is could she…"

"I think I know what you're trying to say," interrupted Veronique. Her troubled mind caused her to pre-empt Karl's statement. "You think Susannah killed him."

"I keep telling myself she's dead, yet I keep getting this niggling doubt. I don't want to alarm you but I thought I should let you know."

"Words evade me, being put on the spot like this," said a worried Veronique. "It's three years since you killed her. You were there; you know she's dead. It can't be any other way," remarked Veronique, somewhat agitated at Karl's aspersion. "You can't ring us like this, getting us all worked up," she added angrily.

"I'm sorry, I know it sounds insensitive but…"

"But nothing Karl. Susannah is dead and that is final." No way could Veronique consider the prospect of Susannah being alive. The consequences were too horrific to live with. The years of tyranny from Susannah had to be over.

"Maybe I'm overreacting but I felt it was my duty to inform you," replied Karl. "I'm sorry to upset you."

"No Karl it's me," replied Veronique apologetically. "That woman makes me react aggressively. You were right to warn us. Don't the police have any idea as to who else could have killed him?"

"No, not as yet," responded Karl.

"I'm lost for words," sighed Veronique heavily. "Please no more. That bitch has got to be dead. You won't mention any of this to Gavin, will you, I don't want him getting upset, not when he's been doing so well."

"Of course not Veronique. I'll let you know if I find out anything. By the way how is Gavin? I know it's Greg's anniversary," said Karl.

"He had another nightmare last night. The same one of Susannah singing at Calypso Tavern and stabbing him to death," remarked Veronique, hating having to say her name.

"Why don't you have a holiday at this time of year? Help to take Gavin's mind off things. You can always come to Norway," suggested Karl.

"Are you psychic? We said the same thing last night. Whether it actually happens remains to be seen. I know Gavin likes to be left alone on Greg's anniversary."

"Well I'll leave you to it. And I will let you know if the police find out who did kill Tor Hegland. Take care," said Karl.

"Yes do keep us informed. I'll speak to you soon," replied Veronique and replaced the receiver. She turned to face Loretta. The perplexed expression on her face was noticeable. It prompted her mother to comment:

"You look concerned Honey, and I couldn't help but hear that woman's name being mentioned."

"Oh Mama, I sure hope I'm overreacting," exclaimed Veronique. "That was Karl on the phone. The medic who dealt with Susannah's body has been murdered, and Karl thinks Susannah may be responsible, which means she is not dead."

"Nonsense! Of course she's dead," retorted Loretta, perhaps out of a desire for Susannah to be deceased rather than any rational judgement. "It's understandable that you feel suspicious, but a doctor wouldn't be tangled up against the law like that and in cahoots with Susannah, not when it comes to murder."

"We have been so happy these last three years," reflected Veronique. "This could so easily ruin everything."

"Now don't go upsetting yourself. You feel tired, your mind can play tricks when you feel like that."

"If being tired was the only problem. I somehow feel things will never get better. One day you feel all is well, the next everything is up in the air, full of uncertainty. That woman cannot be alive," stressed Veronique.

"Now let's not start fretting. Why don't I have a word with Detective Martinez? See what he can find out," suggested Loretta.

"That's a good idea Mama. He could liase with the Norwegian police. The sooner they find out who did kill the medic, the sooner our minds will be at rest."

"In the meantime there is no need to worry Gavin about this," affirmed Loretta. "In fact Honey, I'm gonna ring Detective Martinez right now," stated Loretta decisively.

"Thank you Mama."

CHAPTER TWO

The Beach Party

Everyone was hysterical. "I now have a matching pair," she said.

The Caribbean Sea began to sparkle as the summer sun rose above the horizon. An appearance of flickering lights shimmered across the water as it reflected the sun's rays. The gentle waves caressed the shore as if coaxing the sandy beach to wake up. Nature's beauty witnessed another dawn. Palm trees fanned their open branches as they swayed in the gentle breeze, almost as if they were giving a modest greeting to the morning sun. Birds flew in the clear blue sky as if partaking in an early morning exercise. A gull dived into the sea, catching a fish for breakfast. The Mount Pelee volcano slowly withdrew its shadow over the island as the sun rose higher.

Sebastian and Dominic's open plan beach condo became doused in the morning sunlight. Sebastian yawned and rolled over in bed, putting his arm over Dominic's naked body. He greeted him with a kiss.

"Happy anniversary my love," he said. Dominic opened his eyes and turned to face Sebastian. He smiled at his Caribbean partner.

"Happy anniversary to you too, our third official anniversary," replied a contented Dominic.

Although they had been an item for nearly nine years, they only made their monogamous relationship official three years ago. Their marriage ceremony had been a very happy occasion. July 24th had been their wedding day. Sebastian and Dominic's family and friends had witnessed this joyous event. Amongst the guests had been Gavin and Veronique. Thank goodness for all concerned that Susannah was history. No longer could she blight the Harrison household. Her death certainly made Sebastian feel more at ease. He was beginning to get paranoid that he would end up in the crossfire. Sebastian may be physically stronger than Dominic, but he did fret over the slightest problem. Dominic, being more level headed was a stable cornerstone in their relationship. Now in their thirties the romantic gay couple enjoyed life.

The rising temperature echoed the rising passion that Sebastian and Dominic now felt. They lay naked on their bed and began to make love. The sun's morning rays penetrated a nearby window and came to rest on their naked bodies. The darkened skin of Sebastian's buttocks glistened in the sunlight. His muscular arms embraced Dominic as they fervently kissed. Being their anniversary neither of them were working today. The only plans they had were to prepare for tonight's party to be held at their beach condo. Dominic, being a chef would be creating a Caribbean style buffet. He enjoyed entertaining with his culinary talents. Never the sort to boast but he did revel in praise as one complimented him on the tasty delights. Sebastian's duty for the day was to organise the sporting activities. This included beach volleyball and the sand chase party game. Judging from previous parties most of the guests will end up in the Caribbean Sea, some unexpectedly.

After their anniversary romp Sebastian and Dominic lay naked in each other's arms. They exchanged pillow talk.

A Certain Dilemma

It was a very lazy start to the day. They remained in bed until hunger pangs forced them to get up and eat. The late brunch consisted of toast and cereals, washed down with several glasses of mango juice. Given the heat of the day they remained naked, it satisfied their naturist inclinations. They were not overlooked, no adjoining neighbours so why not be totally free. Wearing clothes would only cause discomfort. It also meant they could save money and energy by having the air conditioning on a lower setting.

In between preparations for the party they managed a swim in the sea. The water was warm and inviting as always. Dominic pumped up their double lilo. They lay together, holding hands as they drifted on the sea. Both wore sunglasses, enabling them to gaze up at the cloudless sky. Sebastian had just finished rubbing suntan lotion over Dominic's white body. His pale skin easily burned in the sun, unlike Sebastian whose native skin tone darkened naturally.

"It will be Gavin and Veronique's wedding anniversary in three weeks," commented Dominic.

"Don't remind me, the wedding that almost wasn't," replied Sebastian. "It is Rebecca I feel sorry for, she should have married Greg."

"If truth be known that is why she declined our invitation," said Dominic.

"Wedding anniversaries are bound to be awkward and upsetting for her," added Sebastian. "Anyway, she is probably looking after Gregori."

"Come to think of it, we never get asked to baby-sit. We too are Gregori's godparents."

"Are you complaining? When do we have time? We have each other. Rebecca has no one. I think looking after Gregori helps her," surmised Sebastian. Dominic turned to face his beloved.

"You are so soft and gentle. I love you," commented Dominic.

"It is just as well you love me, because it's me and you till we are old and grey," replied Sebastian. Dominic splashed some seawater over Sebastian.

"Oh you want to fight," remarked Sebastian. He sat up and pushed Dominic off the lilo.

"Help me, help me, I'm drowning," joked Dominic. "I need a strong man to come and rescue me."

"How like a 1930's Hollywood film, a damsel in distress," responded Sebastian. He rolled over and reached out for Dominic. "Take my hand and pull me ashore."

"In a bit, let's just relax some more." They remained floating on the water with Dominic holding the side of the lilo. Surreptitiously he pulled out the stopper. The lilo began to deflate. "Imagine being on the Titanic, floating in the water and about to drown," reflected Dominic.

"At least this water is not icy cold," stated Sebastian.

"In that case you won't mind getting wet," added Dominic. He pulled the lilo over. Sebastian rolled into the sea. Dominic laughed.

"I thought you were never gonna do it," said Sebastian. They kissed and swam ashore, pulling the lilo behind them.

<>

The morning ritual of the Harrison household transpired uneventful. Gavin got up at 7am, showered, had breakfast and arrived at his office by 9am. Veronique had taken the morning off work so she too had a lazy start, except for attending to Gregori. By no means was he a difficult child, but as with any two-year-old they need constant attention. Gregori sat in his high chair. Veronique fed him his wheat and coconut cereal. He chuckled in between mouthfuls, largely due to Veronique's humorous anecdotes that accompanied every spoonful. For Veronique, Gregori provided a useful distraction. One must not underestimate how devoted Veronique was to her son, but the notion that Susannah may be alive gnawed at her subconscious. That woman had wreaked such havoc on the person she loved the most. Not to mention the times she almost killed the two of them. The possibility that yet again Susannah had faked her death caused a considerable amount of concern. After receiving Karl's telephone call over three weeks ago, informing them of Tor Hegland's murder, Veronique could not rest. Not that she divulged her perplexities to Gavin. She made a conscious effort to remain calm and at ease in his presence, masking her dilemma. Behind the scenes though, Veronique and Loretta had been in contact with Detective Martinez. They had asked him to investigate if Susannah was alive. Loretta had also confided in Tobias. He too appreciated their concern, and agreed to keep the matter away from Gavin.

A second informal meeting with Detective Martinez was due to take place this morning. He had taken their concerns very seriously. Had it been any other person with such an elaborate tale he would have pacified them, implying the laws of probability were against their fears coming to fruition. However, given the complexity of this case so far, and knowing how devious Susannah had been in the past, he could not dismiss this line of enquiry. Therefore Detective Martinez had agreed to contact the Norwegian police to find out the exact details pertaining to Tor Hegland's murder and the subsequent investigation. Not only that, but he wanted to question what happened to Susannah's body.

The meeting was scheduled for 10am. Veronique finished feeding Gregori his breakfast when Loretta arrived at the house.

"Morning Veronique," she said, entering the abode. "And how's my little baby boy," she stated, fixing her attention on Gregori. His chubby face looked at her, his eyes widened, and with a cheeky smile he chuckled at her.

"G'mama, G'mama," he uttered, unable to pronounce the correct term of grandmother.

"That's right it's your G'mama," replied Loretta, lifting him up out of his high chair.

"I'll just clear away the breakfast things," stated Veronique, picking up the used utensils.

"Has my baby boy eaten all his breakfast," remarked Loretta, focusing her attention on Gregori.

"Yes he has, he's been as good as gold," replied Veronique. After a pause she continued, "I do hope we're overreacting. Susannah has to be dead."

"I hope so too Honey. Let's hope Detective Martinez has some useful information for us," commented Loretta. Veronique disappeared into the kitchen, allowing Loretta to sing *The Mango Tree* nursery rhyme to Gregori.

Sit beneath the mango tree.
Gazing at the sunny sea.
See an egret soaring high.
Soon my boy you'll touch the sky.
Soon my boy you'll touch the sky.

Flying high just like a bird.
Flap your wings just coo and chirp.
See below that mango tree.
Sitting there is you and me.
Sitting there is you and me.

Veronique and Loretta arrived at the police station a few minutes before 10am. Veronique carried the overactive Gregori in her arms. His face quivered with excitement as they entered the building. Gregori was completely enthralled by the surrounding hubbub; officers talking aloud; telephones ringing; the noise of a printer printing out a document, not to mention the numerous computer workstations. Gregori stretched out his arm, indicating that he wanted to play on one of the computer terminals. He wrestled in Veronique's arms, anxious to be put down so he was free to explore. He called to his mother in his baby language, but Veronique did not respond. They stood at the reception counter, informing the officer on duty that they had an appointment with Detective Martinez. The officer on duty asked them to sit down whilst he alerted his superior. As they waited, nerves began to set in and Gregori became more agitated. He wanted to run around and explore. Veronique kept him sitting on her lap, dreading the news Martinez would deliver. The respected detective appeared and escorted them to his private office. His short grey curly hair edged his brown rugged and handsome face. He had never married, although the admirers were there but the job always got in the way. Now in his early fifties he looked forward to taking early retirement.

The ongoing daily noise of the main office diminished to a murmur when Detective Martinez closed his office door. His private office was in disarray. It contained a mismatch of furniture. Three untidy bookcases with boxes of files on various shelves lined the far wall. There was quite a large aspidistra in the corner which had seen better days and in urgent need of watering.

"Please sit down," mentioned Detective Martinez, indicating to the two chairs that were positioned opposite his desk. "You must excuse the untidiness. It may look unprofessional but believe you me I know exactly where everything is. Since Wilson's promotion I am left to deal with everything."

"Oh we understand," replied Loretta, being polite. Detective Martinez sat in his chair. Veronique and Loretta sat opposite with Gregori standing between them. Veronique held him firmly to her side.

"Thank you for coming to see me. I do have further information for you," began Detective Martinez. "Yesterday

I received the official report into how Susannah escaped from prison, enabling her to travel to Norway where she tried to kill you and Gavin and also Karl."

"We are intrigued to know how the escape happened, but our main concern is whether she is still alive," stated Veronique.

"Unfortunately, I can't say that for certain," responded Detective Martinez. "However, I have liased with the Norwegian police and I have informed them of our suspicions regarding Susannah. I can clearly state that they were not impressed with my insinuation. Although they are still seeking Tor Hegland's killer, to try and incriminate a dead woman did not carry much clout. I can reveal that his body was mutilated beyond recognition. It was only through DNA tests that provided the link to his identity. His family had reported him missing several months earlier. Due to the severity of the crime, the police have obtained a psychological profile of the perpetrator, and they are convinced it is a man. They have submitted a report to me, which is what I have here," he stated, picking up the document from his desk. "You can both read it if you like, but the gist of it focuses on what a respectable person Tor Hegland was; from a good background; never in trouble with the law; no previous criminality, and that he was not the sort of person to be a cohort with an escaped convict wanted for murder."

"I don't like it one bit," retorted Loretta. "Such apathy."

"Well maybe we are jumping to conclusions," replied Detective Martinez. "Apparently Susannah's body was cremated. The Norwegian authorities were unable to make any contact with any relatives in England, so they saw to matters themselves. I have a copy of the death certificate and the cremation authorisation here." Detective Martinez passed the Norwegian documents with an English translation attached over to Veronique and Loretta. They glanced at them.

"But these are countersigned by Tor Hegland. Isn't that a bit suspicious? Especially as he could be involved, in cahoots with Susannah," remarked Veronique.

"When I challenged that with the Norwegian police they became very defensive. They maintained Tor Hegland would not have gone to such lengths of deception. The idea I was implying was too improbable. He has a most upstanding reputation," relayed Detective Martinez.

"When it comes to Susannah nothing is improbable," said Loretta. She was clearly not impressed with this news and ensured Detective Martinez knew how she felt.

"Let's look at this rationally," said Detective Martinez, trying to allay their fears. "If Tor Hegland and Susannah were working together then why would she kill him? Susannah would need all the allies she could get."

"I am not at all convinced by this information," stated a concerned Veronique. "What about Kirsti Løvik? You said the police could not trace any relatives."

"She was only related by marriage, not a blood relative. However, I did take the liberty of contacting her. She maintains she has not seen or heard from Susannah since she won her appeal and was released from prison. According to Kirsti Løvik, she was not aware that Susannah had died until after she had been cremated," relayed Detective Martinez.

"And how can anyone believe what she says after the lies she told in court during Susannah's trial," retorted Loretta.

"I came here for reassurance, to be told that Susannah was definitely dead. Now I'm more disconcerted than ever," mentioned Veronique.

"Where do we go from here?" asked Loretta. "Are we to be on the lookout for Susannah? Will you be investigating this matter further?"

"Firstly, I am inclined to accept that Susannah is dead. Secondly, if she isn't, she cannot return to Martinique or even the Caribbean. I have alerted all ports and airports to her identity, and for custom officers to be vigilant. I suggest you both try and relax. You really are quite safe," remarked Detective Martinez.

"Then why don't I feel safe?" questioned Veronique. "Will I ever be rid of that woman? Alive or dead she is still the bane of my life."

"Out of curiosity, how did she escape from prison?" enquired Loretta.

"That was a process which took several hours and careful planning," began Detective Martinez. "She obviously had inside help as well as help on the outside. Unfortunately the inmates have remained silent, but we are aware of how the escape occurred. She took advantage of the procedures for early parole. Now Susannah would not be eligible for parole for thirty years, but she used the system to aid her escape. In brief, Susannah was able to infiltrate the security codes that keep sections of the prison separate. This allowed her to reach unsecured areas where those facing parole are housed. She managed to remain hidden until the postal van arrived. All over the prison there are numerous close circuit television cameras in operation. However, some of the inmates arranged a power failure on the day the postal van arrived. This wiped out the functioning of all the CCTV equipment. It seems Susannah hid in the postal van and was driven away. No doubt she would have climbed out of the van the moment it became stationary, probably at a set of traffic lights. The alarm was raised the moment her absence was noticed, but she was already long gone. What concerns me the most is how she managed to leave the country without being detained, allowing her to travel to Norway where she nearly killed you and Gavin." Detective Martinez paused for breath before continuing. "I was not going to tell you this for fear of alarming you, but it is our belief she had a fake identity. That would explain why she was not apprehended at any of the airports."

"So she travels under an assumed name!" exclaimed Veronique. "Which means she can return to Martinique whenever she wants. You'll be none the wiser." The tone in Veronique's voice became agitated.

"Then why tell us she can't return to the Caribbean? Why tell us that we are safe, when clearly we are not? You know full well you cannot stop her from entering the country," responded a disgruntled Loretta.

"Like I have said, I didn't want to alarm you, but I do believe Susannah is dead. The reputation of Tor Hegland convinces me of that," reiterated Detective Martinez.

"Someone had a grudge against Tor Hegland or why kill him so brutally, and it bears all the hallmarks of Susannah," stated Loretta emphatically.

"She is cunning, deceitful, and a master of disguise. Just what can we do?" wondered Veronique.

"The best advice I can give is to go about your normal routine, just be extra vigilant. You already have a fervent security system at the house, the plantation and Calypso Tavern, so stop worrying," replied Detective Martinez, trying his hardest to pacify them. He understood their concerns, but he also trusted his professional knowledge. Tor Hegland did not fit the criminal fraternity. Detective Martinez accepted the Norwegian judgement that Tor Hegland would not be mixed up with Susannah's ruthless and indiscriminate revenge. The cremation certificate also confirmed Susannah's demise.

"Maybe you could lend us some body armour for protection," commented Veronique. He took her request light-heartedly, but Veronique was serious.

"You really are overreacting. I will remain in touch with the Norwegian police and as soon as I have further information regarding who killed Tor Hegland, I will let you know," assured Detective Martinez.

"Thank you," remarked Loretta. "I know you are doing your best. Perhaps we are being overcautious, but who could blame us."

"Yes I am grateful. Sorry if I got a bit angry," added Veronique.

"Don't mention it, I fully understand," replied Detective Martinez.

"We had better be going. We're off to a beach party this evening," mentioned Veronique, giving Gregori a cuddle.

"That's a good idea, relax, I'm sure all will be fine," stated Detective Martinez in a reassuring voice.

"Oh just one more favour," added Veronique as they stood up to leave. "Don't mention any of this to Gavin. I don't want him troubled by this, especially if we are overreacting."

"Point taken. You go and have a pleasant day," replied Detective Martinez.

<>

That evening saw an air of jollification at Sebastian and Dominic's beach condo. People, laughter, and music, all added to the festivity. Friends and family huddled in various groups. Conversation overpowered the background reggae music. A dozen of the guests were playing volleyball on the beach. The floodlighting Sebastian had erected provided adequate light now that night had fallen. It also helped to create that holiday atmosphere one likes to experience. For the romantic, as Sebastian and Dominic were, the setting was perfect to celebrate their anniversary. Amongst the gay soiree were Gavin, Veronique, Loretta and Tobias. Rebecca had declined her invitation. Attending a wedding anniversary so close to the time when she and Greg should have married was not something she wished to do. Besides, Rebecca was more than happy to remain at the house and baby-sit Gregori.

Dominic mingled with the guests and was the dutiful host. He could not contain his excitement of travelling to Hawaii tomorrow. He and Sebastian had booked a two-week holiday on the South Pacific island. It was their anniversary present to each other. The guests listened politely as Dominic spoke, not wanting to steal his thunder. He was a natural socialite and could make the most boring story sound interesting. The guests also congratulated him on his homemade delicatessens. Give credit where it was due; he was a fine chef. Everyone loved his mouthwatering morsels.

Sebastian entered the condo, having played a quick game of beach volleyball. Somewhat breathless and hot, he grabbed a cool lager. His psychedelic shorts and lycra top accentuated his virile body. The cool lager was refreshing. He turned to face his guests, making eye contact with Gavin. Food in one hand and drink in the other, Sebastian watched as Gavin and Veronique approached him.

"It does not seem three years since we attended your wedding," commented Veronique.

"And by all accounts you only just made it, thanks to Susannah," replied Sebastian regretfully. He always tried so hard to avoid the subject of Susannah, and now he had plunged in with both feet. He realised how insensitive his comment was so he fumbled for an apology. "Sorry, I didn't mean to cause offence. My mouth just runs away and before I know it I've said something I had every intention not to say."

"Don't worry, we have known you long enough," replied Gavin. "A few inappropriate reminders does not bother us, not after all we have been through. Susannah came so close to killing us but thank God she did not succeed, and thank God she is dead." Gavin spoke with such ease. His often troubled mind over Greg's murder drew comfort from Susannah's death. She could not yield any further grief in seeking her revenge. Veronique noticed the improvement in Gavin's emotional state. The sleeping tablets he now took had improved his temperament. It was imperative for her to remain relaxed, for fear of alerting Gavin to her concerns. Perhaps she was being paranoid. Well let paranoia win the day. Veronique yearned desperately for Susannah's death to be true. Who could blame her?

"How long have you and Dominic been together in total?" asked Veronique, trying to be light-hearted.

"Nine years in November," informed Sebastian. "This is our official and public anniversary, but we have our own private celebration in November."

"A bit like the Queen having two birthdays, you have two anniversaries," remarked Gavin, displaying a modest amount of humour at the gay innuendo.

"I can safely say we are nothing like the Queen," responded Sebastian in a droll tone of voice. The three laughed.

"What's so funny?" enquired Dominic as he approached them. He put his arm around Sebastian and calmly stood by his side.

"We are," replied Sebastian. "Apparently we are very queen-like because we have two anniversaries as she has two birthdays."

"What's good enough for the Royals, is good enough for us," remarked Dominic, imitating a royal accent. "Anyway, I've come to tell you that the volleyball game is over, so we can now start the beach chase."

"The beach chase!" repeated Veronique. "Sounds ominous."

"It's quite simple, and all couples have to take part," began Dominic as he continued to explain the rules. "We've marked out a circuit on the beach for each person to run around whilst being chased by their partner. If your partner catches you, then you are thrown into the sea. But if your partner does not catch you then you throw your partner into the sea.

To make it fair each couple takes a turn of being chased or doing the chasing."

"So if I chase after Gavin but do not catch him, he then throws me into the sea. Then when it is his turn to chase after me, and catches me, he throws me into the sea again," recapped Veronique.

"You got it," confirmed Dominic.

"So I could lose out twice," said Veronique.

"That's what makes it so much fun," stated Gavin with a smug laugh.

"Sounds unfair to me. You better let me catch you," rebuked Veronique. Of course she did not mean that. She wallowed in Gavin's masculinity.

Dominic informed the guests of the beach chase game. Swiftly they all converged onto the beach. Several participants removed their outer clothes, revealing their swimwear. It was evident to see they expected to get wet. Neither Gavin nor Veronique had played the game before so were not as prepared. In joyous spirits, the couples taking part awaited their turn. The circumference was similar to the area of a baseball pitch. Four deck chairs marked the circuit. Sebastian and Dominic were first to go with Sebastian doing the chasing. Being physically stronger he was confident of catching his beloved. Their starting position was twenty feet apart. Sebastian stood behind Dominic and poised to give chase. One of the guests blew the whistle. The chase was off. In bare feet, Dominic fled across the sand, hotly pursued by Sebastian. The crowd participation soon intervened as they jeered and clapped. Some of the guests shouted out for Dominic to win, others for Sebastian. At the halfway mark Sebastian had narrowed the distance between them quite considerably. Despite the difficulty of running in sand, Sebastian was soon within arms reach of Dominic. The guests were enthralled by the chase, and when Sebastian caught hold of Dominic they let out a cheer. Sebastian picked Dominic up and carried him to the water's edge. A hysterical Dominic could not prevent Sebastian from dropping him into the calm sea. Dominic's attempt to redeem himself was unsuccessful, but equally as enjoyable. Having failed to catch Sebastian, an impromptu tug of war developed as Dominic tried to prevent Sebastian from picking him up again. Instead, they playfully dragged each other into the sea. They got completely drenched.

A few more couples followed before Loretta and Tobias took their turn. Tobias was under strict instructions from Loretta not to catch her. Did he heed this warning? No he did not. Within a split second of the whistle blowing, Tobias was in hot pursuit of his middle-aged wife. Loretta's stout legs seemed to move like lightening, kicking up sand in all directions. Her arms flapped crazily like a bird learning to fly. She struggled to run as fast as she could. Yet despite all this effort, she did not have the speed to maintain the distance from Tobias. Periodically she looked over her shoulder, shouting out various comments.

"Tobias! You're gaining on me. You slow down, you hear," she panted.

"I've got to catch the woman of my dreams," Tobias shouted back. The comical couple provided much entertainment for the guests as they cheered them along. Tobias remained firm in his chase. He easily advanced closer to his wife.

"Don't you get coming any closer, you ain't the bionic man," shouted Loretta.

"I'm like an eagle soaring down to pinch his prey," responded Tobias.

"You just remember what I said, Tobias. Think of your hernia. Remember Valentine's night and our wedding day," called out Loretta, in reference to the previous attempts Tobias had tried to carry her.

"You know you want me to catch you," he replied. Tobias was within arms reach as they approached the final quarter.

Inevitably, he narrowed the distance and grabbed his wife. Loretta shrieked as Tobias lifted her up into his arms.

"No, no, don't you drop me," she cried. "I don't wanna get wet." Ignoring her many pleas, Tobias carried her into the shallow waters.

"I thought you said you had lost weight," uttered Tobias. He soon dropped her into the sea. A huge cheer went up from the guests. Loretta was indeed a good sport and took it all in good humour. The laughter increased when she emerged from the sea with a clump of seaweed caught in her blouse.

"Just call me Neptune," she remarked as she staggered up the beach.

After a few minutes rest Loretta had the opportunity to balance the score. Tobias ran off and she chased after him as fast as her chubby legs would allow.

"You slow down," she shouted to him. Tobias, having increased the distance between them, began to tease Loretta. He turned to face her and started to run backwards.

"You can't catch me, you can't catch me," he stated, like a typical child playing in the school playground. Tobias then began to jump on the spot, doing a couple of star jumps. Due to him acting the fool, Loretta narrowed the distance. She was determined to catch him. However, Tobias soon turned around and resumed running.

"You'll let me catch you if you know what's good for you," shouted Loretta.

When Tobias crossed the finishing line ahead of Loretta, he turned and chased after her.

"Oh no you don't," panicked Loretta, who quickly did an about turn to run away. It was in vain. Tobias grabbed his wife once more and carried her into the sea. They fell into the water. A wave lapped over them. Loretta became submerged for a few seconds. When she stood up a clump of seaweed was caught in her hair. Tobias laughed at his wife. He helped her out of the water. They staggered up the beach, their clothes dripping wet. Loretta still had the seaweed on her head. Everyone was hysterical. "I now have a matching pair," she said.

Unfortunately for Veronique, she lost out both times. This enabled Gavin to drop her twice into the sea. Outwardly she appeared the damsel in distress as Gavin carried her to the sea, but inwardly Veronique revelled at his masculinity. It proved to her and everyone else how macho Gavin was, and she liked that.

The evening concluded with a karaoke contest. Loretta did a stupendous performance of the Ertha Kitt classic, *'I'm just an old fashioned Girl'*. Tobias sang an unusual rendition of the Nat King Cole classic *'What a wonderful World'*. Some people thought he had a sore throat and commented as such. Veronique took on the pop princess Whitney Housten and sang *'I wanna dance with somebody'*. Of course the only person she wanted to dance with was Gavin. She enjoyed making eyes at him during her performance. Gavin sang the romantic James Bond theme, *'From Russia With Love'*, originally performed by Matt Munro. His voice suited the soft melody. Veronique floated in a romantic fantasy. She felt he was singing the song about her. Sebastian and Dominic sang the love duet by Benny and Bjorn, *'I Know Him So Well'*. Clearly everyone noticed how devoted they were to each other.

Sebastian and Dominic's anniversary party was a hoot. Everyone thought so. The jollification of the evening helped to quell Veronique's fears about Susannah being alive. Veronique embraced any activity to occupy her worried mind. Any distraction was welcomed. She scarcely knew what life was like without the Susannah burden. That woman had blighted her happiness for more years than Veronique cared to remember. However, Veronique's reservations could now be eradicated. The following morning, just after 9am, Veronique received a call form Detective Martinez. The news could not have been better. The Norwegian police had arrested the man responsible for killing Tor Hegland. Apparently, the assailant was a schizophrenic who had failed to take his medication. Veronique did not hesitate to tell her mother the good news. This information immediately put their minds at rest. They had made the right decision not to tell Gavin their fears as to whether Susannah was alive. This would only have caused him unnecessary anguish. To Veronique's utmost relief she could finally accept that Karl had killed Susannah.

Chapter Three

Conspiracy

Why we didn't think of it sooner I can't imagine.

The Caribbean sun was high above the horizon. Gavin's Mediterranean style home lay nestled within nature's rich tapestry, helpless to the sun's intensive rays. The surrounding palm trees reached out to the tips of their branches, embracing nature's heat. Birds fluttered from tree to tree, endeavouring to remain in the shade. Gavin stepped out of the shower and dried himself. His bronzed body was the envy of any white person seeking a suntan. He had overslept due to last night's beach party going on into the early hours of this morning. Humorous thoughts occupied his mind, causing him to smile as he reflected on the funnier moments. From his wardrobe he obtained fawn coloured shorts and a lime coloured short-sleeved shirt.

The tranquillisers he now took each night ensured he slept well and helped him to remain relaxed during the day. The sixth anniversary of Greg's death had transpired with its usual amount of sadness. Perhaps taking a holiday in future would be better. It was time to embrace life and enjoy the merriment. Greg would not want him to be miserable.

A Certain Dilemma

Casually dressed, the suntanned Englishman descended his mahogany staircase. In the living room below sat Veronique. She looked up at her husband as he approached. Gregori was playing happily in his playpen.

"I thought I'd let you sleep in after last night's festivities," remarked Veronique, discarding the magazine she was reading. The telephone call from Detective Martinez over an hour ago had made her feel so relaxed.

"It's almost 11 o'clock," replied Gavin. "Tobias will be wondering where I am." He yawned before continuing. "Mind you, we did have lots of fun last night. Seeing your mother being chased by Tobias, it was unimaginable," added Gavin, greeting his wife with a kiss.

"Too true, we all had a good time. Those two sure know how to put on a party," said Veronique, in reference to Sebastian and Dominic. "They seem a perfect couple."

"No point in breakfast, I'll have lunch with Tobias," stated Gavin. Turning his attention to Gregori he continued, "And how is my young man today?" Gavin went over to the playpen and picked Gregori up. His son chuckled as he revelled in the attention. "You be a good boy for your Mama." Gavin kissed his son on the forehead and put him back in his playpen.

"We received another nanny application today, from a woman named Natasha," informed Veronique, reaching for the letter. "She is in her early thirties and from what she states she seems very suitable. I have already phoned her and arranged an interview for tomorrow morning."

"That sounds promising, but I thought you had decided not to have a nanny," responded Gavin.

"Well between me and Mama taking turns, and her being able to work around my shifts, we can manage. But it won't be a bad idea to get someone for emergencies. Judging by Natasha's letter we would be foolish to pass her by."

"Whatever you think my sweetest. At least we can afford one. Anyway, I really must get to the office. See you later." Gavin kissed Veronique and left the house.

He casually walked the hundred-yard stretch across a gravel pathway edged with tropical ferns, numerous hibiscus shrubs and other foliage. There was a driveway accessible by car but Gavin enjoyed the leisurely exercise. The short daily stroll enabled him to view his estate and absorb the wonder of his surrounding world. It was great to be living amongst nature's colourful mosaic. Gavin never took any of it for granted. He appreciated the life he had attained, and was immensely grateful for his fortune.

Gavin soon arrived at his office. It was a single wooden construction that resembled a log cabin. In the heart of the Caribbean stood a fragment of Gavin's Norwegian ski resort. The tropical surroundings replaced the snow covered fjords and mountains. The office was located to the far edge of his land, not far from the cabana and close to the neighbouring forest. In the foreground stood the processing mill and the vast expanse of sugarcane fields.

Tobias was deep in thought and sitting at his desk. He had arrived at 9am, and was in the process of dealing with a crisis when Gavin entered the office. After receiving a damning report on yesterday's sugar despatch, the day was progressively getting worse. Tobias had already made various telephone calls in an attempt to resolve the problem. Thankfully, today's dire straits were unprecedented. There were stringent measures enforced daily to ensure a top quality produce. Yet last night something somewhere had drastically gone wrong. A sugar despatch riddled with ants was definitely not good for business. The whole consignment had to be destroyed, incurring financial consequences. Public health was paramount. There was no alternative but to destroy the whole despatch. The penalties were far too great to do otherwise. One could not salvage any of it for contravening health and safety regulations. The environmental health agency would not hesitate to close down the business if Gavin allowed contaminated produce, or even suspected contaminated produce to be sold.

Tobias looked up at Gavin as he entered the office. A happy and relaxed Gavin closed the door behind him.

"Sorry I'm a bit late this morning. I see you did not indulge in a lie in after last night's festivities," mentioned Gavin, walking over to his desk. "Or did you just get here five minutes before me," he said jokingly, but Tobias was in no mood for general banter.

"I've been here since 9am, and given the crisis I have been confronted with this morning, it is a good job one of us was here," he curtly stated, picking up a print of an e-mail he had received earlier from Carter's International Distribution Company. Carter's being the transport company Gavin employs to deliver the sugar worldwide. Tobias handed the e-mail print to Gavin. "You had better read this," he said. Gavin took the print and read it. He sensed from Tobias' cold reception that the situation must be serious. Seconds later Tobias gave him the gist of the problem. "To get to the point, yesterday's despatch has been destroyed, due to an infestation of ants."

"What!" exclaimed Gavin, skimming through the e-mail. "You have got to be kidding me! How is this possible? We adhere to strict hygiene standards." Gavin looked at Tobias, expecting him to give the gist on how this had happened, but Tobias was none the wiser. All he could do was inform Gavin of what had transpired.

"The environmental health agency carried out a spot check at Carter's yesterday evening. That is how the ants were discovered. Carter's are fuming and are eager to exonerate themselves."

"Well someone has let the side down and I can't for one minute think the problem is our end. I want a thorough investigation into how this has happened," demanded Gavin sternly, looking at his father-in-law.

"So do the environmental health agency," added Tobias. "They will be arriving here this afternoon to inspect the site."

"This is all we need," sighed Gavin. "We have orders to fulfil. Without that consignment we can't meet demand for at least two months." Gavin could not keep still. His thoughts anxiously searched for a rational explanation. They could not be at fault. He was so agitated. "I want an immediate inspection of the mill; the processing plant; packing and despatch done now, before environmental health get here," he ordered.

"I knew you would, that's why I have already instructed Detsen to carry out a thorough check of the site. He is working on it as we speak," responded Tobias. "You don't need me to tell you that this is a serious matter, not just for our reputation but financially too. We shall have to authorise overtime to the staff to replace the consignment and limit the damage. We cannot renege on our orders. Luckily, we are ahead of ourselves with production so I feel confident we can ride out this problem," assured Tobias.

"If we have ants, I want them all destroyed now, before the environmental health officer gets here," stressed Gavin. "Hopefully the problem lies at Carter's end, and if that is the case we will claim compensation."

What had started as a leisurely stress free day soon reached the opposite end of the spectrum. Anxious moments passed whilst they waited for Detsen's inspection report. Gavin and Tobias worked on a rota for staff overtime and a productivity forecast. It was not as if they were unaccustomed to a setback of this nature. However, previous loss had been due to storm damage, which they were insured against. Storm damage is an act of God and no one is responsible or liable, but an infestation of ants is due to lack of hygiene and health procedures. The latter being an adequate reason for the environmental health agency to shut down production, at best for just a limited period, at worst, they have the power to revoke Gavin's business licence.

Patience was never one of Gavin's virtues as he eagerly awaited Detsen's report.

"Hurry up Detsen, I need that report," stated Gavin anxiously.

"He has been on it for almost three hours. I told him we need it by midday," said Tobias.

"We can't have ants," sighed Gavin. "If we do, certain people will lose their jobs."

"I'll page Detsen, see how much longer he will be." Tobias noticed Gavin's calm and relaxed demeanour had disappeared. When Gavin had arrived at the office he was quite jovial. Last night at Sebastian and Dominic's party was the first time in many years Tobias had seen Gavin happy. Now by some admin or human error that happiness had quickly withered away. Tobias picked up his pager from his desk and bleeped Detsen. A few seconds later, Detsen appeared at the office door. He was about to enter when he had received Tobias' bleep.

"How's that for timing," said Detsen satirically as he opened the door. The youthful looking well-built Caribbean entered the office. Neither Gavin nor Tobias appreciated Detsen's composed and jovial mien.

"Well what is the verdict?" asked Gavin bluntly.

"No trace of ants anywhere," responded Detsen. "I've spoken to all the staff, they haven't seen any ants, and all assure me that all the health and safety checks and procedures have been carried out. I've inspected all the equipment myself and checked all logbook entries, no downfall anywhere. I am 100% confident we do not have ants."

"Thank the Lord for that!" exclaimed Tobias.

"Then the problem must be with Carter's," added Gavin. "At least now I can relax. Let's hope the environmental health officer agrees with your findings."

They did not have much longer to wait. Hezron, the environmental health officer arrived promptly at 2pm. The trio team of Gavin, Tobias and Detsen applied their business charm as they welcomed Hezron into the office. They were quite relaxed in the light of Detsen's report. They could confidently and professionally conduct themselves. Hezron, a West Indian man in his fifties, explained the purpose and details of his visit. He estimated that the inspection would take approximately two hours, with a further night-time check to be carried out this evening. Ants were highly intelligent as well as nocturnal insects, and knew when to avoid humans.

The trio team led Hezron around the site, each taking a turn to explain the various functions of a specific feature of the sugarcane plantation process. Hezron was impressed with what he saw. He made various complimentary remarks during the inspection. No one was more relieved than Gavin when Hezron gave a positive preliminary report. The environmental health officer accepted the standard of hygiene was adequate. All that remained was tonight's inspection, to be carried out by Hezron and another colleague.

Gratitude was an understatement as Hezron bid farewell. The moment he had left the premises, Gavin broke open a bottle of whisky to steady his nerves. Tobias and Detsen joined in. They needed to unwind.

Gavin's business and reputation remained intact as the night-time inspection also proved negative for ants. It was a huge relief. They had survived the major hurdle of the environmental health agency. Now there was the arduous matter of increasing production to replace the destroyed consignment. It was imperative to keep on target and deliver the orders. Most of the employees accepted the overtime.

The increased measures would limit the financial loss. Unfortunately, one did not predict further complications.

Within less than a week there had been a further incident of ants. The sugar consignment had to be destroyed. Gavin's prosperity and reputation was at stake. Two incidents of ants within as many weeks had certainly damaged their business. Orders were being cancelled. Gavin and Tobias were still baffled as to how the infestation occurred. The environmental health agency also carried out a further inspection. Again this proved negative for ants. A warning was given and further checks would be carried out. Carter's International Distribution Company was also inspected. Gavin was adamant the problem was with them, but they also received a positive report. Carter's were not to blame.

Somewhat drained by this current problem, Gavin entered his wooden panelled office. Tobias glanced up at him as he stepped inside. From Tobias' physiognomy Gavin could see it was bad news.

"Don't tell me we have more ants, not another consignment destroyed," said Gavin despondently. He could clearly see the document Tobias was holding in his hand.

"No, not ants, thank goodness. But have you ever heard of Global Incorporations Limited?" stated Tobias.

"No I have not," replied Gavin. "Why? Who are they? What do they want?"

"I have never heard of them either, but they want to buy us out," responded Tobias.

"What!" remarked Gavin impatiently. "They want to buy my business!"

"Apparently they do. They want to arrange an inspection visit with a view to making an offer for the whole plantation, including our job and everyone else's."

"Well you can tell them, no!" Gavin emphatically replied as he moved towards Tobias. "We are not for sale."

"I would imagine they have read our latest news reports, the bad press, and think we are an easy target to take over at a rock bottom price," said Tobias as Gavin took hold of the document. After a few seconds perusal Gavin became dismissive.

"I don't even intend to reply. We have more important matters to deal with," stated Gavin as he disposed of the document in the wastepaper basket. Gavin completely disregarded Global Incorporations Limited, along with any notion of selling his company. He sat at his desk, turning his attention to current matters. "Have we had a reply from our insurers as to whether they will underwrite our loss?" asked Gavin.

"As it happens they have not said no or yes. I received an e-mail from them confirming they have received the report from the environmental health agency. They will be informing us of their decision once we have submitted an audited account for the financial loss. Of course we have to wait for Sebastian to return from his holiday with Dominic, for him to work out our exact financial loss," said Tobias.

"I have checked our policy, they have to cover the loss. Our policy clearly states we our covered for all detrimental consequences beyond our control."

"With the environmental health report stating no blame or negligence on our side, it should go in our favour," said Tobias. "But we all know what insurance companies are like. If they can find a way of not paying they will. Nevertheless, should that happen we must appeal."

"Too right we shall appeal, which reminds me to contact Chester Hargreaves. He can check the legalities of our insurance policy in preparation for any appeal," said Gavin. He proceeded to e-mail their solicitor. Gavin and Tobias' desks were positioned in close proximity and at right angles to each other. Gavin sent the e-mail to Chester Hargreaves, outlining the need for a speedy reply in their favour. "What was

Donaldson's reaction when they discovered their consignment was not ready for despatch?" questioned Gavin.

"Thankfully understanding," answered Tobias. "But that does not alter the fact that whoever is sabotaging our sugar had better be caught soon, else our clients will be forced to defect to our competitors," he added with due concern.

"The man's a saint," said Gavin. "I've just had a reply back from Chester. He has already checked our legal position and we do not have any cause for concern. The insurers will have to recompense us."

"Good old Chester, he never lets us down. At least that is good news for us," replied Tobias.

"Still, I will be happier once it is all settled and the culprit is apprehended," stated Gavin.

"I will ring the police later to see if there's any update. Maybe this ant business is not as damaging as we first thought. Donaldson's have been very understanding. If we can make our next despatch to them on time and include some of the deficit of not meeting their previous order, we won't incur any financial penalties."

"That is kind of immaterial as long as the insurers bear the brunt," added Gavin.

"I have also drawn up the overtime schedule required to complete the next order, and make up for what we have failed to deliver. We can utilise the outer field for further propagation. Loretta has even offered to help plant the stem cuttings. You know how she likes working in the fields with the others. We shall be resilient," said Tobias, quite proud of himself. Gavin looked cordially at his adopted father.

"Where would I be without you?" he remarked.

<>

Veronique drove her white Dodge estate up the palm-fringed driveway. It was midday and she was returning from her morning shift at the hospital. The white walls and rustic red roof of their lavish abode appeared in full view. The dwelling was cradled by the surrounding tropical landscape. Even after four years of marriage the novelty of being Mrs Harrison, Gavin's wife, had not dissipated. She felt elated at being lady of the manor. She was convinced this feeling of joy and contentment would always remain. The occasions it did not were due to unwanted memories of Susannah. But even so, Veronique was convinced matters would now improve with Tor Hegland's murderer being caught. Detective Martinez had been right. Tor Hegland would not have been involved with a murdering maniac. Susannah was dead, and those unwanted memories would disappear forever. At least this is what Veronique believed.

Veronique parked her car outside and ascended the veranda steps. Loretta sat on the sofa. She attempted to read through some Egyptian holiday brochures, whilst Gregori played on the floor with his train set. Every so often he required his grandmother's attention. He wanted her to see his train set in operation. The intermittent demands of baby-sitting prevented Loretta from reading her holiday brochure in any detail. Veronique entered the living room. Gregori stood up to greet his mother. He precariously ran across the room. Veronique reached out for him and swung him around as she lifted him up into the air. Gregori's joyous giggly sounds filled the room.

"How has my big boy been for Grandma?" remarked Veronique.

Amidst chuckles and laughter, Gregori managed to convey his excitement with his train set. His baby talk words all mixed up, to a stranger inaudible, but to his mother understandable.

"You've been playing with choo choo trains," stated Veronique.

"Choo chooo, choo chooo," murmured Gregori.

"How has he been?" Veronique asked Loretta. She put him down and pleasantly obliged her son's demand to sit on the floor and play with his trains.

"He has been as good as gold as always," commented Loretta. Being the gloating grandmother, she remained on the sofa, watching her offspring play and being happy. "It gives me such pleasure to watch you both," she remarked.

"I hope he is not too much of a handful," said Veronique. "But I do prefer for us to look after him rather than a stranger, even though Rosie and Natasha would make excellent nannies."

"My sentiments entirely," agreed Loretta. "And it's my pleasure. I enjoy looking after him. Working these half-day shifts has worked out perfectly. Why we didn't think of it sooner I can't imagine. Maybe we can use Rosie and Natasha as occasional babysitters. We just don't need a nanny do we," concluded Loretta. She paused for a brief second before changing the subject. "Anyway!" she stated in an emphasised voice. "I have been looking at holiday brochures of Egypt, that's where your Pa is taking me."

"Egypt sounds like a wonderful place for a holiday; those pyramids and the ancient artefacts," replied Veronique. Gregori's attention was once again consumed with his train set. He began to rearrange the track. His preoccupation left Veronique to converse quite freely with Loretta.

"I can just imagine myself dressed as an Egyptian. Adorned with gold and lavish jewellery," said Loretta.

"Funny, I spoke to Pa earlier and he never mentioned it. I even asked him if the two of you had decided where to go."

"Oh well he doesn't know yet, but I shall tell him later," replied Loretta coyly.

"Oh Mama, what are you like. Well as long as you tell him before you book it," said Veronique. Without any further prompting from her daughter, Loretta gave a running commentary of the Egyptian tourist attractions; the pyramids and ancient artefacts; the various hotels she would love to stay at, not forgetting the mini cruise down the River Nile. Veronique was amused by her mother's enthusiasm. She allowed her to rattle on like an over-excited child. The reality of the day soon returned.

"Oh my goodness, look at the time," stated Loretta as the grandfather clock chimed 2pm. "I need to get going to the craft shop else I will be late." She dashed out of the house and grabbed her bicycle. The dainty two-wheeler was leaning against the veranda. "You enjoy the afternoon," she said to Veronique, who now stood in the doorway. Loretta mounted her bike. "I wonder if this is the same way you mount a camel?" she uttered. Veronique laughed. "Don't mention anything about Egypt till I've persuaded your Pa to take me," she added.

"I won't Mama."

"I shall have to pedal fast," shouted Loretta as her stout little legs spun into action. "See you later." She gave a brief wave.

"You look as though you're training for the Olympics," responded Veronique as she waved back. Loretta cycled down the driveway and disappeared beyond the tropical foliage. She failed to recognise the car as she fled past. Seconds later a pale blue Mercedes came speeding up the driveway. The car came to a sudden halt. The driver was dressed in new clothes, her attire a mixture of muted pastel colours with striking sunglasses. The proud occupant stepped out.

"Well how d'you like my new car," announced Rebecca in her Texan drawl. The sun's rays ricocheted from its pristine polished surface.

"I wondered who it was for a moment," remarked Veronique. "The car looks mighty fine. What happened to the convertible?"

"It was time for a change," replied Rebecca. "It felt awkward parting with the convertible as it was Greg's and I was very fond of it, but the mechanics were becoming problematic so I thought what the heck, let's get a new one, and this is it."

"It looks very sophisticated but expensive," stated Veronique as she descended the steps. Veronique noticed how happy Rebecca seemed. She really was succeeding in rebuilding her life since Greg's death.

"You're Ma makes me laugh. I just passed her on the way. Her face puffing away as she pedalled," remarked Rebecca.

"Don't remind me, I was laughing as I watched her go," replied Veronique.

"And guess what?" announced Rebecca. "My Ma and Pa have decided to pay a visit, they arrive tomorrow. I kind of mentioned it would be ok if they stayed at the house."

"Of course it is fine for them to stay here. You know they are always welcome and it would be good to see them again."

"Great!" affirmed Rebecca.

"I know Mama has been meaning to ring Ursula for the coconut flapjack recipe," remarked Veronique. "She seems to have misplaced the recipe Ursula gave her when your folks were last here."

"You don't need a recipe for flapjacks, it was the first thing Ma showed me how to make," responded Rebecca.

"The ones your Mama makes taste divine, mine never seem to come out like hers."

"I have to confess, as a kid I was for ever sneaking a flapjack or two whenever Ma was not looking. I couldn't get enough." Rebecca opened the car door. "Why not sit inside and view my supersonic four wheels," stated Rebecca. Veronique obliged and sat in the driver's seat.

"I love the smell of a new car," said Veronique. Rebecca moved around and sat in the passenger seat. She began informing Veronique of the controls and gadgetry attachments.

"It has satellite navigation; a trip computer; rear parking sensors so I have no excuse now; as you can see, leather upholstery and electric windows; power assistance steering and speedtronic cruise control. This button retracts the electro-hydraulic vario roof, and of course not forgetting the air conditioning and stereo system with MP3 compatibility. And a lot more besides," said Rebecca.

"It is very impressive but am I suppose to know what you're going on about?" stated Veronique. Rebecca laughed.

"I am so over the top but what the heck. I haven't had this much excitement in ages."

"As long as you know how it all functions and I'm glad you're having fun," said Veronique. "Anyway, do you think your folks would mind babysitting Gregori while they're hear, just to give the chance for me and Gavin to have a night out."

"I am sure they would be delighted," replied Rebecca. "I take it you've not had any joy with finding a nanny."

"No," sighed Veronique. "There are two likely candidates but I just don't seem comfortable leaving him with a complete stranger. I did not expect to feel like this. I was all for hiring a nanny and working full time, but I can't bring myself to do that. I won't mind your Ma and Pa helping out. In fact I think Ursula would make a very good nanny," remarked Veronique. "Well I certainly like your new car," she added. The digital sound of Beethoven's Moonlight Serenade became audible, not from Rebecca's twin speaker car stereo, but from her cell phone. Rebecca grabbed her mobile from its new car phone compartment. The view display read 'Marcus', the head barman at Calypso Tavern.

"Hi Marcus," answered Rebecca in a calm voice.

"Rebecca, you need to get here straight away," stated Marcus hastily.

"What's wrong?" she questioned.

"The police are everywhere, searching your office. They are anxious to talk to you. You need to get here now," informed Marcus.

"Is anyone hurt? What do they want?"

"I can't say over the phone," replied Marcus. "You just need to get here, now."

"Ok. I'm on my way," she cordially stated and finished the call.

"Is everything all right?" asked Veronique.

"Apparently not. The police are at Calypso Tavern and they want to see me. I shall have to go."

"The police! Why? What has happened?" quizzed Veronique. She acquired a sudden sense of fear. The sort of panic feeling she often got from Susannah.

"Well I don't know, Marcus wouldn't say. He mentioned the police were searching my office. I'm completely baffled. Honestly, I only left there thirty minutes ago," said Rebecca.

"Ring and let me know what it is," said Veronique, getting out of the car. "I can't help but feel worried."

"Oh don't worry, it can't be anything too serious." Rebecca moved into the driver's seat. "Just another storm in a teacup. I'd better get going. I'll call you later." Almost as hastily as she arrived Rebecca drove away. Veronique returned to the house. Gregori was still playing on the floor with his train set. Why was Susannah on her mind? Veronique entered the living room and intuitively looked up at the integral balcony. The same balcony where Susannah had stood when she first shot Gavin on his return from Norway, then again on their wedding day. Susannah had proudly stood there holding a gun with the intention to kill them. How Susannah had enjoyed her moment of superiority, looking down on them as they entered the house, with a condescending smirk on her face. Veronique had shuddered with fear at that moment on her wedding day, but why should she feel like that now? Especially now that Susannah is dead.

"Stop being paranoid," she muttered. "I'm overreacting."

Rebecca sighted several police cars parked outside Calypso Tavern. She parked the Mercedes at an uneven angle, partially blocking one of the police cars. No sooner had she stepped out of her car, a police officer approached.

"I presume you are Rebecca Chambers," spoke the female officer.

"Yes I am," replied Rebecca. "What is the matter? Why are you here?"

"We are acting on information we received earlier today," informed the officer curtly.

"What information? My business is above board. Why didn't you ring me if you had some concerns or following up a complaint?" questioned Rebecca.

"Now that would have been foolish of us to ring and forewarn you," replied the officer sternly.

"Foolish?"

"If you could just sit in my car," requested the uniformed officer. She led Rebecca over to her police vehicle and opened the back door.

"Am I not needed inside? Will someone tell me what is going on!" exclaimed Rebecca, beginning to feel agitated. The burly stern-faced female officer took hold of Rebecca's arm as she engineered her on to the back seat of her patrol vehicle. Reluctantly Rebecca obliged, she could do little else. The police officer sat next to her. In the driver's seat sat a male officer. He glanced over at her. A youngish looking man, dressed in uniform. His attire was so clean and pressed it gave the impression it was his first day on the job. "Will someone explain what this is all about!" demanded Rebecca.

"That is exactly what we are here to find out. Hopefully you won't have to wait much longer. We are currently making a thorough search of Calypso Tavern," replied the male officer in a well-mannered fashion. He was clearly well educated.

Although he was a true Caribbean he spoke with an Oxford English accent.

"What are you looking for?" asked Rebecca. At that moment the female officer's personal radio sounded.

"Go ahead Reece," she said.

"The search is affirmative. We have found exactly what we came to look for in Rebecca's office," came a static but coherent voice.

"Message understood," replied the female officer. She turned to face Rebecca and spoke harshly. "Rebecca, we have found a stash of heroin in your office. Therefore I have no alternative but to arrest you." The officer retrieved her handcuffs and placed them on Rebecca's wrists. "You do not have to say anything but it may harm your defence if you do not mention when questioned something which you later rely on in court. Anything you do say may be given in evidence."

"Arrest me! Heroin! This is so not true!" protested Rebecca. "You can't do this to me!"

"Yes we can. You have the right to an attorney which we can arrange once we get down to the police station," remarked the dutiful male officer. Rebecca sat back in her seat, seething with anger but wise enough to remain calm. The male officer started the engine and drove off. Rebecca glanced back at Calypso Tavern, only to see several other police officers emerge from her establishment. She noticed one of them carrying a bag. Rebecca surmised it was the heroin, but how did it get in her office?

CHAPTER FOUR

Incriminations

"Yes Parker, operation homeward bound. I came out without my compact mirror."

Rebecca had been questioned for several hours. She did not fare too well under the constant questions from both the arresting police officers. Their interrogative technique was well rehearsed as each fired questions, scarcely giving Rebecca time to reply. The moment she answered a question the other officer would deliver another, forcing her to give quick answers. The well-spoken voice of Officer Jennings did not weaken his stern approach. What could Rebecca do but deny all of the allegations. It soon became apparent the stash of heroin had been concealed behind her bookcase. To Rebecca it seemed obvious someone had set her up. Would any drug dealer be so flippant as to leave their contraband where it could be so easily found? Rebecca stated as much, but this only fuelled further questions. Neither police officer was willing to accept her innocence. Perhaps they had targets to reach and required a further conviction. Finally, after an endless endurance of cross-examination, Rebecca signed her very detailed statement. Officer Jennings gathered up the

A Certain Dilemma

papers and stood up to leave the room. Rebecca looked at the female police officer sitting opposite.

"Do I get to go home now?" pleaded Rebecca.

"Not yet," replied the female officer with a disgruntled expression on her face. She would have preferred a signed confession from Rebecca, to rap the case up. Instead, the result was more administration and further days of questioning the staff at Calypso Tavern.

"How much longer will I be here?" questioned Rebecca. "I'm hungry and thirsty and I can't say anymore than what I have already said. I know you have a job to do but don't you have any sense of character judgement. You know I haven't done this. I have obliged by answering your questions, but if you are going to continue then I want my lawyer here. In fact I think you have taken advantage of me to question me without my lawyer present."

"We won't be long," said the female officer. She followed Officer Jennings out of the interview room.

Rebecca was relieved the not so philanthropic duo had left the room. She sighed heavily, wondering if she would be charged and imprisoned, or whether she would be going home tonight. It was already after 6pm. Dusk was beginning to fall, not that Rebecca could see out of a window, for the baron room did not possess any. The raised miniscule windowlet on the one wall denied anyone a decent view. The stark interior complimented the four plain walls. The sparse furnishings were a light oak table with three padded upright chairs. Thank goodness the chairs were comfortable to sit on. Rebecca yawned and rested her head in her hands, with her elbows on the table for support. She could only imagine the state of her office after the police scrutiny. Her tidy little empire demonised by their search, and also violated by the drug dealer who had planted the heroin. She only hoped it was not a staff member, that betrayal would be disappointing.

Officer Jennings brought the case to the attention of Detective Martinez. Jennings would appreciate his learned superior's opinion regarding the drug offence now hanging over Rebecca. He knew Martinez had previous dealings with Rebecca. The plight of Gavin and Susannah was a well-known topic throughout the police station. Any crime of such magnitude would be hard to forget. The staff had even placed odds on whether Susannah would eventually kill Gavin. Their crude behaviour was short-lived, and their minor sweep terminated with Susannah's death.

Detective Martinez became suspicious when his colleague informed him of Rebecca's arrest. He did not usually deal with drug offences for his remit was homicide, but as he knew Rebecca from his prior involvement with the Harrison household he felt obliged to take an interest. He did not believe that Rebecca was a drug dealer. Even so he could not let the matter rest. He had to interview her. Officer Jennings welcomed this. Yet perhaps Detective Martinez had an ulterior motive. All previous contact with the Harrison household was due to the criminality of Susannah. Yet this current situation with Rebecca could not be linked to Susannah. He had taken on board Veronique and Loretta's concern that could Susannah be alive, following the murder of Tor Hegland; implying had Susannah killed him? The Norsk authorities had assured Detective Martinez that Susannah was not only dead but had been cremated. In any case, they had now caught the perpetrator of Tor Hegland's murder. One could be forgiven for being paranoid in thinking Susannah was alive. Her ferocious attempts of trying to kill Gavin and whoever else got in her way of seeking revenge would linger in anyone's subconscious. Only the passage of time would eradicate the paranoia. Yet despite the evidence to the contrary, Detective Martinez acknowledged the similarity to when Gavin was arrested at Oslo airport for carrying heroin, which we now know Susannah had planted. The similarity was disconcerting.

Detective Martinez entered the interview room. Rebecca looked up. She was not expecting to see him. Detective Martinez closed the door. Rebecca broke the silence.

"Am I glad to see a familiar face. I take it you know why I am here," she said.

"Hello Rebecca," said Detective Martinez as he sat opposite her. "I am aware of the situation."

"I am completely baffled as to what has happened. I do not have any involvement in drugs."

"You have no explanation or inclination as to how a considerable quantity of heroin was found in your office?" stated Detective Martinez sympathetically.

"None whatsoever," replied Rebecca, her puzzlement showed in her face. "Are all the staff at Calypso Tavern being questioned?"

"They are, but as of yet no positive results," remarked Detective Martinez. He looked at Rebecca with compassion and enquired, "How are you feeling?"

"Completely annoyed, frustrated, tired, and I just wanna go home," she remarked in a demonstrative manner.

"I'm sorry but I was referring in general, with life after Greg." Rebecca looked at him, sighed and replied:

"Not too bad. It has been difficult, especially at this time of year. It's the sixth anniversary of his death. The anniversary should be our wedding. How can it be that the man you are about to marry ends up being buried on what should have been your wedding day," she paused. "I'm so glad that bitch is dead."

"Susannah!" stated Detective Martinez. "She certainly knew how to cause optimum grief." Detective Martinez could see the emotional pain in Rebecca's face. Tears were beginning to swell in her eyes. "Just for the record, I believe you do not have any involvement in drugs," he stated reassuringly.

"Thank you, it's a comfort to know someone believes me," replied Rebecca, wiping a tear away.

"But if you could be vigilant and watch your staff and let us know of any unusual behaviour, it would be appreciated," remarked Detective Martinez.

"Most definitely, it goes without saying. I do not want Calypso Tavern being dragged down into the depths of depravity from corrupt staff and drug dealers."

"You take care of yourself and give my regards to Gavin," said Detective Martinez.

"Does that mean I am free to go?"

"Yes it does. If you like I can give you a lift back to Calypso Tavern," suggested Detective Martinez.

"You bet your bottom dollar you can," said Rebecca with a smile. She eagerly stood up to accept his generosity. "For a moment I thought I was gonna be spending the night here."

"Between you and me our cells are full at the moment," said Detective Martinez.

"Gee, in that case you must thank the criminals on my behalf," joked Rebecca. Martinez laughed.

"At least we know they are guilty." In contrast to her arrival, Detective Martinez pleasantly escorted her to his car.

"If ever you need a deterrent to keep people on the straight and narrow, arrest them for a crime they did not commit. The uncertainty of being imprisoned is terrifying," commented Rebecca.

"I think our democratic way of life will not allow us to do that, but I do understand your reaction. The short sharp shock treatment does have its merits," replied Detective Martinez. He opened the car door for Rebecca.

"Thank you Parker," she remarked humorously in reference to the Thunderbirds. The relief of going home roused Rebecca's comic side. She enjoyed a little humour with the detective. She sat elegantly on the passenger seat, imitating Lady Penelope. Her pink blouse suited the moment. The detective smiled as he closed the door. Once he sat in the driver's seat she added, "Drive on Parker, but not too fast," she said, imitating a posh English accent.

"Yes my Lady," returned Detective Martinez, acknowledging her wit. "Is this to be another mission, my Lady?"

"Yes Parker, operation homeward bound. I came out without my compact mirror." They laughed.

Later that evening, just before 9pm, Rebecca arrived at Gavin's house. The visit was purely to inform them of her arrest. Veronique had already enlightened Gavin that Rebecca had been called away by the police. The possible reason had led to wide speculation. Anxious for the full details Veronique greeted Rebecca on the Veranda.

"Was it anything serious?" asked Veronique.

"I should say so. Can you believe the interrogation I went through," said Rebecca as she entered the house.

"Not bad news was it?" enquired Gavin who was lying back on the sofa.

"I have been on tender hooks wondering what it was all about," said Veronique as she followed Rebecca into the living room.

"Tender hooks!" remarked Rebecca. "I have been read the riot act and arrested for possessing heroin."

"Heroin!" stressed Gavin, sitting up on the sofa. Veronique was stunned. She immediately made the connection to Susannah, who had previously planted heroin in Gavin's suitcase. Had Gavin also thought the same? But this is ludicrous, she thought. Susannah is dead.

"Apparently, the police had been informed that drug dealing was rife at Calypso Tavern, so had planned a raid," explained Rebecca. "The place was crawling with cops when I got there. They found a quantity of heroin hidden in my office, behind my bookcase. Consequently, they had plenty of questions to ask me. I've only just been released."

"And do they know who is behind this?" asked Veronique.

"They have questioned all the staff. To begin with they thought I was the offender, but I think I have convinced them otherwise. Lucky for me that Martinez showed up. He accepts I'm innocent," stated Rebecca. "By the way he sends his regards. He is a good sport. As he drove me home we pretended to be Lady Penelope and Parker from the Thunderbirds."

"Fancy that," said Gavin. "Martinez as Lady Penelope."

"Ha, ha very funny," said Rebecca. "It seems good to laugh now but I really thought I was spending the night in jail."

"It sounds like Martinez may have spoken in your favour," added Veronique.

"Yes I think he did. He said he believed me," relayed Rebecca.

"So is Calypso Tavern open tonight or have the police closed it down?" questioned Gavin.

"Open!" exclaimed Rebecca, implying it was a foolish thing to assume. "The place is closed. The customers this afternoon had to leave under police orders. The area was completely cornered off. There are still cops there now searching. I have been told we can open up as normal tomorrow, unless any further problems arise. If ever I find out who has done this, being handed over to the cops will be a blessing for them, given what I feel I may do if I get my hands on them," stated Rebecca angrily.

"Well at least they know you're not involved." said Gavin. "Drugs is more widespread today than it has ever been. I know exactly how you felt Rebecca. I still remember Officer Søli and the way he interrogated me."

"Yes of course you do. I had forgotten about that. But that was all to do with Susannah. This is probably an organised gang from South America. I saw a programme on TV about it recently. It predicted the drug problem would get worse. Why do people do stuff like this? Are people born without any sense? Anyway, I could murder a coffee," said Rebecca, sitting back in the armchair.

"You could have something stronger," suggested Gavin.

"Good idea. I'll have a rum and coke," remarked Rebecca. She rested her head back on the armchair and sighed heavily.

"You can relax now," said Veronique. "Drugs are a worldwide problem. I guess no one can escape it. At least they know you are innocent." Veronique then purposely changed the subject. "What time are your folks arriving tomorrow?" she briskly asked. Gavin went over to the drinks cabinet in the far corner of the room. He prepared himself a whisky and soda as well as a rum and coke for Rebecca.

"Veronique, shall I do you a drink?" asked Gavin.

"Of course, I will have a vodka and lime," replied Veronique.

"Coming up," he responded.

"My folks will be arriving by 5pm," informed Rebecca. "Wait till they hear about today's drama. They will insist all the more about me returning to Texas."

"Oh I think they gave up on that one long ago," mentioned Veronique. "By the way, I have their room ready, so as soon as they arrive they just need to make themselves at home."

"Are we collecting them from the jetty?" asked Gavin as he brought the drinks over.

"It was mentioned," replied Rebecca, "but I shall fetch them, after all, they are my parents and besides, I want to show off my new Mercedes."

"That reminds me," said Gavin. "Talking of holidays, Sebastian and Dominic return from their second honeymoon tomorrow or the day after."

"It's tomorrow night," corrected Veronique. "I only know because Sebastian sent me a text earlier to let us know when they will be returning so we can meet them at the jetty. I had to tell them we were busy, what with your folks coming, but I have arranged for Jake to fetch them. They have had a fantastic two weeks in Hawaii."

"I would love to go to Hawaii," said Rebecca. "The native music, the South Pacific Ocean. It always seems cleaner than the Atlantic."

"Did I mention Gavin that Mama and Pa are going to Egypt this year," commented Veronique.

"No, I don't think you mentioned it. I know Tobias has not said anything," remarked Gavin.

"Ah!" murmured Veronique. "Best not to say anything, I don't think Mama has told him yet."

"I can just imagine Loretta on the back of a camel, wedged between two humps," joked Rebecca.

"My vision entirely, only with a red fez on her head," remarked Gavin. They all laughed.

The evening transpired light-heartedly, giving a much-needed release for Rebecca after her stressful few hours with the police. Yet she knew it was an interim measure. The press at this very moment were publishing the story. Tomorrow, the morning papers would feature the drugs raid. Calypso Tavern may be open as normal, but the day would be far from its usual routine.

The morning papers that graced every household had various headlines, all depicting a disgraced Rebecca:

'Drugs raid at Calypso Tavern.'
'Casino deals drugs.'
'Calypso Tavern a drug dealers paradise.'
'Owner arrested for possessing heroin.'
'Chips, cards, cocktails and drugs.'

An unflattering photograph of Rebecca being led into a police car accompanied the headline. Gavin read through the article over breakfast. It certainly depicted Rebecca as an unsavoury character. Her reputation had been dented. The press had not pulled any punches in its onslaught of Rebecca and Calypso Tavern being a drug dealer's paradise. However, neither Rebecca nor Gavin were going to hideaway in shame. On the contrary, Gavin intended to utilise the press to counteract these slanderous reports.

Rebecca descended the mahogany staircase, having slept over last night. She had consumed too much alcohol, a mixture of rum and coke and dry white wine. She was too intoxicated to have driven back to her apartment. The last thing she needed was a drink driving charge adding to her current dilemma. Regrettably, she nursed a mild but annoying hangover as she sauntered into the dining room. An elegant dining table stood centrally, large enough to seat twelve people. A golden edged mirror hung on the adjacent wall against a crimson wall covering. Rebecca saw her reflection as she entered the dining room. Gavin sat at the table eating toast as he read the newspaper.

"Well just how bad is it?" she stated, pulling out a chair. Gavin looked up and saw the raw blurry-eyed Rebecca, no makeup, her hair dishevelled and wearing casual clothes. He applied humour and made a comparison to her photograph in the newspaper.

"It's a good thing the press took your photo yesterday and not this morning," he remarked.

"Ha ha, very funny," she replied, sitting down on the dining chair. "Can I read what they have written; do I have any self-respect left," came her sullen Texan drawl.

"Most of it is hype," replied Gavin. "But I've taken the bull by the horns and arranged a press interview for this afternoon, at 2pm. That will help to exonerate us. We can state something on the lines of how shocked we were at the discovery of heroin on the premises, and how we are helping the police with their investigation in this matter."

"Gee! You did not waste any time," reacted Rebecca, rather taken aback by the thought of speaking to the press. "What makes you think I wanna do that?"

"I'm willing to speak alone if you do not want to. I don't mean to force you, but I think it will be advantageous for you if you are there," responded Gavin.

"Well what have I got to lose," she reflected. "I guess it is kind of a positive thing to do, so long as you are there with me. I don't wanna talk to the press on my own."

"Don't worry, all will be fine," affirmed Gavin confidently. "We must show a united front and hit the problem head on. Show the world we have nothing to hide."

"If you say so," replied a tired Rebecca, yawning. "This afternoon huh! At least that gives me a few hours to recover from this hangover and make myself presentable."

"Are you sure a few hours will be long enough?" responded Gavin in a subtle voice. Rebecca looked at him. Words were not needed. The disdainful expression on her face said it all. At that moment Veronique entered the dining room, carrying Gregori.

"Say hello to Aunty Rebecca," she said to Gregori, in a babyish voice. Gregori chuckled and stretched out his one arm to Gavin. "You wanna go to Daddy," remarked Veronique as she moved towards her husband. Gavin stood up and took hold of his son.

"How is my big boy doing?" he said. Gregori laughed as he hugged his father.

"You wanna read the paper," suggested Rebecca to Veronique. "I'm famous at last," she added sarcastically, passing the newspaper to Veronique. Rebecca helped herself to a bowl of coconut wheat flakes. The box of cereal was already on the table, next to a jug of milk.

"Front page news I see," mentioned Veronique, sitting down opposite Rebecca.

"Yep!" remarked Rebecca. "And we are giving a press conference this afternoon at 2pm, so no doubt we will be front page news tomorrow as well."

"Rather you than me. I could not take all the fuss and publicity," commented Veronique. "But aren't your parents coming this afternoon?" she questioned as an afterthought.

"Not 'til 5pm, that's when they shall arrive at the jetty, so I shall have plenty of time to address my public," said Rebecca, the latter part of her sentence she spoke in a blasé fashion.

"No doubt we will get through this, heaven knows we have suffered far worse," stated Veronique. A melancholy pause occurred as one's mind suddenly drifted to thoughts of Susannah. How her wrath of evil still shrouded them in the wake of her murderous onslaught.

"I think we can safely say we can handle this," remarked Gavin, who had now sat down with Gregori on his lap. Veronique had already prepared his mashed up cereal of wheat and coconut with a variety of dried fruit. She handed the bowl to Gavin, who began to feed Gregori.

"Is your Daddy feeding you breakfast," said Veronique to her son. Gregori managed a few chuckles as he ate, but he was too interested in his breakfast to be distracted by his doting mother. Veronique watched with pleasure as she prepared her breakfast.

When the task of feeding his son breakfast was over, Gavin left the house to join Tobias in their office. Veronique had taken charge of Gregori by placing him in his playpen. She had free range to clear the breakfast things away. The little infant played happily with Marmajuke, Teddy and his toy helicopter. Rebecca indulged herself in a long hot bath in preparation for the afternoon press release. The scented bubble bath eased her hangover. She sipped a black coffee as she lay back in the heated water.

During the short walk to his office, Gavin's mind was on the forthcoming press release. He made a few mental notes of what to say. He entered his office, eager to jot down some sentences. Gavin believed the media coverage would be favourable. Tobias was already present and had just finished a telephone call as Gavin arrived. Tobias sighed despondently as he looked up at Gavin.

"Don't look so concerned Tobias," said Gavin, assuming his troubled expression was due to the drugs raid on Calypso Tavern. Gavin could see the morning newspaper on Tobias' desk, the front page displaying Rebecca's arrest. "I've arranged a press interview for 2pm this afternoon. That should quell the public fears and re-establish our credibility," informed Gavin.

"Perhaps we can kill two birds with one stone and announce the closure of our sugarcane plantation," responded Tobias bluntly.

"What!" exclaimed Gavin. "Don't tell me more ants."

"Correct, and as well as ants we have had yet another e-mail from Global Incorporations Ltd about their takeover bid, and why we haven't replied to their earlier correspondence."

"This can not be happening," sighed Gavin as he approached his desk. "Let me see this e-mail." Tobias turned his laptop towards Gavin. The e-mail was on full screen. "Just who is this company," remarked Gavin angrily as he read the e-mail. "Have you replied back?"

"No, not without speaking to you first."

"My position is quite clear. We are not for sale," stated Gavin as he commenced typing his reply to the same effect. "I would rather go bankrupt than sell out," he remarked as he sent his brief but curt reply to Global Incorporations Ltd.

"Be careful what you wish for," said Tobias. "Going bankrupt is not at arms length. The environmental health officer is on his way over, and I fear he will temporarily close us down until this problem with ants is resolved."

"But they can't do that? We have adhered to their regulations, they have checked us over, they know we are not at fault," defended Gavin. "The problem must be with Carter's."

"I said as much to Hezron when he rang just now, that's who was on the phone when you arrived. He will be here within the hour," informed Tobias.

Punctuality was one of Hezron's qualities. He arrived forty minutes later to dispel his official duty. He handed Gavin the temporary closure warrant, suspending all operational activity until the matter regarding the infestation of ants was rectified. The warrant was not a determination of guilt. It bore no relevance as to who may be at fault. Public health and safety was paramount. The risk of allowing the business to continue would be to compromise public health and safety. The environmental health agency would be found negligent if they allowed Gavin's sugarcane plantation business to continue, knowing there was a serious breech of hygiene, either by error or by intentional means by person or persons unknown. It was not the duty nor intention for the environment health agency to make any business go bankrupt. But they had to exercise their responsibility. They will offer any guidance necessary to ensure a business can continue without jeopardising public health and safety. Hezron was sympathetic. His only advice was for them to contact the police, and let them investigate who is causing this problem. Could it be a disgruntled ex-employee?

Hezron left the office. Gavin and Tobias contemplated their next course of action. Gavin sat at his desk, the closure warrant still in his hand.

"I'll call the police," said Tobias. "They have got to treat this as urgent. Too much is at stake."

"There's not much else we can do," reflected Gavin.

"We can still continue to plant new crop, we just can't harvest," stated Tobias.

"We shall have to have a staff meeting and let them know the situation, probably have to stand some people down," mentioned Gavin. "I'll go and tell Detsen the news and to stop further production." Gavin stood up, leaving the closure warrant on his desk. "Sebastian comes back from his holiday tonight, could you send him an e-mail to request an urgent meeting first thing tomorrow. This is going to financially cripple us, and I don't fancy the outcome. Let's hope Sebastian can work a financial miracle," finished Gavin as he walked towards the door. He hesitated and turned to face Tobias. "I would appreciate it if Veronique and Loretta don't know what is happening, not until we have spoken to Sebastian at any rate. There's no point in worrying them unnecessarily."

"I agree," said Tobias. "Mind you it won't be long till tongues are wagging once the staff know."

"No doubt the press will have yet another field day at our expense when they find out," responded Gavin before leaving the office. Tobias bleeped Detsen to put him in the picture.

The press entourage gathered outside Calypso Tavern. The time was approaching 2pm. Rebecca and Gavin had arrived an hour earlier to prepare their statements. They now stood at the entrance proud and confident, giving the illusion of innocence and a victim of someone else's criminality. Rebecca was smartly dressed, wearing a lemon top with a flora sarong. Gavin wore business shorts and a turquoise short-sleeved shirt. Chester Hargreaves, being their legal representative stood by their side. The native Caribbean wore a full business suit, quite inappropriate in this summer heat, but essential for the professional image he wanted to portray. Yet for some that image symbolised oppression in men's fashion. The worldwide fashion industry with its fashion magazines clearly catered for women first and men second. How the male fashion market was treated unfairly. Where was the entrepreneurial approach that had transformed women's fashion, and why had it not succeeded for men?

Rebecca, Gavin and Chester Hargreaves stood side by side. They faced the group of avaricious journalists who were eager for some scandalous confession. They were going to be disappointed. Gavin was ready to address them. Unwelcoming as this event was, it did give Gavin a temporary respite from his concerns over the plantation closure.

"I am sure you have all read today's newspapers," began Gavin. "Half of you probably wrote the articles," he added, attempting to apply a touch of humour. "We were shocked and disappointed that someone was using our premises for their illicit gain. We can assure everyone that Rebecca and I are not involved, and are glad to help the police with their enquiries. We do not take drugs, have never taken drugs, and are not dealing in drugs. I cannot emphasise that enough."

"Do you have any idea who is behind this?" asked a reporter.

"No we don't," replied Rebecca. "But we are as eager as you are to find out who is responsible."

"What measures have you taken to prevent any further drug dealing at Calypso Tavern?" asked another reporter.

"We have increased our security measures. As you can see we have CCTV cameras just about everywhere," informed Rebecca, indicating to a nearby CCTV camera.

"The police are also sifting through hours of CCTV footage already taken, to see if they can detect a likely suspect," added Gavin.

"This is not the first time you have been arrested for possessing heroin is it?" asked a reporter. "Weren't you arrested at Oslo airport a few years ago Gavin for possessing heroin?"

"That was a completely different matter and not related to this in any way," responded Gavin harshly. He did not like being reminded of Susannah's plot to kidnap him. "You all know about Susannah's several attempts to kill me and how she planted heroin in my suitcase. I take a dim view of using that to try and discredit us."

"I was merely comparing the two incidents, and as the saying goes, lightening never strikes twice," commented the same reporter.

"We can only reiterate that we are fully cooperating with the police. They seem to think we are innocent, so why should you think any different," remarked Rebecca.

"Now if you can excuse us," interrupted Chester Hargreaves. "My clients have nothing further to add. You can rest assured we will keep you informed of developments. In the meantime it is business as usual. Calypso Tavern will function as before," relayed Chester Hargreaves with an air of importance. He acknowledged the journalists, then silently ushered Gavin and Rebecca into Calypso Tavern. Once all three were inside they quickly closed the doors behind them, keeping the press outside.

"Relief!" sighed Rebecca.

"All went as planned," said Gavin. "Except for their reference to Susannah. How dare they rake that up!"

"Indeed," added Chester Hargreaves. "That is the press for you, eager to make the innocent person the vilest offender, but do not worry, with me acting on your behalf you can't go wrong," he said triumphantly. Secretly, Chester Hargreaves was revelling in the limelight. Being photographed and the possibility of his words being quoted in tomorrow's newspapers sent a surge of excitement. He was enjoying his brief moment of fame.

"Well thank you Chester," remarked Gavin. "We will see you shortly but right now I need to get back to my office."

"Of course, you can rely on me," replied Chester Hargreaves.

"I have a few things here to sort out," mentioned Rebecca. "Then I've got to meet my folks at the jetty, so I will see you Gavin back at the house. And Chester, thank you for your support."

"It was nothing really, just doing my job," he replied in a demure fashion.

<>

After finishing her morning shift at the hospital, Veronique was preparing Ursula and Godwin's room. She placed a decorative floral arrangement on the dressing table. Gregori was happily playing in his playpen in the nursery, which was opposite the guest room. A typical boyish nursery, pale blue décor with teddy bears, cars and plenty of soft cuddly toys. He seemed a happy child and showed traits of independence and creativity. Every so often one would hear him attempt to sing *The Mango Tree* nursery rhyme. His speech was not fully developed but that did not deter him from using his vocal cords. He enjoyed his gurgling sounds and the attention it brought him.

Veronique had finished preparing the guest room and stood in the doorway of the nursery. She watched her son clutching Marmajuke, his toy monkey. In his own babyish voice Gregori tried to recite *The Mango Tree* nursery rhyme to Marmajuke, as if imitating the times when the nursery rhyme had been sung to him. He did not spot his mother standing in the doorway, for his back was towards her. Veronique watched, proud and happy. These special moments would soon disappear as he grew older. This was all the more reason not to have a nanny. Unfortunately the telephone rang, causing Veronique to leave the nursery. She headed into her bedroom to answer the upstairs extension.

"Hello, Veronique speaking."

"Hi Veronique, it's Karl here," came his abrupt reply.

"Hi Karl, haven't spoken to you for a while. If you want Gavin he's in his office," she stated, sitting down on the bed. "Is everything ok you seem..."

"No! It is you I want to speak to," interrupted Karl. Veronique noticed the urgency in his voice.

"I see, well that means it has nothing to do with the ski resort, so what is the matter?" asked a cautious Veronique.

"No easy way to say this, but you know when I rang a few weeks ago about Tor Hegland being murdered, and it made me think Susannah could have killed him." Karl paused, which allowed Veronique to respond.

"Look Karl, we have been through this before. Susannah is dead. She could not have killed Tor Hegland. Besides, the police now have the person who did kill him."

"Not so Veronique, the police have let him go. Apparently the forensic evidence they have rules him out. It proves the guy they arrested for Tor Hegland's murder did not do it. Although this guy confessed to begin with, he has now retracted his confession. His doctor has vouched that he suffers with a psychotic illness where he admits guilt to attain attention," informed Karl.

"I do not like what I am hearing Karl," retorted Veronique, her happy and content feelings of a moment ago had quickly vanished. "You were there. You killed Susannah. You stabbed her to death with a ski stick. She cannot be alive. How is it possible?" demanded Veronique. "You should not ring here and stir up old wounds, it is just too painful."

"Hey I'm sorry Veronique, I felt I had to tell you, warn you," stated Karl.

"There is nothing to warn us about. Susannah is dead. Detective Martinez has even investigated further, so there is no need to worry. We have moved on with our lives. For goodness sake Karl don't mention any of this to Gavin."

"I do not mean to be insensitive," replied Karl. "I won't say anything to Gavin, that's why I thought I should speak to you."

"That woman is dead, full stop, end of story," reiterated Veronique. "I'm sorry for sounding harsh, but just when I have peace of mind I don't want to be reminded of the last eight years of hell that woman put me through," stated Veronique angrily. Karl sighed, he knew he had riled Veronique.

"Perhaps you are right. I still have nightmares over killing her at the cable car station, only in my dreams she doesn't die," remarked Karl.

"Maybe you need sleeping tablets as well as Gavin. Let Susannah be alive in your dreams, but in real life she is now dead," concluded Veronique.

CHAPTER FIVE

The Ransom

She will kill him! She will kill him!

Veronique and Loretta were putting the finishing touches to their welcome buffet for Ursula and Godwin. Veronique's spirit had lifted since her stern reply to Karl. She had not mentioned the telephone call to anyone, including Loretta. How many more times will she suffer mental anguish at the thought of Susannah being alive? She was practically tormenting herself. No matter what Veronique did, be it housework; seeing to Gregori; or her nurse's shift at the hospital, her mind would wonder if Susannah was alive. Had Susannah killed Tor Hegland? Veronique used the buffet preparations as a distraction. She made every effort to dispel her pessimistic connotations.

Tobias sat in the living room watching early evening television. As he flicked through the channels his mind pondered the effects of the temporary closure warrant. In all the years he had worked on the plantation, business had never been as dire. There had to be a lifeline somewhere. The business was strong and well established. Surely it would not crumble in a matter of a few weeks?

Gavin was upstairs, spending time with Gregori in his nursery. The worries of the plantation business were still troubling him, but he intended to keep matters to himself. He and Tobias had decided not to inform their spouses until they had a positive solution. Hopefully Sebastian will provide a financial window of escape, once he returns from his holiday. Gavin stood by the nursery window, holding Gregori in his arms. The doting father sang Gregori's favourite nursery rhyme.

Sit beneath a mango tree.
Gazing at the sunny sea.
See an egret soaring high.
Soon my boy you'll touch the sky.
Soon my boy you'll touch the sky.

Flying high just like a bird.
Flap your wings just coo and chirp.
See below that mango tree.
Sitting there is you and me.
Sitting there is you and me.

Gregori sang along in his babyish voice. He was more than familiar with the rhyme for Veronique and Loretta sang it to him almost everyday. He was eager to learn all the words so he could sing it to Marmajuke. The view from the nursery window was picturesque. The sun rested on the surrounding treetops as it gently eased downwards. The entrance to Gavin's estate was also in view. Moments later Rebecca's blue Mercedes drove up the palm-fringed driveway.

"Look Gregori, Aunty Rebecca is here with Ursula and Godwin," stated Gavin.

"Urs, Urs, G'in, G'in," uttered Gregori in excitement as he attempted to pronounce their names. Gavin carried Gregori out of the nursery and stood at the overhanging balcony.

"They're here," he shouted down to Tobias, who seemed engrossed with the documentary he was watching on the television. Gavin descended the stairs with Gregori lying in his arms, pretending to be an aeroplane. Gavin gurgled, trying to imitate the noise of the engine. His son found it highly exciting.

"Rebecca's here," called out Tobias to Veronique and Loretta. They were still in the dining room. Tobias turned off the television. Seconds later Veronique and Loretta emerged.

"We know Pa, we saw them coming up the driveway," remarked Veronique, moving over to the entrance hall to welcome them. Loretta followed her out on to the veranda in her usual excited disposition. Rebecca's pale blue Mercedes pulled up outside the house. During the drive from the jetty, Rebecca had informed her parents of recent events. How does one react when told their daughter had been arrested for drugs? And had become a journalistic target with negative press reports on the front page in all the local papers. As predicted, Ursula and Godwin reinforced their request for Rebecca to return to Texas. They maintained life in Martinique was too cut and thrust with too many problems and too much grief. Rebecca refuted their concerns. Life is full of problems where ever you happen to live.

The Mercedes roof was concertinaed back. Both parents had felt like celebrities being driven through the streets in such an exclusive vehicle. Ursula and Godwin saw Veronique and Loretta on the veranda as they approached the house. They made eye contact and waved at them. Veronique and Loretta returned the acknowledgement. Rebecca parked and the occupants soon vacated the vehicle. At last the journey was over. A joyous moment filled the air as they all greeted each other with hugs and kisses, laughter and merriment. This was a moment to be cherished and appreciated for it seldom occurred, but unbeknown to the Harrison family the merriment would be short-lived. Within less than twenty-four hours utter turmoil would grip the family.

"You all look so well," commented Ursula as she embraced Loretta. "It is so kind of you to let us stay at the house."

"Consider it your second home, it's good to have you staying," responded Loretta.

"Well Godwin and I must take you all out to dinner one night, perhaps that Mexican restaurant I have heard so much about," stated Ursula.

"Tobias, have you driven Rebecca's new Mercedes?" asked Godwin as Tobias appeared on the veranda.

"No Pa he hasn't," answered Rebecca. "No one else has driven my Mercedes and that's how it will remain, including you."

"Not even a little drive around the estate," teased Godwin. Ursula was quick to reply.

"The only driving you'll be doing is driving me around the bend. He has gone on about nothing else since Rebecca met us."

"You don't need to tell us what men are like," reflected Loretta. "Anyway, come inside. We have a buffet waiting to be eaten."

"How is your job as a nurse Veronique?" enquired Ursula. "I simply must give you credit. I could not do that job, can't stand the sight of blood."

"You get use to that, and after awhile nothing seems as gruesome. But my job is even better now I am part-time," she replied. Gavin stepped on to the veranda carrying Gregori on his shoulders.

"Doesn't he look a picture, an absolute angel," commented Ursula.

"Thank you Ursula. The years have been kind to me. I have retained my youthfulness," replied Gavin humorously.

"Oh aren't you the one. I was referring to Gregori," laughed Ursula.

"Take no notice of him," added Veronique.

"How are you Gavin?" asked Ursula.

"I can't complain," he replied. "This one here keeps us busy, never a dull moment. Did you have a pleasant journey?"

"Yes we did, and we are looking forward to having a relaxing time now we are here. A rest from the ranch," informed Ursula.

"We can't guarantee you'll get much of a rest with Gregori," added Veronique. "He likes to be up very early."

"Oh that won't be a problem, trust me. I'm used to Godwin's snoring keeping me awake," remarked Ursula.

"I do not snore," retorted Godwin.

"Remember the tape recorder," replied Ursula, glancing at her husband.

"Tape recorder?" questioned Veronique.

"Yes, I taped him snoring one night. He would not believe me otherwise," stated Ursula.

"What a good idea," remarked Loretta. "Tobias did you hear that? He too thinks he doesn't snore."

"Will we be eating this buffet tonight?" questioned a hungry Tobias and purposely changing the subject.

"When ever he loses the argument he always changes the subject," commented Loretta. Ursula laughed again.

"Perhaps he and Godwin should have a snoring competition," joked Ursula.

"Let's not encourage them," responded Loretta.

"Are you still working at the craft shop?" asked Ursula as they mounted the veranda steps.

"Yes I am. You can come and work a shift with me if you like," suggested Loretta.

"I think I may just do that. I know I must buy me a souvenir," replied Ursula.

Introductions abated as they all poured inside the house. Tobias was eager to devour the buffet. He headed straight to the dining room. He disobeyed Loretta's command of aperitifs, his stomach demanded otherwise. Tobias viewed the layout of food on the dining table with awe. A Papaya salad with crab and prawns; a bowl of boiled Jasmine rice; an assortment of pizza slices were next to a platter of fish cakes; various bowls of nibbles; but the centre piece was a Mexican tortilla cheesecake filled with herbs, mild spices and mixed vegetables between the several tortilla layers. For dessert Loretta had baked a mango cranberry nut crumble to be served with lashings of custard or ice cream. For those unable to divulge in such a delight the second option was a mixture of dried fruits including pomelo, strawberries, peaches and apricots with a sprinkle of shredded coconut. How Tobias would love a portion of mango cranberry nut crumble right now. However, not wanting to be too impolite, he merely sneaked a quick morsel to satisfy his stomach. A couple of vol-au-vents did the trick. Tobias returned to the living room, his cheeks bulging as he consumed his snack. The buzz of conversations filled the room. Gregori now sat on the sofa, clutching Marmajuke. Gavin began to hand out drinks. Loretta had her usual rum-ginger liqueur. Veronique had a small tequila, and Ursula a sherry. Godwin wanted a beer but decided to have a whisky before food. Rebecca abstained as she was still nursing a headache. Gavin poured himself a whisky and soda, and then handed a rum and black to Tobias.

"You can propose a toast," requested Gavin to Tobias as he handed him his drink.

"Those vol-au-vents were divine," he remarked as he received his rum and black.

"I hope you left some for the rest of us," remarked Loretta, throwing her beloved a humorous but scornful glare. "At least I know how to resist food. That's why I am so slim and elegant."

"My good woman have you not looked in the mirror lately," came Tobias' reply.

"It's a bit difficult, you always seem to be in it," replied Loretta. "At least the yellow and red hair has gone," she added as an afterthought. After a few seconds of laughter, Tobias proposed a toast.

"To good health, happiness and may sadness be a thing of the past," he proclaimed.

"Good health and happiness," muttered everyone.

Several hours later, the buffet had been eaten and far too many drinks had been consumed. Loretta was quite merry after her seventh or was it eighth rum-ginger liqueur. She eagerly told various stories and humorous anecdotes, despite her lack of sobriety. Godwin made a reference to the good old days when women obeyed men and life was strictly organised. He was not a male chauvinist but was trying to persuade his daughter to let him drive her new Mercedes. Cars belong in a man's world. The plentiful comments from the females soon curtailed his argument. Tobias came to his rescue by advising him to admit defeat before he dug an even bigger hole for himself. Over the years Tobias had acquired the knack of a sapient comment.

The evening unravelled with more food being consumed. All sat in the living room, too bloated to move as if they had finished running a marathon. The only person who was not feeling lethargic was Gregori. He was still full of energy and enjoyed being centre of attention. Yet even his energy levels faded as midnight approached. It was way past his bedtime. He sat beside Veronique on the sofa, his head resting against her arm. His eyes closed as he began to nod off.

"I think Mummy needs to put Gregori to bed," said Veronique.

"No, no, no," uttered Gregori, forcing himself to keep awake. Seconds later his eyes closed and his head flopped downwards.

"Is Gregori going to sleep in his own bed tonight?" mentioned Veronique to her son. He did not reply. His eyes were shut. The little infant had fallen asleep. "He often ends up sleeping in our bed, but at the same time keeping us awake," explained Veronique.

"They do at that age," commented Ursula. "You must show me his nursery."

"Of course, you can come with me when I take him up," replied Veronique. "And thanks for offering to baby-sit, it will be a great help. I seem unable to choose a nanny at the moment."

"The ones we have interviewed seem very capable, but Veronique can't allow herself to let a stranger nurture Gregori. Her maternal instincts are too strong," remarked Loretta.

"Well that's to be expected," responded Ursula. "And it gives me the pleasure of looking after him whenever you want, while we're here."

"Thanks," said Veronique. "I hope you don't regret saying that. I have some double shifts I need to do at the hospital due to staff holidays, it's that time of year again."

"Talking of holidays," chirped in Loretta. "Tobias and I are off to Egypt this year."

"Are we?" questioned Tobias.

"Yes we are, and there's no need to look so vague; I told you about it the other night," relayed Loretta.

"Sounds like you're goin' to Egypt," mentioned Godwin to Tobias. "I wouldn't mind seeing the pyramids. I often thought we should go some day."

"Since when were you interested in all things Egyptian?" questioned Ursula.

"Never took you for a historian, Pa," stated Rebecca.

"Now just because I like being a cowboy on a Texan ranch, does not mean I don't appreciate other lifestyles, especially historical ones," informed Godwin.

"We went to England a few years ago, didn't we Godwin. It was a lovely seaside town. There were plenty of attractions and the beach was inviting. It was my first time in England. I always wanted to go," informed Ursula.

"Where did you stay?" asked Gavin.

"I can't remember the name. It was a short name and unusually spelt, some beautiful countryside too. Mind you there were a lot of Germans about, least I think they were German," remarked Ursula. "We went on a day trip to a castle that was called…now not Cassidy…oh Godwin what was it called?"

"You have a memory like a sieve my dear. It was Cardiff Castle and we stayed at Rhyl," informed Godwin. Gavin began to laugh.

"You said it was your first time to England?" questioned Gavin still laughing.

"Yes," replied Ursula. "We must go again some day. But do tell the joke."

"Sorry to disappoint, only you were not in England. That country was Wales, which is next to England," stated Gavin. "And they have their own language which you may have mistaken for German."

"You mean we were not in England? I'm all confused," responded Ursula. "I thought that little island was all England."

"You are not the first to make that mistake. Scotland is at the top with England underneath and Wales to the left," commented Gavin.

"That was your fault Godwin. I said we should have gone to London, now that is England," remarked Ursula.

"It was too expensive," retorted Godwin. "Besides, we had a lovely time, didn't we? You said you wanted to return."

"Well that's neither here nor there," acknowledged Ursula.

"We haven't discussed our holiday plans yet," said Gavin.

"No we haven't," replied Veronique. "Not sure if we can go on holiday at the moment with Gregori."

"Ah look at him," said Rebecca. "He has fallen asleep." All eyes turned to see Gregori. His head lay against Veronique's side, his eyes were closed and his mouth slightly open. He looked like a Cherub from a religious painting.

"I think it is time for bed," said Veronique as she gently lifted him up. "I'll show you the nursery Ursula, if you like."

"Certainly," she replied.

Not long after Gregori had been put to bed the others soon retired. It was almost 1am. Loretta and Tobias strolled back to the cabana, arm in arm as they walked in the moonlight. The air was still and fresh. Rebecca drove back to her apartment above Calypso Tavern. Unlike last night she had refrained from drinking any alcohol. Ursula and Godwin settled into the guest room, which was opposite the nursery. They had not yet unpacked their suitcases. They quickly put away some of their clothes before getting into bed.

"Isn't this such a lovely house? I feel like royalty every time we stay here," said Ursula.

"Is that a hint for me to redecorate the ranch?" questioned Godwin.

"It would take more than a pot of paint to match this exotic abode. But please feel free to redecorate," responded Ursula. "And they are such a lovely family. Greg would have made a good husband for our Rebecca, I'm sure of it."

"Do you want me to leave the light on?"

"The sidelight will do fine," replied Ursula. They got into bed. "Goodnight Godwin."

"Goodnight Ursula."

"Goodnight Loretta, Tobias, Gavin and Veronique," said Ursula.

"Goodnight Ursula and Godwin," called back Veronique.

"Goodnight too Rebecca," added Godwin, not that she could hear.

"It's just like an episode of The Waltons," finished Ursula. She lay in bed. Within seconds Godwin was snoring.

Veronique and Gavin embraced each other as they lay awake. Neither said a word. Gavin's mind deliberated over the plantation problems, whilst Veronique could not shun thoughts of Susannah.

<>

By 7am dawn had broken. The morning birds were chirping as they nestled in the surrounding trees. Perhaps their dawn chorus had caused Ursula to awake, or had she heard an unexplained noise? She lay still for a while, listening to nature's music. Unable to resist the temptation she got up.

"Gregori is bound to be awake," she muttered and gently got out of bed, mindful not to wake her husband. She glanced at the bedside clock. Godwin snored as she reached for her peach dressing gown that lay on an adjacent chair. The design of her dressing gown matched the peach nightdress she wore. It had been last year's anniversary present from Godwin. Peach was her favourite colour and it suited her brown skin. For a few seconds she admired herself in the full-length mirror. Her eyes viewed the decorative lace design. She tied the embroidered belt, and then brushed her hair. She gave a fleeting glance over her right shoulder to see Godwin lying asleep in bed. She smiled, thirty-eight years they had been married. It was a happy marriage with no regrets. They would have liked more children but despite many attempts Rebecca remained an only child, all the more reason why Ursula was overexcited with Gregori. She would enjoy spending time with the little boy. She tiptoed out of the room, careful not to make a noise as she opened and closed the bedroom door. After walking the few paces to the nursery, she quietly opened the door. Not a sound could be heard. On approaching Gregori's bed she viewed the teddies and toys that filled the room. However, her excitement soon faded as she noticed Gregori was not in his bed.

"That'll teach me for being a silly old woman," she muttered. "No doubt Gregori is in Veronique and Gavin's bed, like he often is." Mission unaccomplished she returned to her bedroom, only this time she was less pedantic about making a noise or waking her husband. "Godwin are you awake?" she quietly said as she ambled back into bed, still with her dressing gown on.

"I'm asleep," replied Godwin. Ursula sat upright in bed feeling somewhat disappointed.

"I went to see if Gregori was awake, play with him for a while," recounted Ursula.

"I thought that's where you went," murmured Godwin. "I've been awake for a few minutes. So was he asleep?"

"No, Gregori wasn't in his room. He's obviously sleeping with Veronique and Gavin. I wanted to sing that nursery rhyme to him; you know the one about a mango tree. Loretta says it's his favourite. I've been trying to remember all the words. It has been a long time since I sang it to Rebecca when she was a little girl. Now how does it go?" she paused before attempting to recite the first verse:

Sit beneath the mango tree.
da da, da da, da da dom.
See an Egret soaring high.
Soon my boy you'll touch the sky.

Soon my boy you'll touch the sky.

"I can't remember the second line," said Ursula.

"Sing it again," suggested Godwin. Ursula did just that but still she could not remember the second line.

"I shall have to ask Veronique," uttered Ursula.

"I think I've got it. *Gazing at the sunny sea.*" sang Godwin.

"Why that's it. You never cease to amaze me," complimented Ursula. They spent a few more minutes singing the rhyme several times over, with Godwin harmonising here and there.

7.15am was the normal time Veronique awoke for work and today was no exception, only she was not due in until 10am. Therefore she allowed herself an extra hour in bed. Gavin was still asleep. They had managed a night's sleep without Gregori waking them up, or climbing into their bed. Veronique was in need of the bathroom so got out of bed. Whilst she was up she went to check on Gregori. For a brief moment she became startled when she discovered he was not in the nursery. Her fears were allayed when she heard Ursula and Godwin singing *The Mango Tree* nursery rhyme. She assumed Gregori was with them, why else would they be singing the rhyme. Veronique would have entered but as she was not adequately dressed she decided against it. She knew Gregori would be safe with them and she knew how eager Ursula was to baby-sit. Nothing like being thrown in at the deep end.

"I hope they know what they have let themselves in for," whispered Veronique. "Typical of my little boy demanding attention. Now let's have that extra hour of sleep." She got back into bed.

Gavin awoke at 8am. He left Veronique asleep as he got up, showered and dressed. His mind was still preoccupied with thoughts of the plantation business. It was important for he and Tobias to iron out a survival package with Sebastian. Gavin also intended to contact the police to see if there were any further developments as to who was sabotaging the business. The culprit must be caught and preferably before they went bankrupt. Gavin left the house without any breakfast. He would have a coffee and a light snack at the office.

At 9.10 Veronique awoke from a deep sleep. Torpidly and feeling as though she could still sleep for a week, she looked at her bedside clock.

"Ten past nine!" she exclaimed, pulling back the quilt. "Why did I not set the alarm?" she cursed. "Now I will be late for work." Within ten minutes she had showered, gripped her hair together for quickness and dressed in her nurse's uniform. There was not time for breakfast or seeing to Gregori. Thank goodness Ursula is here to take care of him, she thought.

Veronique descended the mahogany staircase. She saw Ursula and Godwin sitting on the sofa.

"Did you two sleep ok?" asked Veronique, rushing down the stairs. "You must excuse me. I have overslept and am late for work."

"We slept fine and don't you worry about us you get yourself ready," stated Godwin.

"I'm surprised you overslept," mentioned Ursula. "I'd have thought Gregori would have kept you awake."

"Normally yes, but not today," remarked Veronique as she hurried past them towards the kitchen. "I hope he did not rob you of too much sleep. Is he in the nursery?" she called out as she disappeared into the kitchen. Veronique quickly grabbed a glass of mango juice. Ursula and Godwin looked at each other in puzzlement.

"We haven't seen Gregori today," called out Ursula. Veronique quickly backtracked into the living room with a carton of mango juice in her hand.

"He was with you earlier, just after 7am this morning," stated Veronique.

"No, we have not seen him," reiterated Godwin.

"I did go and check on him at about 7am, but he was not in his nursery. I thought he was in your room," stated Ursula.

"But I heard you singing *The Mango Tree* nursery rhyme," responded Veronique.

"Yes we were singing the song but Gregori was not with us," said Godwin.

"I don't understand? It is not like him to be so quiet!" remarked Veronique. There was a noticeable quiver in her voice. She sensed something was wrong. Veronique placed the carton of juice on to the side table and shouted out his name. There was no response. She then ran up the staircase. Ursula and Godwin stood up; both were at a loss of what to do. Veronique ran into the nursery. She called out Gregori's name but only silence followed. She noticed his quilt was pulled back. She looked around the room, everything seemed normal, but where was he? Veronique ran into all the other bedrooms in a frantic search to find her son, but there was no sign of him anywhere. She dashed back to the overhanging balcony. In fear she griped the banister rail as she looked down at Ursula and Godwin.

"He is not up here!" she exclaimed. Her pretty face displayed a fearful expression.

"Now let's not panic," stated Ursula. "There may be a simple explanation."

"Could he be with Loretta?" suggested Godwin. Without uttering a word Veronique grabbed her mobile from her pocket and speed dialled.

"Mama is Gregori with you?" she hastily spoke the second Loretta had answered.

"No," came Loretta's stunned reply.

"He's gone missing Mama," stated Veronique emotionally.

"I'm on my way over," affirmed Loretta. Veronique ended the call.

"I don't know what to do," said Veronique as she rapidly descended the stairs.

"Godwin and I will check all the rooms down here," began Ursula. "You know what children are like, they are into everything. He's probably asleep in a cupboard somewhere, he did have such a late night last night," stated Ursula, attempting to pacify Veronique. Godwin rushed into the kitchen. You could hear him opening and closing all the kitchen cupboards.

"I'll ring Gavin," said Veronique. "Maybe he has taken him to the office?"

"Why didn't we think of that sooner?" replied Ursula. "That is so likely."

"But he has been missing since 7am," pondered Veronique as reality began to dawn. She fumbled with her mobile and rang Gavin, only for him to tell her Gregori was not there. "We can't find him anywhere!" she cried out.

Gavin left the office. He checked outside as he made his way back to the house, calling out for his son. Veronique was in a state of panic. Ursula tried to remain in control.

"Did you look in the wardrobes upstairs?" asked Ursula in a hopeful manner.

"Wardrobes?" questioned Veronique.

"Yes, kids love to play in wardrobes. He is probably asleep in one," assured Ursula. Veronique stood motionless. Her eyes widened with fear.

"Wardrobes," she whispered. "Wardrobes...Wardrobes," she repeated, each time with more emotion and fear. "Susannah hid in the wardrobe!" she exclaimed. The realisation was too much. She screamed out, "Susannah has got my baby!" Her reaction startled Ursula. Veronique began to hyperventilate as she continued screaming out, "Susannah has got my baby!"

"Keep calm Veronique," urged Ursula. She stood in front of the fraught female and placed her hands on Veronique's shoulders. "What is this nonsense about Susannah? Susannah is dead," questioned Ursula. Veronique emitted a deep drawn out groan as she emotionally exclaimed:

"Susannah has got my baby!" Her legs gave way as she collapsed to the floor. Ursula was powerless to support her. Veronique sat on the floor in a semi trance-like state and screamed out yet again, "Susannah has got my baby! She will kill him! She will kill him!" Veronique's emotional screams sent shivers down Ursula's spine. Godwin returned from the kitchen. He shook his head to indicate Gregori was not there. The sight of seeing Veronique sitting on the floor, wailing as if in excruciating agony, was enough to melt the heart or prick the conscience of the most violent offender.

"Godwin, check upstairs and look in all of the wardrobes," ordered Ursula as she tried to console Veronique. Godwin obeyed his wife. He was halfway up the staircase when Loretta entered the house. She saw her daughter on the floor in deep distress and rushed over.

"Oh my God! What has happened? Is Gregori missing?" questioned Loretta. She knelt down and embraced Veronique. Breathing rapidly, Veronique was unable to respond. She kept moaning emotionally how Susannah will kill Gregori. Veronique hyperventilated and fainted. Loretta cradled her daughter.

"We can't find Gregori anywhere," informed Ursula. "At 7am this morning I checked in on him and he wasn't in his nursery. I thought he was with Veronique and Gavin, but apparently not so," explained Ursula.

"Oh this is dreadful," remarked Loretta, rocking gently back and forth to comfort her child. "But what's this about Susannah?"

A Certain Dilemma

"I don't understand? Does Veronique think Susannah has kidnapped him? But how can it be since Susannah is dead?" commented Ursula.

"Oh my God! May the Lord have mercy," sighed Loretta, her voice denoted much concern. "Is that woman alive?" she murmured. Their attention was diverted as Gavin rushed into the house, closely followed by Tobias. Gavin was shocked to see his wife lying unconscious on the floor, her upper body resting on Loretta's lap. Was he to think the worst? He fumbled a string of words together as he uttered:

"Is she ok? What has happened? Where is Gregori?"

"Veronique has fainted," acknowledged Loretta. "And Gregori has gone missing."

"We should call the police," remarked Tobias.

"I think we must, straight away," uttered Godwin as he re-appeared at the overhanging balcony. All looked up at him. He held what seemed to be a letter in his hand. "This is a ransom demand. Gregori has been kidnapped," he informed. He proceeded to descend the staircase. Veronique began to murmur as she regained consciousness.

"Come on, wake up Veronique," said Loretta. Gavin knelt at his wife's side and tapped her face.

"Everything will be ok, I'm here," assured Gavin as he hugged Veronique. His reassurance did not comfort her as Veronique suddenly became aware of reality.

"Susannah has Gregori," she said in a panicked voice. Her voice quivered and became hoarse as she tried to speak further. "He has been missing for hours."

"I'll fetch you a glass of water Veronique," said Ursula and hastened towards the kitchen. Tobias used his mobile and called the police.

"Ask for Detective Martinez to come over," interrupted Veronique.

"Why Detective Martinez?" questioned Gavin.

"It's Susannah, she has Gregori," stated Veronique.

"Susannah is dead Veronique," remarked Gavin.

"Gavin, why don't you read the ransom note." advised Godwin. "I found it under Gregori's bed."

"There's a ransom note?" questioned Veronique. "What does it say? Is it from Susannah? Of course it is, this is the sort of evil joke she would do," sobbed Veronique. Ursula returned with a glass of water.

"Come on drink this, you need to relax so we can focus on what to do next," encouraged Ursula. Gavin read out the ransom demand:

"No need to fret Veronique, your baby is quite safe and won't be harmed. I shall be in touch to discuss the $2million ransom."

"Has Susannah signed it?" asked Loretta.

"No. It is not signed. That's all it says," said Gavin.

"It has to be Susannah," proclaimed Veronique. "She mentions my name, a stranger wouldn't do that. It's her way of gloating over my pain." Tears rolled down her cheeks as she continued. "She will kill him. I know she will. He will need feeding; his nappy changing; he won't stop crying. How is she gonna manage with him? She will just kill him!" cried out Veronique.

"The police are on their way over, including Detective Martinez," informed Tobias.

"That reminds me," said Ursula. "I'll call Rebecca and tell her what has happened." Ursula walked out of the room to phone her daughter.

"Try and stand up Veronique," urged Gavin. "We can sit on the sofa." Gavin and Loretta helped Veronique to stand up. Her legs were still quite weak. Veronique breathed heavily as though she had run an Olympic gauntlet. Alone she would not have managed the few steps to the sofa. Gavin largely supported her weight. Once seated on the sofa, Gavin sat on her right with his arm around her. Loretta sat on her left, holding her daughter's hand.

"All we can do is wait for the kidnapper to call us," assured Gavin, but it seemed little comfort. His son was in the hands of an evil person. He wanted to breakdown and cry but he needed to be strong for Veronique. His wife was emotionally distraught to even walk unaided. This made him feel grossly inadequate. Gavin hugged Veronique as a few tears rolled down his face. Loretta stood up and moved over to Tobias, for she too was in need of a hug. Nobody spoke; the silence heightened everyone's fear as they thought of Gregori, their little boy being so distressed and frightened. The crumpled ransom demand still remained in Gavin's right hand. He glanced down at it to re-read the contents.

"The note does clearly state that Gregori is safe and won't be harmed," mentioned Gavin. "We shall pay whatever money they want. We will soon have our son back."

Chapter Six

The Witness

It certainly bears the hallmarks of Susannah.

The police, including Detective Martinez had arrived at the Harrison household. Veronique had become less frantic, but still deeply upset. She sat on the sofa, tightly held in an embrace with Gavin. Loretta sat on her other side with Tobias standing behind them. Ursula sat on the adjacent sofa feeling perplexed at the kidnapping. She began to wonder if she had heard a noise when she had awoken. Could she have rescued Gregori from the hands of the kidnapper? She should have gone to check on him sooner. Ursula was a stranger in the house, would Veronique cast aspersions?

Rebecca had arrived and sat next to her mother. The problems at Calypso Tavern, worrying and serious as they are, seemed insignificant to this latest plight. Godwin stood next to Tobias behind the sofa; both looking like a mischievous pair, though no one conveyed comical banter. Veronique appeared deeply distraught, as any mother would be. The whole family were anxious. They expected the kidnapper to call with every second that passed.

A Certain Dilemma

A female police officer sat on the edge of her seat. She made notes of all that was being said. Occasionally she would speak to clarify a statement. Detective Martinez, who sat in the armchair, asked the questions. Two other police officers stood and listened. They had already checked the nursery to see if there had been any forced entry through the window, but as Gavin pointed out, they often left the window open. All other doors and windows were checked, but neither had signs of being forced open. A forensic officer was now dusting the window frame and doorframe of the nursery, hoping to get a fingerprint of the culprit. They had already dusted the ransom note and had retrieved two sets of fingerprints. Unfortunately, it was assumed they were Gavin and Godwin's as both had touched the note. It was doubtful that the culprit had left any fingerprints, but procedures had to be followed. The whole family would have to submit fingerprints in order to be eliminated. A cumbersome process, and given the minds of today's criminals, often futile.

"I can see how deeply upset you are Veronique, as all of you are," began Detective Martinez. "I want you to know that kidnapping a child is very serious and is our number one priority."

"You must help us with this," urged Loretta. "If ever there was a time when we needed you most, it is now."

"Of course, and rest assured, I won't do anything else but to ensure Gregori is returned safely," informed Detective Martinez. Veronique became very emotional again and repeated her dreaded assumption.

"Susannah will kill him. I know she will," cried Veronique. Gavin pulled her closer to him.

"Why do you think Susannah is behind this? She is dead," remarked Detective Martinez.

"Is she?" uttered Veronique. "Or have we all been duped yet again? You tell them Mama, about the telephone call from Karl."

"You're upsetting yourself Veronique," responded Loretta. "You know Detective Martinez checked out the murder of Tor Hegland, after we had the call from Karl."

"What phone call? Who is Tor Hegland?" questioned Gavin.

"Weeks ago Karl rang us," began Loretta. "Tor Hegland was the medic who disposed of Susannah's body from the ski resort, after Karl had stabbed her to death. He has since been murdered, in fact mutilated beyond recognition. They had to use DNA to identify him. Isn't that right, Detective Martinez."

"Yes," agreed the detective. He would have said more but Loretta continued.

"Karl wondered if Susannah could have killed him, in which case she is not dead. Karl only wanted to warn us. We did not tell you because we did not want you to worry. But we saw Detective Martinez and asked him to check the matter out, which he did, didn't you?" relayed Loretta, aiming the final comment at Detective Martinez.

"Yes I did, and it since transpires that the Norwegian police have caught Tor Hegland's murderer," replied Detective Martinez.

"Oh no they have not," interrupted Veronique solemnly. She glanced at Loretta; she looked at Gavin and then continued. "Karl rang me yesterday. Apparently, the person who had been arrested has been set free. The forensic evidence the Norwegian police have proves he did not kill Tor Hegland. The man is innocent. He has a psychotic illness which makes him want to confess to crimes he has not done. He is an attention seeker. So you see, I am right. It can only be Susannah. No one else would do this to us. It is just too much to be coincidental," confessed Veronique.

"Why didn't you tell me any of this?" questioned Gavin sternly.

"Because I could not accept what Karl was implying. I wanted Susannah to be dead, but she isn't, is she. I should have listened to Karl. I should have told you Gavin. Gregori would be safe. We would have better protected ourselves," cried Veronique, giving yet a further emotional outburst.

"Let us not forget the ransom note," reminded Godwin. "It clearly states that Gregori is safe and won't be harmed." He was anxious to add any helpful comment he could.

"Correct," stated Detective Martinez. "To some extent the kidnapper, be it Susannah or not, clearly wants money. Let us remain positive."

"Do you think the problems I'm having at Calypso Tavern with the drugs etc are connected?" questioned Rebecca.

"What makes you say that?" asked Detective Martinez.

"I just think with what happened yesterday and this today, it strikes me as a bit unusual, as if planned, don't you think so? Two acts of criminality aimed at this family in two days. By the laws of probability I would say they were connected," mentioned Rebecca.

"You may have a point Rebecca," stated Loretta. She would have said more, but she noticed Gavin glance over at Tobias. Loretta turned to face her husband. Instinct told her they were hiding something. "What was that look for?" she questioned, fixing a momentary glare at Tobias before turning to face Gavin. "Well come on you might as well tell us." Tobias sighed before confessing.

"We are having problems at the plantation. For some weeks someone has been sabotaging our sugar dispatch with ants," informed Tobias.

"The environmental health agency has temporarily closed us down until this problem is resolved," added Gavin.

"And on top of that we are being pursued in a takeover bid, not that there will be much business to take over. If things continue we shall be bankrupt," said Tobias.

"Oh my God! It goes from bad to worse," sighed Loretta. "I knew there were problems with the ants but did not think it was this severe."

"You see I am right, this just reinforces my belief that Susannah is behind all of this," responded a melancholy Veronique. "No one else hates us."

"I am inclined to agree," remarked Rebecca. "But what the heck are we gonna do?"

"How can that woman be alive?" retorted Loretta. "She must have the devil on her side. Will nothing kill her?"

"The whole family is crumbling," stated Rebecca. "Greg's murder, the plantation, Calypso Tavern, and now Gregori kidnapped. Is there anything else left to hurt us even more?"

"My head on a plate," responded Gavin. "Susannah was never a religious person, but that biblical story with John the Baptist, she would love to re-enact."

"Now, now, let's not get melodramatic," intervened Detective Martinez. "Personally, I believe Susannah is dead. Problems can be like public transport, no bus on time then three come at once. What we need to do right now is concentrate on getting Gregori back," stated Detective Martinez, attempting to steer the family on to a positive course of action, instead of negative paranoia.

Detective Martinez had already orchestrated the recording of all telephone calls to and from the house. If they could trace the call when the kidnapper rang, it could lead to a speedy arrest. He had also sanctioned for two police officers to remain at the house at all times. This would provide protection, as well as a hands-on approach to relay the plan of action, whatever that action plan would be to bring this matter to a satisfactory conclusion. Detective Martinez then tried to allay their fears from assuming the problems were connected.

"I know you are innocent of the drug problem at Calypso Tavern Rebecca. You are not the first nightclub owner to experience these problems. The police will get to the bottom of this, you'll see," he stated.

"I certainly hope there are no more instances. If there have been several attempts of ants in the sugar dispatch, then there is likely to be a repeat performance of drugs planted at Calypso Tavern. I don't want to be arrested again," voiced Rebecca assertively.

"The CCTV footage should help incriminate the culprit so you are safe Rebecca," replied Detective Martinez. He then turned his attention to Gavin. "And Gavin, with regard to the troubles you are having at the plantation, have you informed the police?"

"Yes I have but it still did not stop the environmental health officer closing us down," answered Gavin abruptly.

"The environmental health agency is only following government guidelines. You let the police find the perpetrator, and then you will be able to run your business as normal." Gavin looked blank at the detective. He was not re-assured by his simple and logical explanation.

"If you remember," began Gavin, "Susannah planted heroin on me, so there's a connection straight away with the drugs found at Calypso Tavern. We need firm evidence that Susannah is dead before she can be eliminated."

"I have the cremation certificate, what more proof do you need!" remarked Detective Martinez, rather annoyed by the family's repeated insinuation that Susannah could be alive. He had already been ridiculed when trying to imply the very same thing to the Norwegian authorities.

"Anyone could have forged that cremation certificate," remarked Loretta. Detective Martinez was about to adversely reply. His temper was being tested and negative paranoia would not help the situation. However, the telephone rang. Fear griped the household, coupled with hesitation. Everyone thought could this be the kidnapper? Veronique suddenly came to her senses. She got up from the sofa and dashed across the room to answer the call. If it were Susannah, she would recognise her voice. Despite the hatred she had for her, Veronique would apologise for her previous behaviour. She would reason with her and beg her to let Gregori come home. Surely Susannah must have a maternal streak and not harm him? Detective Martinez grabbed Veronique for a second.

"If it is the kidnapper, keep them talking for as long as possible," he said. The telephone continued to ring. Veronique was eager to answer it. The police officer gave the all clear. They were ready to intercept the call. Veronique broke away from Detective Martinez and reached for the telephone.

"Hello," she quickly said.

"Is that you Veronique? This is Sister Jamima. Are you coming to work today only you're late for your shift?" Veronique was disheartened that it was not the kidnapper. She quickly explained the situation to her supervisor. Veronique also implicated Susannah as being the culprit. She had no qualms in telling Sister Jamima. It was an attempt for Veronique to exonerate herself for the time when she tried to kill Susannah in the hospital. That incident had led to Veronique being suspended from work. Sister Jamima had severely reprimanded her then, now let the authoritarian supervisor feel guilty. Detective Martinez gesticulated to keep the call brief. Veronique made her excuses. Sister Jamima expressed her sympathy and asked Veronique to keep her informed of the proceedings.

Until they had heard from the kidnapper, Detective Martinez pointed out that all other calls should be kept to a minimum. The line must be available for the kidnapper to call.

<>

The refreshing jet shower helped to waken Sebastian. The droplets of water glistened against his black skin. The torrent of water cascaded down his muscular torso. The water droplets turned white as Sebastian applied the shower gel. The abundance of white lather glided down his body like an avalanche crashing down a mountain. He had retained his physique that had won him the gay competition of 'Mr Chic Martinique' several years ago. It was most likely he would win again if he ever re-entered. He and Dominic had returned to their beach condo late last night. They had spent a relaxing time in Hawaii. Their anniversary holiday had surpassed all expectations. The couple were true romantics and enjoyed spending quality time together, sightseeing, eating at various restaurants of as many different cultures as possible. They even tried surfing and water gliding.

Sebastian finished his shower, dried himself and left the ensuite. Dominic was awake and sat up in bed. He was not required to work until tomorrow, so took the liberty of having a lazy day. A naked Sebastian came and sat at his bedside.

"Morning gorgeous," said Sebastian as he greeted Dominic with a kiss.

"You off to see Gavin now?" replied Dominic.

"That's right, see what problems they will give me today. Gavin's e-mail seemed urgent," reflected Sebastian. "But don't you worry, I will be back as soon as I can, so we can spend our last day together before we get sidetracked with our jobs."

"I will be waiting," said Dominic. Sebastian's stomach rumbled. Neither of them had eaten since their meal on the return flight, nor had they had chance to do any shopping.

"We have no milk or cereal, and I'm feeling quite hungry," stated Sebastian.

"I'm hungry too," moaned Dominic. "Only it isn't food I want," he added seductively. Sebastian lowered his body and kissed Dominic.

"I know what you want and you will have to wait till later. Business beckons and I don't have the energy or the time," replied Sebastian. Nothing would please him more than to make love with Dominic, but he was too hungry and was already running late. Sebastian stood up and dressed himself. Gavin had not specified a time to meet, but Sebastian knew from previous experience to be as early as possible. If he were not at Gavin's by 10am, he would be receiving a telephone call from him. Sebastian kissed Dominic farewell and left their beach condo. Dominic had been left with strict instructions to stock up with food. That was the only chore required today.

Sebastian drove his black Mariah motorbike and sped through the streets. In need of urgent sustenance his hunger pangs forced him to stop off at the local store. He could easily buy some milk and cereal to have breakfast at Gavin's, along with a sandwich for lunch. That would see him through the day until he could return home to his beloved.

Sebastian parked his motorbike outside the food store. He removed his crash helmet and placed it in the rear compartment. He entered the store and grabbed a shopping basket. He briskly walked to the relevant aisle. He was familiar with the layout as he often shopped there. He quickly obtained a carton of milk, a tuna mayonnaise sandwich and a dried fruit box of cereal. In haste he made his way to the checkout. It was after 10am and he knew Gavin would not be pleased if he were much later.

It was customary for music to be playing in the store. Today was no exception, only as well as the music there was a child crying. Sebastian approached the checkout and could see the child in the arms of a woman ahead of him. In his haste, Sebastian gave a fleeting glance at the child as he passed by. Moments later he stopped dead in his tracks. He suddenly realised the child was Gregori, his godson. He turned and retraced his steps. Gregori was looking at him,

A Certain Dilemma

and immediately stretched out his arms towards Sebastian. His little hands alternated from a clenched position to his petit fingers being outstretched.

"What is all the fuss about?" said Sebastian to Gregori in a cordial tone. The woman who was holding the little infant backed away. "Oh it's ok, there's no need to worry. I am Sebastian, his godfather and a friend of the family. You must be the new nanny," assumed Sebastian. He placed the shopping basket on the floor and went to take hold of Gregori. "Come to your Uncle Sebastian," he said. "You should not be giving your new nanny a hard time." The woman would not let go of Gregori. "There's no need to be alarmed," said Sebastian to the woman. "You can see he knows me." He finally managed to take hold of Gregori. The woman looked agitated and nervous.

"I should not let you take him, you could be a complete stranger. What sort of nanny would I be if I let anyone hold him? I have a responsibility," said the woman intermittently.

"You know me don't you," said Sebastian to Gregori, who had now stopped crying. "I think you want your Mama. I'm on my way to see your Daddy. I could take you with me only…"

"No you can't," interrupted the woman. "I have my orders and besides, you won't have a child seat in your car," she hastily assumed.

"I also don't have a car, I ride a motorbike," joked Sebastian, but he could see the woman was nervous. "There is no need to look so concerned. Is it your first day at being his nanny?"

"Yes it is," replied the woman, trying to appear relaxed. "I just want to make a good impression for Veronique and Gavin. I don't want them to think I can't control Gregori."

"Quite right. I am sure you will make a fine nanny once he gets used to you," replied Sebastian. "He likes ice cream, that should keep him quiet and enable you to get into his good books. You will soon be his Mary Poppins." He then spoke to

Gregori. "Well then my little friend, you must stop crying and be a good boy for your new nanny." Sebastian kissed Gregori on the forehead and passed him back to the woman. "I will probably see you at the house," he remarked, picking up the shopping basket. Gregori became agitated again and started to cry. Sebastian stood and looked at him. "Now be a good boy," he said.

"Thank you," said the woman. "I will take him back to the house now." She quickly left the store carrying Gregori in her arms.

There were three other customers at the checkout in front of Sebastian, so it was a further fifteen minutes before he left the store. He rushed to his motorbike, retrieved his helmet from the rear compartment and replaced it with the shopping. He mounted, revved and sped off.

Sebastian appreciated the velocity breeze. It provided a brief respite to the sun's heat. He zoomed up Gavin's driveway as if he were in the Grand Prix. A cloud of dust and gravel dispersed from beneath his rear wheel as he braked sharply. He paused before descending. Why were there two police cars parked outside? He removed his crash helmet and left it on the seat. He took the food from the rear compartment and turned to ascend the veranda steps. He momentarily stopped as a male police officer stood in the doorway.

"You are Sebastian?" he questioned firmly.

"Yes. What has happened?" The officer did not reply. He merely stepped aside to allow the financial accountant to enter the house. All heads turned to face him as he walked into the living room. Sebastian could see Veronique was upset and embraced by Gavin. Duly concerned Sebastian commented, "Has someone died?" Insensitive as the comment might be, it was not meant in a malicious way. Veronique cried out, her worst nightmare was coming true.

"No! No! No! He can't be dead." She firmly believed Susannah was going to kill Gregori. Sebastian froze to the spot, still holding his shopping. He did not know what else to say or do. Tobias then provided the explanation.

"Gregori has been kidnapped," began Tobias.

"Kidnapped!" repeated Sebastian. "But when?"

"At least three hours ago," informed Tobias.

"But I have just seem him with the new nanny," responded Sebastian, suddenly realising the enormity of what he had witnessed. His comment triggered simultaneous remarks from around the room.

"You've seen him where?" demanded Detective Martinez, standing up from his armchair.

"You have seen him?" whimpered Veronique.

"Where?" questioned Gavin.

"What!" exclaimed Loretta, Ursula and Godwin.

"I was in the food store twenty minutes ago. The 7-11 food store on the edge of town," began Sebastian. "I heard this child crying. He was in the arms of a woman. When I walked past I noticed it was Gregori crying. Naturally, I stopped and introduced myself. This woman, whom I assumed was the new nanny, she said she was his nanny, I think?" relayed Sebastian, feeling considerably awkward.

"Could she still be in the store?" requested Detective Martinez.

"No she left before I did," replied Sebastian. Everyone hung on every word Sebastian said.

"Do you know where they went? Which direction? What car she drove?" urged Detective Martinez.

"No," replied Sebastian. What a feeble answer to give. Detective Martinez ordered one of the police officers to radio headquarters and begin an immediate search of the area.

"We can check the store's CCTV footage," stated Detective Martinez. "Officer Keston, you go to the store to check it out." The police officer promptly obeyed and left the house.

"Was it Susannah?" asked Veronique.

"I don't know. I never met her, except at the trial. I don't think it was her," replied Sebastian. "But Susannah is dead so how could it be her?" he said as an afterthought.

"Describe her, what did she look like?" begged Veronique. Sebastian tried to reply. He was feeling extremely nervous being put on the spot. He always hated too much fuss and attention. His words would not flow as easily as he would have liked.

"She was youngish, white, short dark hair or was it blonde? She spoke with an accent, not American but a foreign accent like German, I think?" uttered Sebastian.

"Well that rules out Susannah," mentioned Detective Martinez.

"Oh don't be fooled by that. Susannah is a master of disguise. It could still be her," interrupted Gavin. Attention soon re-focused on Sebastian as he struggled to continue.

"I was more concerned with Gregori. He was crying and reached out to me. Now I can see why she was so reluctant for me to hold him. But I did, I took him from her to stop him from crying, which he did, he did stop crying."

"You held him in your arms and then gave him back to her," voiced Veronique angrily, almost as if she were accusing Sebastian, making him feel responsible. "You let that woman take my baby," she cried out.

"Veronique it is not Sebastian's fault," remarked Loretta, trying to comfort her daughter.

"I'm sorry, but I really thought she was the nanny, she said she was his nanny. How was I to know?" replied Sebastian. Emotion overwhelmed him. He felt so guilty. He had ignored his instincts. If he had not been in such a hurry he could have rescued Gregori. Sebastian walked over to the armchair feeling ashamed. He could not bear Gavin and Veronique looking at him. He sat down trying his hardest not to cry. He let the shopping bag fall to the floor. He was no longer hungry.

The hunger pangs had evaporated, instead, his stomach churned with fear.

"It's ok Sebastian," remarked Gavin. "At least we have evidence that he is still ok."

"You are a vital witness," said Detective Martinez. "It was a good thing you went to the store. This will help to focus our investigation. The sooner we view the CCTV footage the better." The detective moved to the far side of the living room, taking one of the police officers with him. He also made a phone call on his mobile to HQ, to orchestrate proceedings. He was also going to arrange a press conference at the house.

"I don't understand?" questioned Veronique. "It does not make sense. Why would Susannah go public in broad daylight? She would know she would be captured on a surveillance camera."

"Then maybe it is not Susannah," added Loretta.

"Why would it be Susannah?" uttered Sebastian. "She is dead." He paused before continuing in a flippant tone, "Oh this family, it is one nightmare after another and I always seem to get caught up in it."

"We have reason to suspect that Susannah is alive," informed Gavin. "Yesterday, we gave a press conference because there was a drugs raid on Calypso Tavern where a stash of heroin was found, obviously planted to incriminate us. Over the past few weeks we have had problems with ants in our sugar dispatch. Three consignments have been destroyed. Someone is trying their hardest to sabotage the business. The environmental health agency has temporarily closed the plantation down, and now Gregori has been kidnapped. It certainly bears the hallmarks of Susannah. No one else hates us as much," relayed Gavin. Sebastian was at a loss of what to say. It all seemed incomprehensible.

"Not forgetting the murder of Tor Hegland," added Loretta. "He was the coroner doctor who took away Susannah's body from the ski resort three years ago, when she almost killed Veronique and Gavin on the cable car."

"But hadn't Karl killed her?" questioned Sebastian, regaining control of his emotions.

"That's the sixty-four million dollar question!" responded Rebecca. "It would not be the first time Susannah has faked her death."

"It beggars belief the amount of trouble she goes to in order to seek her revenge," stated Tobias. "All because her husband died in the cable car accident."

"That's because she is evil and twisted and likes playing games with us," remarked Veronique.

"You should not feel bad Sebastian, about seeing Gregori with this woman," reflected Detective Martinez, re-joining the conversation after seeing to other matters. "You could be the crucial witness needed to bring Gregori safely home."

"I do hope so," added Veronique. "I want my baby back. I did not mean to upset you Sebastian."

"It's ok, you are going through hell. You don't need to apologise," replied Sebastian. "I guess it was a good job I stopped off at the store."

"Is there anything else we can do?" Tobias asked Detective Martinez.

"No, just wait for the kidnapper to call us. We will be checking the CCTV footage, hopefully get a make of the car she drove. I am confident of a successful outcome. You must all remain here to support each other. We have the situation under control," informed Detective Martinez. "Two police officers will be staying here until Gregori is returned. I assume you don't object to that?"

"No, of course not," replied Gavin. "Thank you for all you are doing."

"Sebastian, I need you to come with me to the police station to identify the woman from the CCTV footage," said Detective Martinez.

"Right, whatever I can do," replied Sebastian, standing up. He left the shopping bag on the floor.

"It will be good if we give a press conference today, so please find a suitable and recent photograph of Gregori. We can use it to hit the headline news with. I shall arrange the press and TV crew, so they will arrive shortly," advised Detective Martinez. He and Sebastian quickly left the house.

"Gavin fetch the photo album from the study," stated Veronique.

"Sure Honey, back in a sec," replied Gavin, getting up from the sofa. Ursula watched him leave the room. She had remained silent, not wanting to impose on the family's grief. Until Sebastian's arrival she had accused herself of not checking on Gregori sooner, she may have saved him. Ursula had feared the family might equally accuse her. Now that Sebastian was the number one witness, it had removed any unwanted attention from her.

"Is there anything we can do?" she asked.

CHAPTER SEVEN

Apprehension

She felt as though a knife had pierced her heart.

Several hours had passed since Sebastian had viewed the CCTV footage and had identified the kidnapper. The surveillance camera only monitored the front entrance so it had only caught the woman entering and leaving the store, carrying Gregori in her arms. The quality of the footage was adequate. Was it Susannah? Detective Martinez could see it was not. The woman's face was smaller and rounder. She wore a blonde curly wig to hide her features, but even in this disguise the bone structure did not match. Detective Martinez arranged for her photograph to be on the front page of all the local newspapers and TV reports. He wanted to flood the public with her identity. Somebody somewhere will know who she is. Yet would this press release endanger Gregori's safe return? Detective Martinez thought not. It was paramount that the woman was caught. Her only motive was money. She had no interest in harming the child. Experience had taught him that criminals are cowards. They perpetrate their crimes in secret, and the punishment within the criminal fraternity for harming children was far greater than a judicial sentence. This woman would not want to be connected to child abuse. She would want a quick resolve, take the ransom and hide away.

After having had a fantastic holiday in Hawaii with the love of his life, Sebastian had felt happy and relaxed when he had left their beach condo this morning. He now felt tensed, drained, emotionally exhausted and extremely guilty. If anything untoward happened to Gregori he could never forgive himself. Deep down he knew Veronique and Gavin would hold him responsible for not rescuing their son when he had the chance. Anyone with an ounce of gumption would not leave a tearful child in the arms of a complete stranger. He was Gregori's godfather. He should have known better. Sebastian truly believed the woman was the nanny. This whole incident merely reflected his trusting nature, but in this case leading to adverse consequences.

Dominic sat in his recliner reading his latest spy novel. He looked up at Sebastian as he entered the room.

"I expected you home hours ago," said Dominic. "I've done the shopping."

"My appetite has vanished. I've not eaten anything all day. What food I bought this morning I have left at Gavin's," replied Sebastian despondently. Dominic noticed the perplexed look on Sebastian's face.

"You've not had a good day have you? Were things that bad at Gavin's?"

"Have you not seen any news today?" questioned Sebastian. His tone of voice was weary.

"No, I have not switched the television on. I have had a lazy day reading my book, apart from doing the shopping," replied Dominic. "Why? What's on the news?"

"Gregori has been kidnapped," informed Sebastian as he flopped down on the sofa.

"My God! That is bad. Do they know who did it?"

"It is all bizarre so you must bear with me while I explain," stated Sebastian. "At first everyone seemed to think it was Susannah."

"Susannah?" interrupted Dominic. "I thought she was dead."

"Apparently she could be alive," replied Sebastian flippantly. "Honestly that family will be the death of me. The more I deal with them the more bizarre the situation gets."

"Don't be so melodramatic my love," said Dominic, getting up from his recliner. He moved over and sat next to Sebastian on the sofa. He greeted him with a kiss. Sebastian began to explain in more detail the labyrinth of events.

"The reason why Gavin wanted to see me was due to financial problems. The plantation has been closed down temporarily due to ants in the sugar. There have been three consignments contaminated with ants, and the environmental health agency had no alternative but to close the plantation down. That's what Gavin wanted to see me about today. How they can survive the economic hiccup of a cash flow problem. Calypso Tavern was closed due to a drugs raid. The police found heroin in Rebecca's office. She was arrested but released without being charged. And Global Incorporations Ltd, whoever they are, are trying to take over the plantation and want to buy Gavin out. Only instead of our prearranged financial meeting, Gregori is kidnapped. There is a ransom demand for $2million. With all that has happened someone clearly hates them, which is why they think Susannah is alive. No one hates them as much as she did or does. The person who took charge of her body in Norway, after Karl supposedly killed her, has been murdered," relayed Sebastian. Dominic listened to this brief monologue. He would normally have replied to various points but the events overwhelmed him.

"My spy novel pales into insignificance compared with this," remarked Dominic, trying to absorb every detail his partner was saying, as well as attempting to water down the

A Certain Dilemma

contents, for he knew Sebastian was prone to exaggerate. "Mind you, poor Gregori. I hope he'll be ok."

"Oh you haven't heard the best of it yet," declared Sebastian. "Guess who is the star witness?" Sebastian's eyes watered with regret. Even Dominic did not expect this reaction from him.

"Hey come on, there's no need to get upset," he stated, putting his arm around Sebastian. In need of reassurance Sebastian turned and hugged Dominic.

"We spent too long in Hawaii. We forgot what normal life was like," said Sebastian. He broke from the embrace and continued to explain. His voice quivered with emotion. "On my way to Gavin's this morning I stopped off at the store. I needed something to eat, as you know we had no food. In there I saw this woman carrying Gregori. He was crying. I went over to him. She led me to believe she was his nanny. I even held Gregori in my arms to stop him from crying, but then gave him back to her. I could have rescued him. If anything happens to him, what will I do?" Tears rolled down his face. Dominic looked at him.

"My love," he said as he hugged Sebastian. "It is not your fault. I take it you have told the police about this, and Gavin and Veronique."

"Yes they all know. In fact I was able to identify the woman from the CCTV footage, so to some extent it was a good job I was there."

"There you go, you should not blame yourself," comforted Dominic.

"Veronique blames me, you should have heard her accuse me. I felt completely helpless and guilty, especially with the whole family looking at me."

"The fact that you were there means they will capture this woman," assured Dominic. "I take it then the woman is not Susannah?" he said as an afterthought.

"No it was not Susannah. That family seems to attract trouble. I know I have said this before, but I feel as though I want to distance myself from them. After today I definitely will."

"But they are good for business," mentioned Dominic.

"The way I feel right now I'd sooner go bankrupt," responded Sebastian. "I was just going about my business, and now I end up in this twisted nightmare. I don't get paid danger money," reflected Sebastian. Dominic gave another reassuring hug.

"What happens tomorrow? Will you be required to see the police or Gavin?"

"Yes!" Sebastian sighed, breaking from the embrace. "I have been given the task to resolve where Gavin can get $2million from for the ransom. Tonight I have to check through all the accounts of Calypso Tavern, the plantation and the ski resort. Tomorrow I meet with Gavin at the house to enlighten him of where the money can be obtained. I know for a fact he won't like my findings."

"You don't seem very optimistic. I thought their finances were solid, after all, Gavin's a millionaire, isn't he?" questioned Dominic.

"If you include all his assets yes, but I am aware of his finances. At the moment his cash flow is eating away at his capital. The plantation with its current problems is losing money. The ski resort made a loss the last two years due to global warming. Norway does not get the snow it used to have. So many ski resorts have gone bust. It is just a matter of time before Snøby suffers the same fate. Calypso Tavern is ticking over, but with drug problems, who knows what the outcome will be. Not forgetting the $500,000 he gave to Susannah in a ploy to get her arrested. If Gavin's empire does not financially improve, he will no longer be a millionaire."

"Well at the end of the day it is not our problem. You and me are all that matter to us. If Gavin loses his millions

A Certain Dilemma

we shall be all right," assured Dominic. "You say you haven't eaten all day; just as well I have baked a pasta and veg pie. Why don't you take a shower, freshen up and I will serve up dinner."

"Thank you," replied Sebastian. "Sorry to drone on but I felt so bad about it."

"You are a vital witness so you should not feel bad. Gavin and Veronique will realise your valuable contribution in Gregori's rescue," consoled Dominic.

<>

Evening drew very coldly over the Harrison household. Agitation was rife between the occupants as they waited for the kidnapper to ring. All afternoon the telephone had scarcely been silent. Various friends and acquaintances that had seen the press release and TV news reports had rung them out of concern. Their intentions were honourable, but this only heightened the tension between the family. Were the public telephone calls preventing the kidnapper from getting through? Hence the abrupt but necessary reaction from either Veronique or Gavin when they answered the telephone, only to end the call seconds later.

Much discussion had taken place as to the identity of the woman. Veronique was adamant the woman was in cahoots with Susannah. That red haired tyrant had plagued her happiness since the first day she arrived on the scene. At the time no one else could see Susannah's deceptive streak, but Veronique was not blind to it. Whilst everyone else applauded Susannah's cabaret charisma and her English sophistication, Veronique inwardly cursed her. Susannah had quickly built a wedge between her and Gavin, and had thrown herself at the man Veronique secretly loved. Veronique's bitterness towards Susannah grew very quickly as she witnessed how easily susceptible Gavin was to her manipulative manner.

Veronique had hated seeing the two of them together. She had been so close to killing Susannah in hospital that she wished for that moment again. If ever she got the opportunity she would ensure Susannah was dead. No more fake deaths.

The family tried to keep a level head and not allow the 'Susannah theories' to cloud their judgement. Tobias and Gavin discussed various business enemies or rivals. They knew who their competitors were and had compiled a list. This information was passed to Detective Martinez to make further enquiries. Gavin sat on the sofa operating his laptop. He was surfing the Web trying to find out more about Global Incorporations Ltd. Who were they? Where were they based? What assets do they have? What was their history? He clicked on a link entitled *subsidiary*. Gavin then discovered who the principal owner was of Global Incorporations Ltd. The company was affiliated to 'Supreme', a brand of Scandinavian cosmetics.

"Oh my God!" sighed Gavin as he looked up from his laptop. "I think you are right Veronique, it is Susannah, or at least her wrath is being continued on her behalf."

"What have you found?" requested Tobias. Before Gavin could respond the others passed various comments.

"I hoped beyond all hope it would not be that woman!" exclaimed Loretta. "She shows no mercy."

"It could only be her Mama," added Veronique scornfully.

"That woman is completely insane and inhumane to do what she has done," stated Rebecca.

"No, Susannah may still be dead," continued Gavin. "The owner of Global Incorporations Ltd is Kirsti Løvik, Susannah's sister–in–law. Maybe she is carrying on from where Susannah left off. After all, it was her brother who was killed in the cable car crash." The female police officer viewed the website. She used her mobile and quickly informed Detective Martinez of the findings.

"So it is Kirsti Løvik who has been sabotaging our business," stated Tobias.

"And no doubt planted drugs in my office," added Rebecca.

"So could she have Gregori?" wondered Loretta.

"It was not Kirsti Løvik on the surveillance tape," replied Veronique. "But perhaps she has an accomplice?" The policewoman re-joined the family group having spoken to Detective Martinez.

"Let me just update you," she began. "Detective Martinez will now contact the Norwegian police and request that they interview Kirsti Løvik. He will stress to them the importance of this case. He said to tell you that developments are proceeding and with this crucial bit of information he is confidant we shall soon resolve the case." The policewoman spoke with authority.

"I do not share your optimism," declared Veronique. "I am so worried. I feel physically sick."

"Let me fetch you some water to help settle your stomach," said Loretta as she stood up to go to the kitchen.

"Wait a minute," stated Gavin, attracting everyone's attention. "I have just received an e-mail entitled *ransom demand*."

"So you have," remarked Veronique, looking across. "Quick open it up and find out what it says," she anxiously added. The policewoman moved over to stand behind Gavin. She had to witness the e-mail. Again the police officer retrieved her mobile and was ready to record the ransom demand. It was vital evidence. Everyone's adrenalin raced as they crowded around Gavin, forming a semi-circle behind the policewoman. Gavin opened the e-mail and read it out:

"Please accept my assurances that Gregori is quite safe. We mean him no harm. You have 48 hours to arrange a $2million transfer of funds. Gavin, you will reply to this e-mail when you

have the money ready to transfer into my bank account. I will then e-mail my account details to you for you to transfer funds via electronic transfer. When the money has been received I will tell you where and when to collect Gregori."

"My heart's beating so fast," sighed Veronique as she viewed the e-mail. Gavin re-read it to clarify its contents.

"Look how they seem to emphasise how safe Gregori is," remarked Ursula.

"I noticed that too," added Loretta.

"Makes me think it can't be Susannah," replied Veronique. "She is not that caring. She would want to cause optimum grief."

"It is a good sign," declared the policewoman. "I have sent the message to Detective Martinez. All you have to do Gavin is arrange the money."

"Sebastian is coming over in the morning so we should be able to sort that out. The bank has already been alerted. I cannot risk anything going wrong. I don't care about the money, let them get away with it, I only want my son back safely," responded Gavin with deep sincerity.

"Please be honest," began Veronique, speaking to the policewoman. "In your experience, we will get Gregori back, won't we?"

"I have every confidence of a positive outcome," replied the policewoman.

The following morning a tired Gavin sat on the veranda bench. Neither he nor Veronique had managed to get much sleep. This was to be expected. Both were anxious and extremely worried about Gregori. It was his first night away from them, away from his usual routine. How would he be? Were his kidnappers looking after him satisfactorily? Most of the night Veronique and Gavin had lain in bed, talking and comforting each other. Gavin had kept his laptop on the bedside table, fully operational in case a further e-mail arrived from the kidnappers. By all accounts it was the two police officers that had slept the most, but then they were not emotionally involved.

Feeling apprehensive, Gavin waited for Sebastian. Everyone else was in the house, practically sitting in the same seats they sat in yesterday. The only person not present was Rebecca. She had stayed at her apartment last night in order to keep a watch on things at Calypso Tavern. She had questioned the staff about the drugs. She practically begged for someone to confess, just so she could eliminate Susannah. Rebecca was desperate for peace of mind. She even offered to protect them from the police, providing there were no more incidents. Sadly, no one admitted to the deed. Susannah remained the likeliest suspect.

Sebastian soon arrived at the house. He dismounted his motorbike and retrieved a folder from the rear compartment. On ascending the veranda steps, Gavin greeted him. They shook hands. Gavin thanked Sebastian for his help yesterday and apologised for upsetting him. Sebastian brushed it aside, saying it did not matter. However, he dreaded seeing the family again. He was apprehensive for two reasons. Firstly, would the family vent their anger at him for not rescuing Gregori in the store, and secondly, the financial news he had for Gavin was not good.

"Hi everyone," said Sebastian as he entered the living room. The family replied with pleasant remarks. Sebastian avoided making eye contact with anyone, especially Veronique. Gavin then escorted him to his study. There was no light banter. It was strictly business, and the matter was too serious for any jokes. Gavin sat at his desk; Sebastian sat opposite and placed the folder in front of him. Gavin looked directly at Sebastian and firmly said:

"Can we meet the $2million ransom demand, yes or no?"

"Yes," replied Sebastian. Gavin sighed heavily and sat back in his chair.

"Thank God for that," he said before continuing. "I knew you would find the money, thank you Sebastian."

"I think I ought to point out where the money is coming from," added Sebastian.

"Of course, go ahead, not that it matters much for we shall do whatever it takes," remarked Gavin. Sebastian opened the folder and read out his prepared financial report.

"The amount of money available from the accounts of Calypso Tavern, the plantation, the ski resort and your own personal finance amounts to $1,200,000. This leaves a shortfall of $800,000. Some further savings could be made but not a significant amount to raise the shortfall. If a loan were taken out to meet the remainder, then given the state of current business we could not afford the repayments."

"So where is the money coming from?" responded Gavin. "I am a millionaire. I don't need any loan."

"You are still a millionaire but in assets only, not in cash. The last two years the ski resort has not made a profit. The plantation is currently closed and revenues are drying up. You have a cash flow problem. Reserves are being spent to prop up the ski resort and to keep the plantation afloat. Calypso Tavern is not doing much better. The recent drugs raid will have an adverse consequence," said Sebastian.

"So where is the money coming from?"

"The only viable option is to relinquish an asset," replied Sebastian.

"Is that really necessary?" challenged Gavin.

"There is no alternative Gavin. You must sell either Calypso Tavern, the plantation, the ski resort or the house and cabana," responded Sebastian, too well aware that Gavin did not like his suggestion.

"Are my finances really this bad?"

A Certain Dilemma

"It's not that your finances are bad. There are not many people who can suddenly take $2million from their savings. Look at the budget reports yourself," replied Sebastian as he handed over the relevant documentation. "The money is just not there." Gavin looked at the reports and soon realised that Sebastian was right.

"I can't sell the plantation, nor the estate because it is my business and home," commented Gavin. "The ski resort?" he paused before continuing, "Thanks to global warming people do not buy ski resorts anymore, not where Snøby is located. That only leaves Calypso Tavern. But how can I sell that? It was Greg's."

"I know this is hard for you Gavin, but you don't have much option, you need to sell Calypso Tavern. It is the obvious business to sell. It won't take much marketing, and it is the easiest and most profitable. The business is worth $3million, so the sale will solve all your other financial difficulties as well as provide for the ransom," stated Sebastian sympathetically, and applying a touch of accountancy advice.

"All this mess because of Susannah," reflected Gavin. Sebastian could see how perplexed he was. The result of Susannah's vengeance had taken its toll. "This won't work! I can't sell Calypso Tavern by tomorrow. It takes time to sell a business."

"I have already liased with the bank. Due to your good credit rating they have agreed to advance the $2million in lieu of the sale. In other words they want Calypso Tavern as collateral," informed Sebastian. "All we need to do today is present a written contract exchanging the business for the advance in lieu of the sale. I took the liberty to prepare such a contract. You may wish to bring it to the attention of Chester Hargreaves for his perusal." Sebastian passed the document across to Gavin.

"You really have thought of everything," responded Gavin, reluctantly accepting that he could do nothing else.

"That is what you pay me for."

"Then I guess there is no choice. I shall have to sell Calypso Tavern," conceded Gavin. "The importance here is to get Gregori back. I shall contact Chester to go over the legalities of the document, but it seems in order. My other problem now is what the hell do I tell Rebecca. She will not like Calypso Tavern being sold." Gavin picked up his study telephone and rang the Texan. She had not long awoken, but was lying in bed. Gavin asked her to come to the house immediately. He told her it was nothing to worry about, just business.

Sebastian listened to the conversation. Oh yes to be a fly on the wall and witness Rebecca's outburst at Calypso Tavern being sold, but he definitely did not want to be present. Sebastian had suffered enough drama yesterday. Rebecca would surely vent her anger at him.

Gavin ended the call. He did not feel proud with himself. The sacrifice was not too great for his son, but he still felt he had betrayed Greg.

"I will contact the bank. I have already pre-arranged a 2pm appointment for us today, for you to sign the exchange contract," informed Sebastian. He could see Gavin was torn; yet he pertained a stiff upper lip.

"What forward thinking you have," remarked Gavin. "As soon as I have the money, I can reply to the ransom demand e-mail and the transfer can go ahead. I will also contact Martinez to tell him it is all systems go." Gavin reached across his desk to shake Sebastian's hand. The gesture was twofold, an admission of gratitude for solving his financial situation, and also for moral support. "This has got to work. We must get Gregori back," commented Gavin.

"The kidnappers are only interested in the money. Gregori won't come to any harm," assured Sebastian, not just out of kindness but also guilt. "If we have finished I shall see you at the bank," stated Sebastian, eager to leave to avoid any further unwanted confrontation from the family. "Oh, yesterday I left some shopping here," he added.

"Yes, see Veronique. I think she put it in the kitchen. Also please ask her to come and see me." Sebastian left the study. He dreaded talking to Veronique, but he could scarcely ignore Gavin's request. All faces turned to him as he asked Veronique for his shopping. She had already fetched his bag and was ready to hand it over. Sebastian stated that Gavin wanted to see her in the study. Thankfully she left the living room. Loretta broke the awkward silence that fell.

"Did you and Dominic have a nice holiday in Hawaii?" she enquired. "With all that happened yesterday I forgot to ask."

"Yes we had a lovely time, thank you. The problem with holidays are that one hates returning to normal life," replied Sebastian, trying not to say anything insensitive. Should he mention if there was any news of Gregori or would that be unwise? He should have asked Gavin but had been too preoccupied with his finances and Gavin's reaction to selling Calypso Tavern. Sebastian stood facing the family. The shopping bag was tightly held in front as if it were a shield. All Sebastian wanted to do was run out but he felt compelled to stay. This emotional trial filled him with anguish. The judge and jury were staring at him as he trembled in the witness box.

"We must thank you once again for your anniversary party. We all had a fantastic time," commented Tobias.

"I have heard all about the beach chase," chimed Ursula. If the overfriendly comments were an attempt to make Sebastian feel at ease, they did not succeed. All he wanted to do was leave and preferably before Rebecca arrived.

"Yes it was a fun night. Thank you for coming, and Loretta do you still have the seaweed?" remarked Sebastian.

"As a matter of fact I do. I have planted them in a rock pool by my front door," she replied.

"Well I won't keep you, I have appointments elsewhere. I hope all goes well," stated Sebastian. He went to leave the house, prompting Loretta to be hospitable.

"When all this is over we shall have a party, both you and Dominic are invited," she informed. Sebastian showed his appreciation and bid them farewell. Loretta was anxious to know the outcome of the meeting. She followed Sebastian out of the house and snatched a few seconds with him on the veranda.

"Do we have the ransom money?" she dutifully enquired.

"Yes we do," returned Sebastian. "By this time tomorrow it should all be over."

"Oh thank heavens for that!" sighed Loretta. "Give my regards to Dominic." Sebastian mounted his motorbike. He revved the engine and drove off. Loretta waved goodbye. Sebastian's black Mariah carried his butch virile body away.

Sebastian passed Rebecca as she drove to the house. Her new Mercedes sparkled in the sunlight. He acknowledged her as he rode past and was relieved that he could not stop and chat. He did not want to be the one to tell her Calypso Tavern was up for sale, and he could foresee her angry reaction when Gavin tells her. That was one argument Sebastian did not want to witness. No doubt Rebecca would fly off the handle and accuse him of influencing Gavin's decision. Sebastian did not want to receive the wrath of her Texan drawl. After the meeting with the bank, Sebastian would have no further need to contact the family in the foreseeable future. It could be several months before he would see Rebecca again, by which time the dust would have settled.

Rebecca drove up the palm-fringed driveway and parked her Mercedes. Loretta had remained on the veranda.

"We have the money for the ransom," informed Loretta.

"Hey that's good," replied Rebecca. "I guess that's why Sebastian was here. He seems to be leaving in such a hurry." Rebecca mounted the veranda steps.

"You know Sebastian, he doesn't like fuss, and with all that happened yesterday it's no wonder he wants to keep a low profile," remarked Loretta.

"It is so easy to like Sebastian. He is soft and gentle yet that strong muscular body of his is to die for. He is such a hunk. He and Dominic make a good couple." The two females entered the house.

In an attempt to boost popularity points Gavin had informed Veronique of his intention to sell Calypso Tavern. It was the only source of money to pay the ransom. It was predictable that Veronique supported the decision; her only objective was to get her son back home. Selling Calypso Tavern was a means to an end. The decision was final, but how turbulent would Rebecca's reaction be?

"Hi Ma, Pa," said Rebecca on entering the living room. Ursula and Godwin were sitting on the sofa.

"How's that new car of yours Rebecca?" asked Godwin, hoping for the chance of a test drive.

"Why perfect of course. And no! I am not giving you the keys," teased Rebecca, knowing full well her father wanted to drive her Mercedes.

"Well said Rebecca," acknowledged Ursula. "Honestly Godwin, you're worse than a boy wanting to play with his go-cart," she stated in a mild chastisement voice.

"You know I would love a new car," responded Godwin. "Only wish I had the money."

"You're the one who took early retirement. Where did you think money was gonna come from," remarked Ursula.

"Oh Pa, you should have said, maybe I can help you out," suggested Rebecca as she sat down in the armchair.

"Never mind all that now, we have more important matters to deal with," rebuked Ursula.

"Oh don't mind us," intervened Loretta. "It's a relief to have a different topic of conversation. These past twenty-four hours seem an eternity, but hopefully for not much longer. Gavin has got the ransom money," she proudly informed.

"That is a relief," sighed Ursula and Godwin.

"And how do you know this?" quizzed Tobias, looking at his spouse.

"Because Sebastian just told me on the veranda," she indignantly replied. At that moment Veronique entered the living room, she saw Rebecca sitting in the armchair. Is all fair in love and war? Veronique needed her son. Who owns Calypso Tavern was irrelevant. Rebecca would realise and accept there was no alternative.

"Hi Rebecca," said Veronique.

"Hi Veronique, how are you feeling?" replied Rebecca.

"I don't know what words to say to describe how I feel," she responded. "Anyway, can you come through to the study, we need to talk."

"Sure, no problem," replied Rebecca who immediately stood up. "When Gavin rang me he said to come over straight away, he did not say what it was about."

"We just need to discuss something," replied Veronique candidly.

A hush of silence filled the living room as Rebecca left followed by Veronique. Heads turned to see them leave the room. No one made any comment, but all wondered what the talk would be about.

Gavin sat at his desk as Veronique and Rebecca entered the study. In the forefront of Gavin's mind was the safe return of Gregori. Perhaps for this reason one could excuse his lack of tact.

"Please sit down Rebecca," he said as though she were an employee about to face a reprimand. Rebecca sat opposite him. Veronique stood by her side. "As you are aware I need to find $2million for the ransom. The only way I can raise the money is to sell Calypso Tavern."

"What!" exclaimed Rebecca. Her explosive reaction was predictable. "You can't sell Calypso Tavern!"

"I have to, I have no choice. It is the only way I can raise the money," informed Gavin.

"You're a millionaire, surely you have the money?" questioned Rebecca angrily. She could see that Gavin was serious but her instinct was to defend herself.

"I know this is awkward for you Rebecca," interrupted Veronique, "But all other options have been considered."

"All other options!" repeated Rebecca, abruptly standing up. Veronique had to move aside and steady the chair from falling over. Rebecca walked a few steps away in disbelief. So many thoughts were buzzing through her mind; thoughts of Greg; their memories; how happy they had been; how shattered she had become after his death; the constant struggle to rebuild her life and how she had still managed to carry out Greg's dream. Against all the odds, she had finally stabilised her life. She had a purpose. Now all that stability was about to crumble. No! She would not allow Calypso Tavern to be sold.

"I know this is difficult but you must see my position," expressed Gavin. The atmosphere was tense. Rebecca turned and faced Gavin as she began her counterattack.

"Difficult does not cut it. It's no wonder you don't have any money, you keep giving it to Susannah," she stated in defiance. "That fiasco at the airport four years ago, paying her $500.000, played right into her hands, and now she's coming back for more money, just like I said she would."

"Don't get irrational Rebecca. Susannah is dead, this is a different matter," remarked Gavin.

"Don't get irrational!" repeated Rebecca. "Have you any idea how I feel? I don't know whether to cry, scream, shout out to the whole world the anguish that strangles me," she stated angrily. "Why do you need to sell Calypso Tavern in any case? Why not sell Snøby, your precious ski resort; after all, that is where this whole nightmare began with that cable car crash killing Susannah's husband. What a shame she wasn't on board as well," uttered Rebecca.

"I have to act quickly to raise the money. I cannot do that with Snøby, and in any case due to global warming and less snow, ski resorts are not the high flying success they used to be," informed Gavin sympathetically.

"Well you can't sell Calypso Tavern in twenty-four hours either so how is that gonna get you the money? And besides, you already have a buyer for the plantation so sell that instead," retorted Rebecca.

"The plantation will not reap enough funds to cover the ransom unless I sell the whole estate and we are all homeless. And the reduced price that Global Incorporations have offered is unacceptable," explained Gavin.

"What an excuse!" seethed Rebecca.

"Calypso Tavern is worth $3million. The bank is willing to advance $2million in lieu of the sale. We sign the documents this afternoon," said Gavin assertively.

"Seems like you've got it all planned without discussing it with me first. I don't know why you even bothered to consider me. It's clear to see you don't care for my feelings," replied Rebecca. She felt completely betrayed. Her emotions became apparent as her true feelings surfaced. "How can you sell Calypso Tavern? It was Greg's; it's all I have of him. It is where we lived, where I still live now," she uttered, returning to the chair. "Please Gavin there must be another way? I can give you a few thousand dollars, so will Ma and Pa. Don't you and your folks have money Veronique," she pleaded, but to no avail. She sat down in the chair as tears rolled down her face.

"If there was any other way I would do it. The only other asset I have is the estate and I can't sell that nor the plantation, it is our livelihood," mentioned Gavin.

"Oh, what do you think Calypso Tavern is for me, that's my livelihood," shouted Rebecca.

"You still own the apartment..." began Gavin.

"It's a good job I own the apartment or you'll be selling that and throwing me out on to the streets," interrupted Rebecca.

"Please don't say things like that. What I was about to say was you will still be living and working at Calypso Tavern, along with all the other staff. The business will be sold as a going concern," appeased Gavin. Rebecca was too upset to comment any further. She felt as though a knife had pierced her heart. What little comfort she had salvaged from Greg's death was now being taken from her.

CHAPTER EIGHT

Deliverance

It is a sad reflection of the world we live in.

Over the next two days the occupants of Gavin's house remained unchanged, almost like a two-day religious vigil. Yet this was far from any peaceful seclusion. None of the Harrison household left the house, with the exception of Rebecca, who needed to keep close reigns on Calypso Tavern. She also needed to recount her wounds from her argument with Gavin. Despite her persistence, she had failed to overturn his decision to sell Calypso Tavern. Rebecca felt emotionally blackmailed, especially when Gavin stated that had Greg been alive he would not have hesitated to sell the business. How could she argue against that? But it was her business now, at least morally. Now some stranger was going to own it. Calypso Tavern had now been surrendered to the bank in exchange for the $2million ransom.

The police maintained their presence, eager to trace the kidnappers. Detective Martinez followed up every lead that was generated by the media coverage. He was confident the woman's identity would be discovered soon. In the grounds of the estate the press gathered, waiting for any further update.

This time Gavin did not object to the journalistic mob. He was grateful for the publicity. He hoped it would lead to the rescue of Gregori.

Rebecca arrived at the house. She was never the sort to sulk. Despite her feelings she was anxious for Gregori's safe return. She did not want to cause any further anguish for Gavin and Veronique, so attempted to respect his decision to sell Calypso Tavern. Her parents on the other hand were secretly pleased with the latest developments. They did not pass up on the opportunity to persuade Rebecca to return to Texas. Her life in Martinique had come full circle. She had no future here. They emphasised that Rebecca would not like working for the new owner of Calypso Tavern, not having been the boss for so long. The only viable option was to return to Texas and make a fresh start. Rebecca was non-committal, but she also did not disagree, unlike previous times. Ursula and Godwin saw this as a positive sign.

Detective Martinez was present and now sat in the armchair. His mobile telephone rested on the side. He had orchestrated the transfer with the bank. The whole process was being closely monitored. He was confident the kidnappers would be caught. Gavin sat on the sofa with his laptop. Veronique was by his side. The adrenalin was running high for Gavin as he replied to the kidnappers' e-mail, confirming the money was ready to be transferred. Seconds later by returned e-mail the kidnappers divulged the bank account details that the ransom was to be paid into. Detective Martinez relayed the information to Gavin's bank manager. None of the family spoke as the transaction took place. Veronique was completely worried. Her arm was linked with Gavin's as she sat next to him. Her mind was in turmoil. She constantly prayed that the kidnappers would be true to their word and return Gregori unharmed.

"Thank you, that will be all for now," said Detective Martinez as he ended his telephone call with the bank manager. "The money has been transferred," he announced to everyone. "My officers at the bank will be investigating further. The bank details should lead to a name and address, but these most likely will be fictitious. However, indications are that the money has been transferred to a bank account in Hong Kong."

"Who the hell do we know in Hong Kong?" questioned Gavin.

"It would seem the bank account has been set up to receive the money, and no doubt will be closed down when the money is transferred elsewhere," stated Detective Martinez. "Fear not, the trail has not gone cold. We will be liasing with the Hong Kong authorities. You have not lost the money yet," assured the detective.

"Hong Kong!" sighed Gavin. "I don't hold much hope in getting the money returned from there."

"Never mind the money, I just want Gregori back," mentioned an anxious Veronique. Gavin embraced his wife; the laptop was still positioned on his thighs.

"We will get him back now they have the money," comforted Gavin.

"All this waiting is churning my stomach," added Loretta.

"Mine too," remarked Ursula. "And I have hunger pangs adding to the problem, but I simply could not eat a morsel right now."

"It is no wonder, it's almost 3pm and we have not had lunch," replied Loretta. "I'll go and make some coffee and refreshments." The stout Caribbean got up off the sofa and headed into the kitchen.

"I'll come and help you," offered Ursula and followed Loretta into the kitchen.

"What time are we expecting a message from the kidnappers?" asked Tobias.

"Any time now I hope," answered Gavin.

A Certain Dilemma

Godwin was standing next to Tobias behind the sofa. Both had similar features and one would be forgiven for assuming they were brothers. Detective Martinez had vacated the armchair and now stood by the hallway leading to the study, talking quietly with the policewoman. A murmured whisper is all that could be heard of their conversation. Rebecca stood up to stretch her legs and silently walked over to the window. The peaceful tropical surroundings that she viewed were in complete contrast to the inner turmoil she felt. She tried to understand and accept Gavin's decision to sell Calypso Tavern, but despite her logical frame of mind, her feelings were raw. In her heart she had lost a bit more of Greg. It would be so easy to return to Texas as her parents wished. Why is life so damn cruel?

"You hear about this sort of thing nearly everyday on the TV or in the newspapers," commented Godwin to Tobias. "Never in a million years do you expect it to happen to you."

"It is a sad reflection of the world we live in," replied Tobias. "The world is a much smaller place to live and crime seems to spread a lot further. I would hazard a guess that there is not a family on this Earth that has not been the victim of a crime, be it minor or major."

"You may be right there," replied Godwin. "To some extent we have been lucky with the ranch, plus we never had any exuberant possessions worth stealing."

"It's here!" declared Gavin. "The e-mail from the kidnappers," he added as he opened the message. Veronique glanced across, eager to read the e-mail.

"What does it say?" questioned Detective Martinez. He quickly moved closer. The policewoman followed behind. Gavin read out the message:

"Be ready to collect Gregori from the jetty at 5pm. Keep your mobile at hand. I will tell you when to leave the house

via a text message. There will be no more e-mails. Thank you for the money."

"That's in two hours time," said Veronique. "Should we go to the jetty now?"

"No!" replied Detective Martinez. "The message clearly states that Gavin will be told when to leave the house. You never know they could be watching so we must go along with their instructions. However, I shall arrange my officers to be in position at the jetty and the neighbouring forest, ready and waiting. The moment the kidnappers arrive at the jetty with Gregori we shall arrest them."

"You keep saying them, do you believe it is not Susannah?" asked Veronique.

"Indications are it is an international syndicate, perhaps that is a good thing. At least you can feel saver knowing it is not Susannah," responded Detective Martinez. He left the living room in order to contact HQ to organise the siege.

"Don't you worry Veronique, it will soon be over," comforted Tobias.

"It cannot be soon enough Pa," she replied. Loretta and Ursula appeared from the kitchen, each carrying a tray of assorted refreshments.

"Any news?" enquired Loretta,

"Yes Mama, we are to collect Gregori from the jetty at 5pm," informed Veronique.

"That is good news," remarked Loretta as she placed her tray on a side table. "Ursula, you can put yours over there," she added, indicating to the adjacent side table. It was the same side table that a framed photograph of Susannah used to stand on. The same photograph that Gavin was holding as he stood in the centre of the living room the day he had returned from Norway, before an unsuspecting Susannah shot him from the overhanging balcony. Needless to say, the said photograph along with all other pictures of that woman had since been destroyed.

"We have coffee, herbal tea, biscuits, coconut cake, mango ice-cream and a few more tasty morsels, so this should keep us going until Gregori comes home, then we can have a proper feast," said Loretta, trying to lift everyone's spirit. Loretta passed Gavin his mug of coffee.

"Thanks Loretta, I am parched," said Gavin. "Wouldn't mind a whisky put I need to keep a clear head for driving."

"Try not to look so worried Veronique, they only wanted the money, they won't hurt Gregori," stated Ursula. Having placed the tray on the side table she stood next to Godwin. "Everyone just help yourself," she added.

The following two hours passed anxiously. Except for Veronique, everyone managed to partake of the refreshments. However, she did allow herself a cup of coffee. Tobias and Godwin indulged further and had a beer. All the family could do was wait. Detective Martinez had left the house. He and several police officers surrounded the jetty. They remained camouflaged within the tropical foliage and were confident in apprehending the kidnappers. From the outset it was prudent to assume there was more than one person involved. International criminality was a well-organised operation. Kidnapping with ransom demands into overseas bank accounts often depicted organised crime involving a dozen or so villains. It seemed unlikely that the meagre woman caught in the store CCTV footage with Gregori was working alone.

Two police officers still remained at the house. They had been on duty since their arrival shortly after Gregori's kidnapping. Extra hours meant extra money, and they quite liked living in such an opulent dwelling.

"It's ten to five," remarked Gavin, somewhat agitated. "Almost time for them to text me." Not only was he on edge about meeting the kidnappers, but also the bulletproof vest he now wore was uncomfortable. Detective Martinez had insisted that he wore the vest. Gavin did not object, having been shot before he did not relish the thought of a repeat attack.

"Anyone want this last coconut slice?" stated Loretta, beginning to clear the trays away.

"Mama, save it for Gregori, you know how he likes them," requested Veronique.

"Why sure thing Honey," replied Loretta. At that moment Gavin's mobile bleeped. He had received a text message. All looked at him in a sudden freeze of animation. Loretta stood upright like a statue holding the tray. Rebecca was seated in the armchair but had leant forward. Tobias and Godwin were standing close by, each with a glass of beer in their hand. Ursula had gone to fetch the other tray so had her back to Gavin, but she quickly turned on the spot to face him. The policewoman and her colleague looked on, eager to alert Detective Martinez of the text message. Almost as if time had stood still they remained motionless as Gavin read out the text message:

"You may leave the house now and drive to the jetty."

"Is that all it says?" asked Tobias.

"Yes," replied Gavin. "And I'm off to fetch my son." He pushed the laptop aside as he stood up to leave the house, still keeping his mobile in his hand.

"Let me come with you!" urged Veronique.

"No, it's best if you stay here," added the policewoman as she used her mobile to alert Detective Martinez. "Remember not to look out for us Gavin. We are well hidden. We don't want the kidnappers sensing a trap."

"Sure," responded Gavin as he exited the house. Veronique followed him on to the veranda. She felt compelled to be with him.

"Gavin I am scared, be careful," she uttered. Gavin turned and embraced Veronique. He looked into her limpid watery eyes.

"Don't you worry, I will be coming home with Gregori," he said. He turned away and jumped down the veranda steps. Veronique watched him run around to the side of the house to where his Mustang was parked. She stood on the veranda, unable to look away. Gavin quickly drove off. She could not take her eyes off the car. She yearned deeply to be going with him. The tropical forest that surrounded their home soon hid the vehicle. Tears rolled down her cheeks. Why did Veronique feel she would never see him again? She sat on the nearby bench and cried. Deep down inside she knew Susannah was alive. Detective Martinez was wrong. There was no international syndicate. Susannah was behind this and Gavin was walking into a trap. Susannah will be at the jetty, ready to kill him. Veronique stood up. What could she do? She felt completely helpless. Her emotions overflowed as she stumbled back into the house.

"I just know something dreadful is gonna happen!" Veronique cried out as she staggered into the living room. "Susannah is alive, she has Gregori and now she will kill Gavin." Veronique collapsed to the floor, her legs simply buckled. The emotional strain was too great. Loretta came to her aid. Veronique looked directly up at the policewoman. "Please do something, it is a trap to kill Gavin," she sobbed.

"Don't upset yourself Honey," comforted Loretta.

"We are there and will do all we can to keep Gavin and Gregori safe," responded the policewoman.

"I have this overwhelming sense that I won't see Gavin again," cried Veronique as she lay on the floor, her upper body resting against her mother. Loretta offered what words of comfort she could as she embraced her daughter.

"Gavin will be fine, he has the bulletproof vest," consoled Loretta. Veronique continued her verbal anguish:

"In an hour from now Gavin will be dead. She will have reaped her revenge. Even if Susannah is caught, if we don't let her go she will never tell us where Gregori is. He will be tied up somewhere in a remote place, crying but no one to hear him. Please do something," wailed Veronique to the police officers. "Don't let Susannah win!"

The journey time to the jetty from the house was roughly fifteen minutes. Five minutes into the journey a further text message appeared on Gavin's mobile. The absence of any identity on the display made Gavin assume it was from the kidnapper. Leaving one hand on the steering wheel he read the text message.

Change of plan. Go to the marina, Southside. You have 7 minutes to get there.

Gavin did not hesitate as he slammed on the brakes. His Mustang skidded to a halt. After a three-point turn he headed for the marina. Gavin was no fool; he half expected all would not go according to plan. The rendezvous at the jetty was an obvious decoy. He also realised that he was alone. Detective Martinez and his officers were all at the jetty. Even if Gavin informed them of the change of plan, they could not reach the marina in time. Plus their presence could jeopardise Gregori's safe return. Gavin was grateful for the bulletproof vest. There was no time to lose. He raced towards the marina, breaking the speed limit. Gavin knew the journey time was at least ten minutes. Every turn he made caused the loose terrain to shoot out from under the tyres. He performed a 90 degrees wheel spin as he turned on to the lane that would take him down to the Southside of the marina. On approaching, Gavin looked around to see if he could spot Gregori. The brake pads screeched as he stopped the Mustang. He got out of the car. There were various yachts and speedboats moored. He saw a couple of people on a yacht. Were they the kidnappers? In the absence of anyone else he ran towards them.

"Do you have Gregori?" he shouted out, running as fast as he could. The Mexican couple looked on, unable to fathom Gavin's statement. They remained silent. "Do you have my son Gregori?" he repeated as he reached their yacht. The two Mexicans gave a blank expression.

"No," said one of them.

"Have you seen anyone with a small boy?" requested Gavin. His temperament was clearly agitated. Again they answered no. Gavin was completely riled. What does he do now? He pulled out his mobile from his pocket. Perhaps there was a further text message, but the display was blank. Next, Gavin ran up and down the various boardwalks calling out Gregori's name. People appeared on deck, their curiosity aroused by Gavin's behaviour. He did not make any hesitation in addressing them. One of them must be the kidnapper. Gavin demanded the whereabouts of his son to every person he met. To his disappointment neither of them were the kidnappers, nor had anyone seen a small boy. Gavin's ranting and raving seemed in vain. There was no sign of Gregori anywhere, but he could not give up. He noticed the time was now 5.45pm. What has gone wrong? He has followed all of the kidnappers' instructions. Where was Gregori?

There was no alternative. He began to search every yacht and every speedboat. Gavin jumped on deck, shouting his son's name. He tried doors and windows but most were locked. The ones that were open he climbed inside or rushed below deck. Frantically he searched for Gregori. Anyone he bumped into he asked if they had seen a small boy, but again to no avail. Out of sheer desperation he stood on deck of a yacht, looked all around the marina and shouted out Gregori's name. The only people he could see were the onlookers he had already approached. They watched out of a sense of duty. One yacht owner even called the police, reporting a crazed man was trespassing on all the boats, acting very suspiciously. Once again Gavin shouted out Gregori's name, but still no response. He grabbed his mobile and replied back to the kidnapper's text message stating:

'Where is my son?' Gavin received a negative acknowledgment. The text had been undelivered.

"No!" cried out Gavin. In temper he kicked the side of the yacht.

"What seems to be the problem?" came a stern voice. Gavin turned to see the marina security guard standing on the boardwalk. A tall broad shouldered black man dressed in uniform. Gavin sighed heavily as he vented his anger.

"I'm looking for my son," he stated. "I've lost my son. He is around here somewhere. He is only two years old." The guard noticed how perplexed Gavin was.

"I assume this is not your yacht?" questioned the security guard.

"No, it is not. I thought my son may be on one of the boats," replied Gavin. "I had to search for him."

"I understand your anxiety, let me help you find your son. This is a dangerous place for a small child, he may have fallen into the water," remarked the security guard. Perhaps not the wisest comment to make.

"Oh my God don't say that, he can't swim," panicked Gavin as he jumped down from the yacht. He ran to the water's edge. The security guard assisted. They looked into the water as they walked up the boardwalk.

"When did you last see him?" asked the security guard. Gavin hesitated on what to say.

"It is kind of complicated. He must be here, we have to keep looking," urged Gavin. He shouted out to the neighbouring folk who were watching. "Look for my son! Check the water by you!" Some did just that; their actions prompted others to do the same.

"Why would your son be here by himself?" questioned the security guard. At that moment Gavin's mobile rang. There was no indication on the display as to who it was.

"Hello," stated Gavin, hoping it was the kidnappers.

"Detective Martinez here Gavin, we have Gregori, he is safe. He is with me at the police station."

"You have him!" cried out Gavin with relief.

"Yes, and we have also arrested a woman. Can you come down to the police station?" informed the detective.

"I am on my way. Thank God, thank God, thank God. See you in a jiff," he said and ended the call. Gavin turned his attention to the security guard. "That was the police, they have found my son. I must go and fetch him." He rushed past the security guard.

"I am glad for you," called out the security guard. Gavin ran off. The bulletproof vest was a hindrance but he did not care. The nightmare was over. No doubt the kidnapper had enjoyed sending him on a wild goose chase. So what! It did not matter now. Gregori was safe and the culprit had been caught. Gavin ran along the boardwalk unbuttoning his shirt. The security guard and the other onlookers watched. Gavin reached his Mustang. He removed the bulletproof vest and replaced his shirt. The cumbersome attire was not needed now. He jumped into the driver's seat, turned the ignition and pressed hard on the accelerator pedal. He drove to the police station a little less frantic than when he drove to the marina. Dusk was falling as the sun touched the oceanic horizon. Nocturnal creatures began to stir as night-time approached. The resting sun shone into Gavin's face. He put on his sunglasses.

Detective Martinez alerted the Harrison household that Gregori was safe. He also informed them that a woman had been arrested. However, the safe return of Gregori was not as a direct result of the police operation. The police officers were lying in wait at the jetty as planned. When Gavin had failed to show up, and there seemed little sign of the kidnappers, Detective Martinez sensed the situation had gone adrift. At approximately 5.30pm, he had received a text message saying a woman had walked into the police station with Gregori. Now that Gregori was safe the operation concluded.

Gavin parked his Mustang outside the police station and ran into the building. At the reception desk there seemed little introduction. The duty officer was expecting him. Although the duty officer had not met Gavin before, he immediately recognised him from the numerous photographs in the public domain. Most people in Martinique had not met Gavin, but there would be few who would not recognise him in public. Over recent years Gavin had received much public attention, largely due to Susannah's trial and the numerous press coverage that had ensued.

"Come through Gavin, we have been expecting you," said the duty officer. He escorted Gavin to a side room. "Wait here while I tell the chief you're here." The duty officer left Gavin alone in the small confined room. The room only contained four chairs and a small coffee table. Gavin seated himself, eager to see his son. Moments later a policewoman entered the room carrying Gregori.

"Daddy, Daddy, Daddy," called out Gregori. His father stood up and reached out for his son.

"Daddy is here to take you home," said Gavin, taking hold of Gregori. He hugged him and Gregori returned the affection.

"If you can stay here for a moment, Detective Martinez wants to see you," said the policewoman.

"Of course. Thank you so much. I am very grateful for whatever it is you did," remarked Gavin. The policewoman smiled and left the room. Gavin sat down placing Gregori on his lap. "Shall we ring Mummy?"

"Yes!" said Gregori gleefully. Gavin rang home. Tobias answered.

"I have Gregori, he is safe and doesn't seem any worse for wear," said Gavin.

"We know, we have already been informed," replied Tobias. "I'll pass you to Veronique, she is standing right next to me." Veronique grabbed the receiver from her father.

"Hello Gavin, are you all right?" she anxiously said. "I have been sick with worry. Could not stop crying."

"We are both fine, and don't upset yourself. Everything is fine now," replied Gavin, he then turned his attention to Gregori. "Say hello to Mummy."

"Hello Mummy," shouted Gregori.

"Mummy can't wait to see you," replied Veronique. "Have you been a good boy?"

"Yes," stated Gregori, who did not seem in the least bit perturbed by his ordeal.

"We will be home as soon as we can," remarked Gavin. "I'm waiting to see Detective Martinez and find out who this woman that kidnapped our son is."

"Of course, now I know you are both safe I can relax," said Veronique.

"We will be home as quick as we can," stated Gavin and ended the call. He turned his attention to his son. "So my big boy what have you been doing?"

"Watching television," stated Gregori. "The lady gave me lots of ice cream and read stories to me. She was a nice lady," relayed his son excitedly. "Will she come to see me again? I want to show her Marmajuke."

"No, she won't be," answered Gavin. He was relieved that Gregori had not been harmed during this dire adventure, but Gavin was rather vexed that his son should have enjoyed himself. After all the anguish the family had suffered it seems Gregori was having a wonderful time, how typical.

"I know Daddy, sing *The Mango Tree*," he excitedly said. "The lady did not know it and I tried singing the words but could not remember the words. Sing it for me Daddy." Gavin could not refuse. He proudly sat his son on his knee and sang the nursery rhyme.

Sit beneath a mango tree.
Gazing at the sunny sea.
See an egret soaring high.
Soon my boy you'll touch the sky.
Soon my boy you'll touch the sky.

Flying high just like a bird.
Flap your wings just coo and chirp.
See below that mango tree.
Sitting there is you and me.
Sitting there is you and me.

"Well someone's having a good time," remarked Detective Martinez as he entered the room. "Smiles all round, what a pleasing outcome," he added as he greeted Gavin. "No need to get up, you stay sitting with this little one on your lap." The detective sat next to them.

"Thank you so much," remarked Gavin as they shook hands.

"I don't mind admitting that I got very concerned when you failed to turn up at the jetty," mentioned Detective Martinez.

"That is because I received a text from the kidnappers urging me to go to the marina," informed Gavin. Gregori sat on his lap looking up at the burly detective.

"I see," he replied. "Well I have to tell you that we were not instrumental in rescuing Gregori. At about 5.30, a woman walked into the police station carrying him."

"You mean the kidnapper gave herself up?" assumed Gavin.

"No, we know from Sebastian's testimony and the CCTV footage that the female kidnapper is white. The woman who returned Gregori is black and early indications imply she is innocent," stated Detective Martinez. Gavin objected to the chief's latter remark.

"There is no way she can be innocent," was Gavin's outburst. "Please don't be fooled by this woman."

"I understand your anger and rightly so. We are still questioning her and checking out her alibi for the past forty-eight hours, and also her bank details. She maintains that as she was walking down the adjacent street to the police station, this little boy ran up to her saying *'take me to my mummy and daddy'*. There was a note pinned to his shirt stating *'my name is Gregori take me to the police station.'* When she picked him up she noticed a car speeding away. She saw the driver, a blonde female, whom she has already identified from the CCTV footage as the woman who had Gregori in the food store. We now have further CCTV footage to view from the neighbouring streets. You can rest assured we want to apprehend the kidnapper as much as you do. I say kidnapper it most likely is an international criminal syndicate who is behind this."

"You will check if there is any connection to Susannah or Kirsti Løvik in Norway," requested Gavin, rather beleaguered by the evasive nature of those against him. "Have you heard any more from the Norwegian authorities? Could Susannah be alive?"

"All investigations take time, but with regard to Susannah, there is no evidence to say she is alive," assured Detective Martinez. "I also intend to travel to Norway and interview Kirsti Løvik. But what I can tell you is that we did not retract any fingerprints from the house except of your family of course, so there we drew a blank."

"Well we have Gregori back that is the main thing. Maybe it is an international criminal syndicate after all, and nothing to do with Susannah," surmised Gavin. "So what happens now?"

"I think you need to take this little one home, relax and spend time with your family. Leave us to do our job in finding his kidnapper and reclaim your $2million," commented Detective Martinez. "You know he aught to be checked out at a hospital, although he seems perfectly fine."

"I understand your concern. Veronique will check him over. He has told me the lady gave him ice cream and read stories. He seems to have had a marvellous time," informed Gavin.

"Let's be thankful for small mercies," remarked Detective Martinez.

Gregori's homecoming was a euphoric occasion. He enjoyed being centre of attention. Veronique's reaction was to keep a constant hold of him, she did not want to let him go, but all Gregori wanted to do was play with his toys. He even said he had missed Marmajuke.

"He seems as happy as ever," remarked Loretta.

"Gregori, look what Mama has got for you," said Veronique, holding out a coconut slice. "Your favourite biscuit." The overexcited Gregori toddled over and happily took the biscuit.

"Can I have ice cream like the lady gave me, and will she be coming to see me again?" asked Gregori earnestly.

"We can have ice cream of course, but the lady cannot see you again because she is a naughty person," replied Veronique.

"She is not a naughty person and I want to show her Marmajuke," stated Gregori disappointedly.

"Why don't I take you into the kitchen and get you some ice cream," suggested Loretta. Gregori's face lit up with excitement. Loretta picked him up from the sofa and carried him into the kitchen.

"At least he seems fine," commented Ursula. "Will you be wanting a nanny?"

"Definitely not!" came Veronique's emphatic reply. "I shall take a career break from work and look after him myself. After the last few days I don't think I shall be able to ever let him out of my sight. Nor shall I leave his window open at night. All doors and windows will be kept securely locked and bolted."

"I am glad things have turned out well," said the policewoman. "Which means our job here is done unless you want us to stay?"

"No, we shall be fine now," said Gavin. "Thanks for all your support. You and your colleague have been here for three days, don't you have homes to go to?" joked Gavin.

"We do, we do, but we also like the overtime," responded the policewoman. "You take care now and keep all doors and windows locked. Enjoy your evening." Gavin and Veronique escorted the two remaining police officers out of the house. They stood on the veranda and watched them drive away.

"It seems Gregori enjoyed his little adventure," remarked Veronique.

"And so we should be grateful," replied Gavin. "I know you feel perplexed but at least he is fine. Life is always ironic."

"After all the heartache we suffered, our little son was having a fabulous adventure. He liked the lady and even missed Marmajuke. You are right Gavin. Life is ironic," said Veronique. They snatched a few seconds alone. After a kiss and an embrace they returned inside.

Chapter Nine

Suspicions

Money was flowing down the drain like water gushing from a burst pipe.

Whatever ordeal Gregori had encountered at the hands of his kidnappers had not marred his chirpy character. The little infant played happily with his toys. Veronique, the doting mother remained by his side at all times. Either they would partake in typical mother and baby games with Gregori revelling in the attention, or she would read a book whilst he amused himself. He certainly seemed contented. However, for Veronique the horror of this dreadful experience would always be in the forefront of her mind. She would never forget the dreaded uncertainty of not knowing if she would see him again.

Gregori's kidnapper or kidnappers were still at large. The black woman who had returned Gregori was allowed to go free. The wonders of CCTV had not only captured Gregori running towards her, but also showed the blonde woman taking Gregori out of her car and pointing to the black woman for him to run to. Unfortunately, despite such excellent pictures of the female kidnapper, her identity remained unknown. The blonde capacious wig she wore succeeded in masking her true features. At least the CCTV images clearly eliminated Susannah, adding credence to the belief that she was dead. All evidence signified Susannah had been cremated. However, Kirsti Løvik's possible involvement was still in question. Detective Martinez was still hoping to interview her, but this had not yet transpired for she was out of the country. The Norwegian police intended to fully cooperate. However, they were powerless to sanction a meeting because they could not locate her. The information that her secretary Lana had given was that Kirsti Løvik was in Europe on business. Detective Martinez will be requiring a stronger alibi when he finally interviews her. The elusive Scandinavian could not remain hidden forever.

Veronique hoped that Kirsti Løvik would supply the missing answers once interrogated. Surely her troubled mind would soon be eased? Setting aside all these issues Veronique picked up her son, sat him on her knee and sang *The Mango Tree* nursery rhyme.

> *Sit beneath a mango tree.*
> *Gazing at the sunny sea.*
> *See an egret soaring high.*
> *Soon my boy you'll touch the sky.*
> *Soon my boy you'll touch the sky.*
>
> *Flying high just like a bird.*
> *Flap your wings just coo and chirp.*
> *See below that mango tree.*
> *Sitting there is you and me.*
> *Sitting there is you and me.*

Gregori enjoyed it so much she sang it several times over. And then when she had decided enough was enough, Gregori continued singing it to Marmajuke.

<>

As the days passed, Gavin's financial status worsened. The plantation remained closed. The environmental health officer had vigorously inspected the process, and was satisfied that Gavin did adhere to health and safety regulations. An inspection certificate of endorsement was issued. This was welcomed news. Gavin assumed they would allow him to re-open his business, but this was not the case. The police investigation was ongoing and the saboteur had not been apprehended. Until matters had been cleared up, the environmental health agency could not authorise the lifting of the temporary closure warrant. They had to be certain there would not be any further reprisals, in other words no more ants in the sugar despatches.

It was inevitable that Gavin reneged on his orders. He had urged his customers to be patient, but of course they had orders to fulfil themselves. The suspension of trade was very damaging. His clients were forced to seek custom elsewhere. Gavin's competitors seized the opportunity to recruit his lucrative orders. His business was in serious jeopardy. The years of hard work that his parents had first initiated were disappearing quickly. The outlook seemed pessimistic. All Gavin and Tobias could do was wait and watch their business decline. They had even stopped planting new crop. It grieved them to see existing crop wither away. Money was flowing down the drain like water gushing from a burst pipe.

Global Incorporations Ltd was still interested in buying the business. However, their latest takeover bid was for a lower amount than previously declared. They justified the reduction due to Gavin's current trading dilemma. They felt obliged to offer Gavin an olive branch for him to surrender and sell the business whilst he still had one to sell. Gavin was defiant as before, and rejected their insulting offer. The plantation was not up for sale. He had not reached the end of the road yet. He was banking on the proceeds from the sale of Calypso Tavern to cushion this financial calamity. That is if Calypso Tavern is sold in the near future. At this moment in time the casino complex remained on the market. Unfortunately though, it had received little interest. However, business at the casino was thriving as always. The drugs affair had not curtailed the profits. It even seemed that the bad publicity had generated further custom. Gavin was grateful for this financial flicker of hope. He had now reached the stage where Calypso Tavern's profits would have to subsidise the plantation. An audit nightmare for Sebastian, but as Gavin was the sole owner of both companies, it ruled out any shareholder complaints.

<>

Detective Martinez was quickly ushered through security at Oslo airport. Kirsti Løvik had resurfaced and had been arrested on her return to Norway. This did not please her at all. Despite Kirsti Løvik being a Norwegian citizen, the authorities agreed for her to be questioned by the Caribbean detective. After all, he knew the full details of his criminal case in Martinique, and the possible connection to the unsolved murder of Tor Hegland. The charge at the moment was kidnapping, but other charges may be made depending on further evidence acquired. Did Kirsti Løvik place drugs in Calypso Tavern? Was she responsible for sabotaging the plantation? Did she have any involvement in Tor Hegland's murder? Could she confirm whether Susannah was alive? The plentiful circumstantial evidence would make the interrogation very interesting.

A police car transported Detective Martinez from the airport to Oslo police station. The second week of August was an autumnal day. The leaves on the trees had already begun to turn. Detective Martinez sat on the rear seat and glossed over the interview agenda. He only planned to stay in Oslo for two days so needed to ensure he asked Kirsti Løvik all the relevant questions. He suspected that she would be uncooperative. His agenda of questions emulated a family tree, depicting her possible replies. This would then lead to a further question. It was essential to apply foresight in the hope of reaching the truth. He read through the pages of his notes like an actor learning his lines. It was imperative not to fluster this opportunity.

Kirsti Løvik, the dominant 56-year-old seethed with anger at being arrested. Her mood was indignant as she sat in the interview room at the police station. She had purposely evaded the authorities, not because she was guilty, but because she objected to having her freedom hindered. Her previous conviction had been squashed having won her appeal, but that did not give the authorities the right to question her over similar matters. During her European business trip, her secretary Lana had informed her she was wanted by the police, all the more reason to delay her return.

Kirsti Løvik's lawyer sat next to her. He had already briefed her on the matters in question. He was a youngish man, the sort Kirsti Løvik desired sexually, but there were no lustful feelings today. During her prolonged absence she had authorised him to contact the police and ascertain the reason why they wanted to speak with her. Perhaps her absence was self-detrimental. She knew she would be questioned on returning to Norway but she did not expect to be arrested. Impatiently she waited for Detective Martinez to arrive. When he eventually entered the room, she glared at him defiantly.

"So we meet again," she said in a sarcastic manner. Detective Martinez did not rise to her indignation. He merely sat down opposite her. Between them was a small table, standing on it a recording device. Formal introductions were not needed. "How long is this going to take?" she stated.

"That depends on how quickly you answer the questions, so it is up to you how long we shall be," responded Detective Martinez. Once he had activated the recorder, he read out her rights. "Kirsti Løvik, you do not have to say anything but it may harm your defence if you do not mention when questioned something which you later rely on in court. Anything you do say may be given in evidence."

Kirsti Løvik stared directly into Detective Martinez's eyes as he spoke. He was not deterred by her intimidating attitude.

"We have many issues to discuss with you, so it is in your best interest to cooperate. I am sure your lawyer would agree," said Detective Martinez. Kirsti Løvik remained silent, allowing the detective to continue. "You are aware we have been looking for you for some time. Your prolonged absence has aroused suspicion. Therefore, if you are innocent it is advisable to be cooperative. Any act of indifference will make you appear guilty."

Kirsti Løvik sat in a dominant pose. Most people would cower under interrogation, but she was not going to be submissive. She coldly stared at the detective as he continued to speak:

"I will state the matters in chronological order."

"Excuse me, in what order?" remarked Kirsti Løvik, breaking from her silence. "My English is limited," she added.

"In date order of when the events occurred," corrected Detective Martinez. "The first matter is the murder of Tor Hegland."

"Why do you think I had anything to do with that?" she remarked flippantly. Her attitude was tiresome and she showed little respect for Detective Martinez. "Anyway, the police arrested someone else for his murder, then they let him go."

"You dealt with Tor Hegland over the cremation of Susannah. Did you find him in anyway unusual?" asked Detective Martinez.

"I was very upset at the time. My mind was on Susannah, my sister-in-law. I was the only family she had, that I am aware of. I did not see anything unusual with Tor Hegland."

"Why did you choose to have Susannah cremated?" asked Detective Martinez.

"I did not," answered Kirsti Løvik, shrugging her shoulders. "At the time I was away on business as I often am," she said, emphasising the latter part of the sentence as if to make a comparison with her recent absence. "When I returned I discovered from the newspapers that Karl had killed Susannah, and that Tor Hegland, the local coroner had charge of her body, so I went to see him. When I got there she had already been cremated."

"Who ordered the cremation?" asked Detective Martinez.

"Gavin. Tor Hegland told me that he had contacted him re any possible relatives. Gavin said she did not have any. When Tor Hegland asked Gavin what to do with her body he replied, *let her burn in hell*, so he cremated her," informed Kirsti Løvik.

"And what did you do then? Were you upset, angry that this had happened without your knowledge?"

"Of course I was upset. Susannah was dead but I was not angry with Tor Hegland, he did not kill her, he only did his job. He had saved Susannah's ashes in a casket, so I arranged for them to be buried in her husband's grave, my late brother. That is what she would have wanted."

"Did you have any further contact with Tor Hegland afterwards?"

"No I did not. I never saw him again," stated Kirsti Løvik. "I was saddened to learn of his murder, he seemed a good man, but I had no reason to kill him so don't you get thinking I did."

Reluctantly she gave her answers, along with the occasional sigh. She could see the many pages Detective Martinez had in front of him, each page containing a myriad of questions. What a pity she did not get any sponsors for this marathon interrogation. She could have raised a fortune.

"You are the owner of Global Incorporations Ltd, are you not?" questioned Detective Martinez. Kirsti Løvik gave a condescending glare as she abruptly replied:

"Yes I am."

"And have you been bidding to take over Gavin's plantation business?" quizzed Detective Martinez.

"Is there a law against it," remarked Kirsti Løvik coldly.

"Why would you want to take over Gavin's plantation business?" Kirsti Løvik sighed heavily as she gave her reply.

"I am a business woman, that's what business people do, invest and buy other companies."

"But why would you want Gavin's business?" urged Detective Martinez. Kirsti Løvik became evasive and did not respond. She looked at her lawyer. That was his cue to intervene.

"I think my client is more than honest with you. She has many business ventures in many companies. Unless you have any firm evidence linking my client to the perils of Gavin's misfortune, I suggest we terminate this interview."

"These matters we are questioning are very serious," responded Detective Martinez. "The murder of Tor Hegland; the kidnapping of Gavin's son; the sabotage of his plantation and drugs planted at Calypso Tavern."

"I know nothing of all that," interrupted Kirsti Løvik.

"Well I hope you haven't any involvement," replied Detective Martinez. "The last thing I want is unnecessary distractions from our investigation of these matters."

"Then stop wasting my time," stated Kirsti Løvik abruptly. "Just because I told a lie in court to defend Susannah, you think I am capable of murder and kidnapping. Honestly! Where is your sense?"

"I can assure you I have plenty of commonsense. I could spend days questioning you over these matters. How would you like that? I too don't want to spend that much time with you. Therefore, for us to eliminate you from our enquiries, I suggest you undergo a polygraph test," said Detective Martinez.

"My client will do no such thing," retorted her lawyer.

"A poly test? What is that?" questioned Kirsti Løvik

"A polygraph test is a lie detector test which is 96% accurate," informed Detective Martinez. Kirsti Løvik looked away. Had she something to hide?

"What concrete evidence do you have that my client is involved?" demanded her lawyer.

"There is strong circumstantial evidence, so we can either keep questioning Kirsti Løvik for as many days or weeks as it takes, or we can spend a couple of hours doing the polygraph test, which if Kirsti Løvik is innocent she will have nothing to fear, and I won't need to question her again," remarked Detective Martinez.

"This is against my human rights. You have no legal right to do this," protested Kirsti Løvik angrily. In a moment of touché Detective Martinez stared into her eyes, like she had stared at him at the beginning of the interview.

"Given that you lied to us before during Susannah's trial when you were on oath, I cannot be too naïve to accept every word you say as the truth. The truth always comes out in the end, so we might as well get it over and done with." He could see she was not happy with his suggestion. Just what was she hiding? His judgement told him she was not a killer, but why did she seem so guilty? However, regardless of his suspicions he did not expect her reaction.

"Oh I will do it," she said flippantly. "Anything to be rid of you. I have nothing to be ashamed of." Detective Martinez was surprised how quickly she agreed. He had expected her to be more emphatic in her refusal. Perhaps she was innocent after all.

The polygraph test had been arranged for the following day. They regrouped in the same interview room. Kirsti Løvik felt annoyed. She must have suffered a moment of weakness to submit to Detective Martinez. Agreeing to the polygraph test was one thing, having the patience to tolerate it another. She was accustomed to being her own boss and did not like being dictated too. Her attitude was clearly demonstrative. She paid little regard for the mechanical device that would determine if she was guilty.

"How can such a feeble contraption be reliable?" she swiftly remarked. A Norwegian police officer had connected the impulse receptor to her finger. He would monitor the recordings as the interview progressed. Kirsti Løvik sat with her lawyer by her side. Detective Martinez sat opposite with a clipboard in front of him, listing all the questions he intended to ask her. To begin with a few general questions were asked in order for the police officer to accurately set the device. Kirsti Løvik was told to curtail her answers to either yes or no. Once the formalities were over, Detective Martinez began his questions.

"Is your name Kirsti Løvik?"

"Yes," she replied. The censor remained constant, indicating she was telling the truth.

"Do you own a perfumery business?" asked Detective Martinez.

"Yes," replied Kirsti Løvik. Again the censor remained constant. She was telling the truth.

"Are you 56 years of age?"

"Yes," she said begrudgingly. The censor remained constant. Now that the general questions were over, Detective Martinez could pose the all too important ones.

"Did you murder Tor Hegland?"

"No," she replied. The censor remained constant. She had told the truth.

"Do you know of anyone else who murdered Tor Hegland?"

"No," replied Kirsti Løvik. She had told the truth.

"Did you have any involvement in the death of Tor Hegland?"

"No." Again she had given a truthful answer. Detective Martinez then addressed the matter of Gregori's kidnapping. Although Kirsti Løvik was not the woman in the CCTV footage, he still followed procedure to eliminate her from the crime.

"Did you kidnap Gregori, Gavin's son?"

"No," replied Kirsti Løvik. She was telling the truth.

"Did you have any involvement in kidnapping Gregori?"

"No," sighed Kirsti Løvik, somewhat bored with the repetitive questions. However, the censor remained constant. She had told the truth.

"Do you know who did kidnap Gregori?"

"No." She had told the truth.

"Did you have any involvement with receiving the $2million ransom?"

"No," she replied, giving a truthful answer.

"Are you the owner of Global Incorporations Ltd?"

"Yes."

"Did you have any involvement in sabotaging Gavin's plantation by putting ants in the sugar consignments?"

"No." To her detriment the censor waved, indicating she had lied. The officer recorded the negative result. Detective Martinez was fully aware of the findings as he posed his next question.

"Did you have any involvement in planting heroin at Calypso Tavern?"

"No!" she affirmed, but the censor waved yet again depicting a lie. Detective Martinez asked a few more questions

A Certain Dilemma

before reaching the all too important one. It was the question that the Harrison household were eager to know the answer to.

"Is Susannah alive?"

"No." She was bewildered. Why would he ask that? However, the censor remained constant. She had told the truth.

The polygraph test was complete. Detective Martinez and the police officer left the interview room to discuss the results. Kirsti Løvik and her lawyer were allowed refreshments as they waited for Detective Martinez to return. Her lawyer sipped a cup of black coffee. He asked if she had been truthful. Her reaction was indifferent.

"No doubt we will soon find out," she replied.

Thirty minutes later the interview reconvened. The police officer remained standing by the door as Detective Martinez discussed the polygraph results. He did not hesitate in confronting Kirsti Løvik about lying over sabotaging the plantation, and hiding heroin in Calypso Tavern. To his surprise she did not deny the results. Perhaps she thought there was little point. In her defence she admitted acting out of grief over Susannah's death. Although it was Karl who had killed her, it was all Gavin's fault. Kirsti Løvik revealed that Susannah had divulged her revenge plan. How Susannah had wanted to destroy Gavin and had told her a few ideas, like planting drugs at Calypso Tavern and putting ants in the sugar dispatch. Kirsti Løvik confessed that she wanted to continue with Susannah's revenge. Her feelings were so strong that she felt compelled to seek justice for Susannah, and also for her brother's death in the cable car crash. She was not remorseful.

Kirsti Løvik signed her confession and an agreement not to pursue any form of reprisal against Gavin. Under judicial law Detective Martinez referred her criminal acts to the Norwegian authorities, for them to consider any penal sentence. He was more concerned in capturing Gregori's kidnappers than any civil prosecution. He did ask Gavin if he wished to press charges. All Gavin wanted to do was get back to business. He was only too relieved when the environmental health agency lifted the closure warrant. His insurance company had finally paid up for lost production, so Gavin referred the matter to them, to see if they wanted to claim any compensation from Kirsti Løvik's perfumery empire. What was more reassuring was the fact that Susannah was dead. Had she been alive Kirsti Løvik would have known this. All thanks to Detective Martinez for orchestrating the polygraph test.

Gavin's financial status began to improve. Sugar production became a 24-hour process in order to make up for lost revenue. Gavin practically worked round-the-clock to re-establish his credibility and secure orders. He gave a press release. The public were made aware that Kirsti Løvik was responsible for the temporary closure of his business, and the drugs at Calypso Tavern. Recovery was sharp and swift. However, Calypso Tavern remained unsold, but Gavin was confident a buyer would surface sooner or later. Especially now the drugs affair had been resolved. At least business was booming, so profits were increasing once more.

Today, August 17th was Gavin and Veronique's fourth wedding anniversary. To mark the occasion Gavin had booked an evening meal at the Mexican Marina Diner. Arm in arm they strolled along, talking casually as they watched the setting sun sink below the watery horizon. A vibrant colourful cloak of orange and purple nestled in its wake. The fiery sky reflected in the ripples of the Caribbean Sea. This occasion was also the first time Veronique had left Gregori since the kidnapping. Ursula and Godwin were more than happy to baby-sit. Their holiday was certainly eventful and was set to continue. They felt unable to return to Texas, given all the problems that were rife. They wanted to be supportive and also protective of their daughter. Every day they pondered over all the sinister entrapments that surrounded the Harrison household. They feared for Rebecca's safety. Not only that but with Calypso Tavern being sold would this prompt Rebecca to return to Texas? Ursula and Godwin certainly hoped so. Perhaps a few gentle hints of persuasion may be all that is required for Rebecca to change her mind.

Gavin and Veronique ambled along like two lovesick teenagers. They continued their early evening stroll via the marina. Various yachts and speedboats were moored. Not far off they saw a local inhabitant sitting on the boardwalk, fishing. A lantern was by his side as dusk fell. Gavin recounted his frightful search for Gregori. The fact that he had leapt aboard many yachts in desperation, then the dread of wondering if Gregori had drowned. Those moments he would never forget. Veronique echoed his anguish. Those forty-eight hours were the worst of her life. Arm in arm they continued their walk, allowing romance to flourish.

"It is so peaceful down here," sighed Veronique happily. "What time is the table booked for?"

"7.30," replied Gavin. "Our fourth anniversary. I hope you are not too disappointed in me just taking you out for a meal. With all that has happened recently I hadn't the time to plan anything special," remarked Gavin.

"You know I don't expect fancy presents. Just being with you is more than enough for me," replied Veronique. She valued every moment with Gavin. Not too long ago she thought they would never be together, thanks to the wretched Susannah. Then with Gregori's kidnapping, she felt convinced it was a trap by Susannah. On reflection this had taught her to appreciate their relationship and not be obsessive with trivial matters or material things. Being wealthy was merely a bonus and nothing more. It certainly was not essential.

"Why don't we book a holiday and get away for a while, with Gregori of course. I am sure he will enjoy the change of scenery," suggested Gavin.

"I can agree to that," replied Veronique. She glanced at her watch. The time was only 6.30. "Aren't we early for the restaurant, the time is 6.30, it's only five minutes away," she said.

"Is that all the time is?" responded Gavin. "I thought it was later than that." There was a note of mischief in his voice. Fortunately Veronique did not suspect. They continued their walk along the Caribbean shore.

"Oh look Gavin, there's a yacht over there with my name on it," remarked Veronique, pointing to the elegant schooner they were approaching. The yacht was brilliant white with a pale blue abstract design running across the bow. It looped around the name *Veronique*, which was painted black in an italic style. The centre mast stood proud and firm, its sail gathered in. The subtle cabin rose up from the deck. This resembled the shape of an open-mouthed shark caught in time as it surfaced the water to devour a seal or some other form of prey. Of course there were no teeth it was just the outline of the cabin that resembled the king of the ocean. "It looks new," added Veronique.

"Well if it has got your name on it then it must be yours," replied Gavin nonchalantly. Veronique turned and looked at him. Gavin smiled. "Happy anniversary darling."

"You bought me a yacht!" exclaimed Veronique, completely euphoric and letting go of his arm. Gavin laughed then coyly added:

"If you don't like it I can always take it back."

"Do I like it, I love it, but can we afford it?"

"Our financial problems are over now business is back to normal."

"I know that but we didn't get the ransom money back," stated Veronique.

"Not yet we haven't, but Martinez is still on the case. Hopefully Calypso Tavern will be sold soon."

"Can I go aboard now?" she said, allowing her excitement to flourish.

"Of course," replied Gavin. Veronique ran the few paces to the edge of the yacht. For a few moments she stood and admired the sheer beauty of the vessel before climbing aboard. She took a firm hold of the handrail. The metal bar was cold to the touch. She quickly mounted the boarding ladder. The deck was finished in teak fibreglass. Veronique did not want to step her dirty footprints on it, but she had to step aboard and investigate further. She turned to face Gavin. She looked down at him as he stood on the boardwalk, his smiling face beaming up at her.

"When did you plan all this?" she said. "I had no idea you were up to something."

"Why don't I give you a guided tour?" said Gavin as he climbed aboard. "It has a headsail reefing system, self-tailing halyard and sheet winches. Manual and electrical bilge pumps, a staunch bowthruster and..."

"Oh don't say all that it doesn't mean a thing to me," interrupted Veronique laughing. Gavin saw how cheerful he had made his wife. He had not seen her this happy in a long time. They walked around the deck. Veronique admired the beauty of her present. They snatched a moment to look out to sea. Veronique's hand clenched the nearby side rail as they glimpsed the diminishing sunset. They stood in front of the cabin, engulfed with romance. Gavin grabbed Veronique and kissed her. She allowed herself to be locked in his arms as his lips pressed firmly against hers.

CHAPTER TEN

Egypt

In a mismatch of coordination he stumbled out of the pool in full frontal of everyone.

What impression would the ancient pharaohs of Egypt have of Loretta? An interesting match for Cleopatra perhaps. Although Loretta could not embrace the company of an asp, she certainly wanted to relax in a milk bath and revel in the company of many suitors, but Tobias was her Mark Anthony. Now the beginning of September saw the Caribbean couple jetting off to Egypt. Loretta had finally persuaded her husband to take her to the ancient land of the Pharaohs. Their three week holiday would see them having a cruise down the River Nile; visit the many bazaars en route; view the spectacular pyramids; stand in awe of a sphinx, and see an Aladdin's cave of artifacts and antiquities. It was inevitable that this excursion would bring them many memories, most of which would be humorous and at Loretta's expense. For example, the few days they spent in the 'Valley of The Kings' would not be forgotten too easily. Loretta wanted to join in with the local inhabitants and their traditions, so insisted on riding a camel. She and Tobias were part of a tourist group. The tour guide, an Egyptian young female with short dark hair that was styled like a pharaoh, proudly escorted her entourage. Bursts of laughter filled the air at those who attempted to mount a camel. Loretta thrust herself on to the animal's back, throwing her arms around its hump.

"Push me a bit further," she shouted to Tobias. "I can't get my leg over." Tobias chuckled as he helped his wife.

"Pull yourself up," he said as he pushed her from behind. The camel retained its crouched position. Loretta manoeuvred her body as best as she could. No doubt the camel was accustomed to the antics of humans. Loretta quickly settled in an upright stance.

"I did it, good boy," she said, patting the camel's hump. "You had better get on your camel Tobias," she called out triumphantly. However, her calm demeanour soon vanished as the camel decided to stand up. Loretta lost complete control of her balance. She almost fell off backwards as the camel pushed itself up on its front legs. In desperation she clung tight to the hump and pressed her legs firmly against its body. Next as the camel's back end rose upwards, she nearly fell head first over the hump. She called out to her husband in a wailing cry for help, but Tobias merely laughed, such was the comical sight. She had begged him for many years about taking her to Egypt, now he was going to get his money's worth.

"Did you call me Dearest?" said Tobias, who was sitting proudly on his camel. Loretta was vexed at how effortless her husband had made of mounting his camel.

"How did you get on your camel so quick," she remarked, having regained her balance but looking somewhat dishevelled.

"It's just like riding a bike," responded a carefree Tobias.

"Oh aren't we the equestrian," remarked Loretta.

Once the tourists had mounted their camels then the entourage moved on. An assistant would take charge of four camels, two at either side, holding the reins to each camel. This ensured that an over-boisterous camel would not go galloping off. The tour guide led the way, riding her camel. She shouted out a running commentary of the area as they gradually ambled along.

"Over to the right you can see the Temple of Luxor, built by Amenophis lll and Rameses ll. It was built to host the festival of Opet. Further on you can see the Abu Haggag mosque with its magnificent architectural features," informed the tour guide enthusiastically. Perhaps the pleasant distraction was to make one feel at ease on the camel. If so it did not have that effect for Loretta. She constantly kept patting its hump, saying things like:

"Go slowly, go slowly, there's a good camel. If I had a carrot I would let you have it." The assistant kept looking up at her, amused by her comical antics.

"You can also see the ruin of a sphinx," continued the tour guide. "The pharaohs built a whole avenue of sphinxes leading all the way to Karnak, sadly most no longer exist."

The brief camel ride lasted for forty minutes, ending at the entrance to a huge pyramid. Tobias knew his wife would be excited to enter such an historical dwelling. Loretta dismounted the camel. The sight was equally as comical as mounting. The moment the camel squatted at the rear, Loretta slid off like a child sliding down a banister. She landed ungracefully on the sandy ground. Tobias helped his wife up.

"That's one way to dismount Dearest," he said gleefully.

"Given time I would perfect the technique," replied Loretta, dusting the sand off her clothes. She took a swig of water from her hipflask. "Anybody would think you had ridden a camel before," she stated emulously.

"By the end of the holiday you will be galloping across the desert," joked Tobias. He too drank water from his hipflask. Loretta refrained from commenting further and moved over to where the other holidaymakers stood. The several assistants took charge of the camels, giving them a well-earned drink of water. The tourists were now on foot for this part of the excursion. They stood at the entrance of an ancient pyramid. They looked up in awe at the magnificent structure.

"In case you were not aware, we are in the Valley of the Kings," declared the tour guide. "Where one can view over sixty-two known tombs that are buried here. These belong to many of the ancient pharaohs, including Rameses the Great, and Tutankhamun the 18th destiny boy king. I am sure you can appreciate the massive construction of this amazing pyramid that stands before us. Even with today's technological advances it would take some planning and expertise. How the ancient Egyptians managed to achieve such is still a mystery."

The tourists absorbed every word the tour guide was saying. It was all so very authentic, as if they had stepped back in time, especially as the tour guide was dressed as a pharaoh.

"Over to my left you can see the famous statue of Rameses ll." All heads turned to where the tour guide had pointed. They saw the ancient sculpture. "You have all heard of Tutankhamun," she said, attracting their attention. Heads nodded in agreement. "Within this pyramid before us lies the body of Tutankhamun."

There was a deathly silence as she deliberately paused, attributing to the suspense as she led her flock on an Egyptian journey they would find most memorable. It was not listed in the guide that they would actually see Tutankhamun's burial tomb. The tour guide continued:

"Over the centuries many explorers came searching for Tutankhamun's tomb, but with little joy. In 1835 a team of Egyptologists did partially excavate the undiscovered tomb, but did not locate his sarcophagus. They knew this was where Tutankhamun was buried by the hieroglyphics on the inner stonewalls, which we shall see in a moment. It was not until 1922 that the sarcophagus of Tutankhamun was discovered by Lord Carnarvon and Howard Carter, two English Egyptologists and their party of explorers." The tourists were enthralled as they listened to the tour guide. "Before we enter the pyramid, it is only fair that I point out the following: Legend has it that a curse lies over the pyramid and will descend on all who enter." A sinister whisper rumbled through the group. "After discovering Tutankhamun's sarcophagus in 1922, Lord Carnarvon became very ill and died 5.4.1923 of blood poisoning. Many at the time thought that he had succumbed to the curse of breaking the sealed tomb. Over the following seventeen years all other explorers of Lord Carnarvon's 1922 expedition, and who had entered the pyramid, died unexpectedly. Was the curse real? People at the time certainly believed so."

"Oh Tobias, maybe we should not go in!" muttered a worried Loretta.

"I think it is safe by now," assured Tobias. Others too made various comments about entering the pyramid. Some had strong reservations and wished to remain outside. Such indecisiveness caused one American guy to speak out:

"It's all nonsense! There wasn't any curse, it's all superstitious waffle."

"Then you can go in first," uttered Loretta.

"The ancient pharaohs used the curse stories as an excuse to kill people. It was their form of capital punishment," voiced the American guy. "You would have to be dense to believe the curse is real."

"I don't see you eager to be first inside," replied Loretta, seeing that the American guy had remained at the back of the group.

"Lady, if it will make you feel better, I will lead the way," replied the American guy as he edged his way to the front.

A Certain Dilemma

"Well on that note shall we all go in?" responded the tour guide.

Fears set aside, the party entered the pyramid with the sceptical American guy standing next to the tour guide. Once inside, one noticed the drop in temperature. The only light source available came from various candles that were periodically placed in alcoves hewn out of the stonewalls.

"Be careful where you walk as the ground is uneven," warned the tour guide. After approximately twenty feet she stood still and switched on her torch, shining the beam across the left wall. "Here you can see the hieroglyphic inscription." All looked up to view the many symbols and drawings of ancient language writing. "Notice the sphinx at the beginning faces right and the sphinx at the end faces left. This signifies the beginning and the end as an everlasting eternity."

"What does the inscription say?" asked Loretta. The tour guide was only too eager to provide the answer.

"It has taken many centuries, but scholars are now able to translate most hieroglyphics. This inscription reads: *Those whose mortal bodies enter will now remain entombed for ever.*"

"Does anyone else feel scared?" questioned Loretta.

"It is a little freaky," said a middle-aged woman.

"How far into the pyramid do we go?" enquired Tobias.

"All the way inside," replied the tour guide proudly. "There is no need to feel scared. I do this tour several times a week," she informed. "Incidentally, you see that block of stone up on the ledge." She pointed upwards. The others looked up to see a huge stone block above the entrance. "Legend has it that many pharaohs weren't always dead when entombed in the pyramid. Not a pleasant way to die but it is only a legend. However, what is not a legend is if this block of stone falls across the entrance, other stone blocks will interlock and there is no way of getting out." The tour guide shone her torch over their heads, highlighting the stone block structure.

"The ledge is on a pivot and should the pivot move, the stone block will fall down blocking the entrance and sealing the pyramid. The ancient pharaohs used a lever on the outside to operate the pivot, thus entombing the deceased or whoever was inside."

"It's a bit like Indiana Jones," said someone light-heartedly.

"Is the pivot likely to move?" asked Loretta, trying not to appear frightened.

"I can assure you it is well secure," remarked the tour guide. "Now follow me."

Slowly they moved into the inner chambers of the pyramid, admiring the many carvings and illustrations on the stonewalls. The temperature seemed to drop even further. A deathly chill filled the air. People felt too awestruck to comment. This was a surreal moment, to be treading where the pharaohs had trod thousands of years before.

"Just behind this wall we shall see a replica of the Screaming Man," informed the tour guide. "The original is in the Cairo museum, but I can assure you that if they were side by side, you could not tell the difference."

"Why is he called the Screaming Man?" wondered Loretta.

"That will become apparent when you see him," replied the tour guide. "Follow me." The entourage slowly moved beyond the wall. Like a haunting horror movie the reaction was predictable. Gasps echoed as the guide shone her torch on the Screaming Man. His realistic corpse lay upright in an alcove. The agony on his face was unmistakeable.

"Did he die like that?" questioned a tourist.

"Yes," replied the tour guide. "It is believed he was poisoned, hence the facial expression. His mummified body was discovered in 1881 by a group of Victorian Egyptologists. When they removed the bandages, they were clearly shocked. Since then scholars have endeavoured to find out his identity.

A Certain Dilemma

From the outset it was accepted he must have been royalty, because he was buried with the ancient kings. Unfortunately, his coffin did not contain his name or any artefacts considered essential to reach the afterlife. His body was also covered in goat's skin, which was a symbol of disgrace, and a certainty you would go to hell. After much deliberation and many theories, the majority of scholars believe that the Screaming Man is Pantewary, the son of King Rameses lll. Records tell us there was a coo to overthrow king Rameses lll by his son, Pantewary. The disgraced prince was forced to commit suicide. That was the ultimate sacrilegious punishment."

"Why would he want to kill his father?" asked Loretta.

"That I can not say for certain, most probably power. One would think being a prince was a privileged lifestyle, but ruling over your kingdom and a harem of wives seemed desirable enough to kill for."

"How long ago was this?" raised Tobias.

"3,000 years ago," replied the tour guide.

"And his body is still preserved after all that time?" questioned Tobias.

"Yes it is. The Egyptian mummification evolved over many centuries, and was very effective. His true corpse is contained in a glass cabinet at an even temperature. There is a coach trip to the Cairo museum for those wanting to see the real thing," informed the tour guide. "Now if we can move along this corridor, we have more sights to see."

Cautiously they followed in the dimness. Soon they all congregated in a square recess within the pyramid, almost like a room but without any doors or windows. They found themselves surrounded by gold statues, ornate carvings and various artefacts. This was truly a rich and impressive sight. The tour guide shone her torch over the treasured possessions. The gold dazzled as the beam glided across the surface.

"These are only replicas of the artefacts discovered in 1922 by Lord Carnarvon. The real ones are now on display in the

Cairo museum," informed the tour guide. Everyone carefully manoeuvred in and around the Egyptian treasures. Even though they were imitation, one appreciated the authenticity of their presence. "However, what is not a replica is the tomb of Tutankhamun right here," she stated, boldly shinning her torch on the horizontal sarcophagus. It lay on a stone plinth. "I am sure you will agree that it is a magnificent feeling to be here."

An eerie silence fell as everyone realised they were inches away from Tutankhamun's coffin, his mummified body still lying within. They gradually approached the Boy King's resting place. For centuries his remains have lain still and preserved. Seconds later a thunderous noise echoed through the chamber. The elaborate imitation artefacts and trinkets shuddered. A golden three-foot statue of an Egyptian goddess rocked back and forth before falling over. The ground trembled beneath them.

"It's an earthquake!" shouted the tour guide.

Dust descended from above, gently falling on the panicked tourists. Some coughed as they inhaled the powdered fragments.

"What do we do?" shouted a voice.

"Get out!" replied the tour guide.

Everyone quickly headed towards the entrance. It was out of sight as they were deep inside the pyramid. The noise augmented into a roaring grinding sound. The earthquake had dislodged the pivot, causing it to release the stone block. The massive stone fell and blocked the entrance. It was as if the pyramid had come to life as the other stone blocks interlocked, and the ancient Egyptian construction entombed everyone.

"The pivot has moved," announced the tour guide. "We are trapped."

Like the ancient pharaohs they were now sealed in death. They would soon succumb to suffocation. More statues fell over as the earthquake intensified. People lost their balance and fell to the ground.

"It's the curse!" panicked Loretta. "We are all gonna die!"

"Look, the walls are about to collapse," shouted the American guy. Part of the masonry from the adjacent wall fell down.

"Let's return to the inner chamber. It will be safer there," shouted the tour guide.

Dust and sand bellowed everywhere like a thick fog roaming overland. They regrouped in the chamber, in front of Tutankhamun's sarcophagus. Then in a split second there was silence. The rumbling had ceased and all became still.

"It's over," said the tour guide. "Is anyone hurt?" Various replies of no came across.

"I have never been in an earthquake before," remarked a youngish woman.

"Me neither," said another.

"Is it the curse? Are we trapped?" wondered a scared Loretta.

"Is everyone all right?" asked the tour guide, her voice conveying fear.

"We are not really trapped in here are we?" questioned Tobias, dusting himself down.

"Of course we're not trapped," said the American guy.

"I have my cell phone, so we shall soon be rescued," stated the tour guide. "It's no good, I can't get a signal." The realisation of being trapped in the pyramid began to dawn on the tourists.

"There must be another way out?" said a voice. Everyone stood by the tour guide, expecting an encouraging sign.

"There is no other way out," she said, shaking her head. "I know all the tunnels and corridors of this pyramid, there is no other exit."

"We're all gonna die like the pharaohs!" remarked a tourist.

"Don't be stupid, we will be rescued. People know we are in her," said the American guy emphatically. One of the candles in the alcove began to flicker before becoming extinguished.

"We are running out of oxygen," commented the tour guide.

"I don't believe it," cried Loretta. "I don't want to die in here." Tobias embraced his wife.

"We must keep quiet to save our oxygen. We will be rescued soon," stated Tobias to everyone. A further candle flickered before dying. The tour guide shone her torch across the group, catching their frightened faces in the beam. A loud muffled noise filled their enclosure. It seemed to come from in front of them. The tour guide shone her torch across the lid of Tutankhamun's sarcophagus as it began to open.

"Oh my God, look!" exclaimed a tourist.

"It is the curse come to take our souls!" shouted the tour guide. Several visitors screamed in fright as the mummified body of Tutankhamun sat upright, its head turned to face them. Loretta screamed with all her might and quickly recited the Hail Mary. Others trembled and clung to each other in fright. Cobwebs fell from the dried bandages that enshrouded the corpse. His jaw lowered as a piercing scream filled the chamber. Loretta fainted; her legs gave way as she slumped into Tobias' arms. He struggled to support her, and blew on her face to revive her. Loretta gasped heavily and coughed as she regained consciousness. Finally, a doorway opened in the far wall, allowing daylight to fill the enclosure.

"I hope you all enjoyed the Egyptian adventure," said the tour guide. "Follow me everyone." The group exited the complex, some were laughing having realised it was a joke, others still rather bewildered about the experience.

"We can get out," uttered Loretta, seeing the daylight. "Quick Tobias let's get out whilst we can."

Outward appearances were authentic as the dusty looking tourists gathered around the tour guide outside the pyramid. They seemed as if they had survived a fate worse than death.

"Hands up those who knew in advance that it was a hoax pyramid," stated the tour guide. Five of the group raised their hand up, including Tobias. Loretta gave him a glare.

"There was no earthquake? You knew it was not for real and did not tell me," she retorted.

"Of course I knew Dearest, why else d'you think I brought you here," he laughed. Loretta caught her breath and quickly replied:

"For that you can carry me back to my camel. On seconds thought I better walk, I don't want to be dropped." Tobias laughed as he embraced her.

It was a couple of days later that Loretta managed to employ her witticism. She had carefully planned her tease on Tobias. They had taken a five-day cruise down the River Nile, stopping along the way at the many bazaars en route. Loretta bought an array of costume jewellery, beads, bracelets and earrings. They were all handmade. She also mentioned to Tobias in a fortuitous manner that she had bought him a new pair of swimming trunks. This one afternoon Tobias was eager to show off his virile body. They lazed semi naked on deck, absorbing the ambience of cruising along the River Nile as if on an old fashioned Mississippi showboat. Tobias proudly wore his new swimming trunks as they sat in deckchairs by the edge of the swimming pool.

"I say Tobias, those yellow trunks do look very fashionable on you," commented Loretta as she soaked up the sun. She wore her floral bikini with matching shoulder rap.

"I am your hunk in trunks," replied Tobias. The nearby tourists could overhear their conversation. They smiled and wondered how gullible one could be. Loretta had given them a nod and a wink.

"They are all the rage with teenagers," she added. "Why don't you christen them in the swimming pool?"

"It's an unusual material for trunks. Don't you think they might shrink in the water," remarked Tobias.

"I asked the shop assistant the same thing, and she assured me the die prevents the wool from shrinking," informed Loretta casually. "Why don't I come in the pool with you?" She proceeded to get up.

"Who's gonna watch the bag and cabin key if we both go for a swim?" remarked Tobias.

"Good point my dear husband. I better stay here whilst you have your swim, then you can guard the bag whilst I have mine," responded Loretta. She silently laughed as Tobias ambled towards the swimming pool. He did not suspect that Loretta had knitted the lemon trunks. The onlookers viewed the Caribbean gent as he stepped into the water.

"It's lovely and warm," called out Tobias. One almost felt sorry for him.

"Enjoy your swim," replied Loretta. She then mouthed in a whisper across to an adjoining couple. "And to think he was worried about them shrinking." They laughed and watched with anticipation.

Tobias began to swim back and forth. There were three other people in the swimming pool. One youthful guy was lounging on an inflatable bed. The other two were diving under water as if exploring the Great Barrier Reef. Tobias gently did the breaststroke mindful not to disturb them. After watching her husband swim leisurely for several minutes, Loretta stood up with her camera and took a few snapshots.

"Tobias, let me take one of you coming out of the water," she said. Tobias obeyed and began to climb up the swimming pool steps, holding on to the rail with both hands, unaware that the knitted trunks had stretched. The water now heavily weighted the garment. As he ascended up the steps the swimming trunks fell down his legs. They rested around his ankles. Loretta quickly clicked her camera. The spectators cheered. Tobias tried to retain his dignity. In a mismatch of coordination he stumbled out of the pool in full frontal of everyone. He then lost his balance as he tried to pull the trunks up and fell backwards into the swimming pool. His precarious entry upturned the inflatable bed. The restful young man submerged beneath the water. Thankfully the youth could swim. Tobias soon regained control from his unceremonious naked aqua dive. His head appeared above the water only to see his lemon swimming trunks floating on the surface. There was raucous laughter everywhere. Tobias did not know what to do. Loretta admitted to the prank.

"I too can plan a joke," she said. Tobias saw the humour. He grabbed the trunks and awkwardly put them back on before ascending from the swimming pool. He clutched the knitted garment against his midriff and bowed to the appreciative audience. They applauded with one or two blowing a wolf whistle.

"Shall I do an encore?" he teased.

"I knitted them one afternoon at the craft shop," confessed Loretta.

Tobias and Loretta enjoyed their holiday. They had acquired many memories to be told once they returned to Martinique.

<>

It soon became a regular routine that Friday evenings were spent on Gavin and Veronique's yacht. They welcomed this opportunity to mend bridges with Rebecca. Overriding the statement two is company three is a crowd they invited her to join them on board. The impending sale of Calypso Tavern had ruptured their friendship. Rebecca was overwhelmed by sentiment for Greg. She thought she had passed those fearful feelings, but the sale of Calypso Tavern had opened old wounds. She could not accept that Greg's pride and joy was going to be owned by someone else. Rebecca had even contemplated her parents' wish to return to Texas. She had gained much by living in Martinique, yet seemed to have lost more. A further gripe to bear was the surplus equity Gavin would be left with after the sale. A tidy profit of $1million once the $2million ransom was repaid to the bank. It was for this reason that Rebecca had shown little interest in the yacht. She felt it had been bought with blood money. She had also made her feelings known to Gavin and Veronique. Yet harbouring negative feelings can be self-destructive, so over the passing weeks Rebecca mellowed towards them. Finally she conceded and accepted their offer. Tonight was her first visit to the yacht. Even Rebecca admitted it was good to have a weekly break from work. Saturdays at Calypso Tavern were so busy and demanding, a Friday night reprieve would help to cushion a hectic weekend.

Detective Martinez was still no further forward in capturing the kidnappers or reclaiming the ransom. A Gabriella Korakova had received the money. Her Russian identity was probably false as there was no further trace of her. Gavin did not know the person, and her Hong Kong bank account was now closed. Nevertheless, Gavin's financial position had been boosted now the plantation was up to date with production, and the insurance company had reimbursed their loss. It felt good to relax once more, and the yacht enabled such pleasure.

Gavin gently eased the yacht towards the shore. The three of them had spent a few hours cruising the vicinity, at times allowing the yacht to drift with the current.

"Back to the fray," commented Rebecca.

"I could get used to living on a yacht," added Veronique. "It is so peaceful and relaxing." The two females sat below deck in the compact but adequate cabin. Its teak design incorporated sky blue furnishings in the seat upholstery with matching curtains at the narrow but essential windowlets. Bijou cupboards and drawers were stringently placed to make optimum use of the space. At the foot of the steps leading up to the deck were two ornate wooden pillars running from the gallery to the deckhead above. The purpose of the pillars is to allow one to loop ones arms around them, keeping your hands free yet retaining your balance. A feature that is essential if navigating through rough seas. Equipped with kitchen facilities, shower room and a moderately spacious lower cabin, the luxury twin berth yacht became Gavin's pride and joy. Rebecca and Veronique sipped their glass of wine as they wallowed in the ambiance. Gavin was at the helm steering the yacht gently to its moorings.

"Should we be helping Gavin to lower the sail or something?" wondered Rebecca.

"I think he will have already lowered the sail," informed Veronique. "You can take it from me he prefers to do it all himself. I have asked several times for him to show me but he still hasn't. Here am I thinking he bought the yacht for me."

"You should ask him if he bought it for you or himself," stated Rebecca.

"Oh I have, his reply was does the Queen of England drive her QE2."

The yacht drifted to a halt as Gavin secured it to the moorings. Moments later he descended the steps into the cabin.

"You certainly know how to handle her," was the greeting he got from Rebecca.

"You are quite right Rebecca, I do," responded Gavin proudly. "She knows exactly how to obey my commands, don't you Veronique," he added light-heartedly. Her eyebrows rose as she threw him a glare.

"I was referring to the yacht," corrected Rebecca.

"And so was he, weren't you my darling," added Veronique.

"Of course I was," replied Gavin. "I see you two have finished off the wine," he remarked, picking up the empty bottle from a side table.

"We knew you wanted us too," stated Rebecca. "Which reminds me to mention that I need to stay at yours tonight. I've had too much to drink to drive back to the apartment."

"No worries, anyway your Ma and Pa return to Texas in a couple of days, so they will appreciate your company," stated Veronique. "I hope they have enjoyed baby sitting Gregori. I feel as though I have leaned on them too much."

"Oh they have loved it," confirmed Rebecca. "You don't need to worry on that score."

"With all the drama we have encountered it was good of them to stay and help out," remarked Veronique. "I certainly could not have left Gregori with anyone else."

"Ursula has really enjoyed being a surrogate nanny whilst Loretta and Tobias are in Egypt," mentioned Gavin as he stood at the cabin entrance, his arms looped around the wooden pillars. "Incidentally, they return tomorrow morning."

"I bet they will have a few stories to tell," assumed Veronique.

"I will just ring Marcus, check everything is ok at Calypso Tavern," stated Rebecca, inadvertently changing the subject.

"You always do that on your night off," said Veronique. "Don't you think Marcus would contact you if there was a problem."

"True, but it puts my mind at rest. Anyway, I can tell him I won't be home tonight," replied Rebecca. After making her brief telephone call they vacated the yacht.

"Bye bye Veronique," said Veronique as she gave one last look at her yacht. All three linked arms with Gavin in the middle as they strolled homewards.

"I owe you an apology," remarked Rebecca as they meandered across the boardwalk.

"No you don't Rebecca," replied Gavin.

"Yes I do for giving you such a hard time over selling Calypso Tavern."

"It has not sold yet. If we don't get a buyer soon I may have to lower the price or rethink matters," replied Gavin.

"I only wish I could afford it. I feel it belongs to me. It's just that I miss Greg so much," reflected Rebecca.

"We all do," stated Veronique. "But difficult decisions have to be made. Life is never easy but it sure is hard enough."

"ABBA," mentioned Gavin.

"ABBA what?" questioned Veronique.

"They wrote a song entitled *Life is never easy but it sure is hard enough*," stated Gavin

"Did they," remarked Veronique.

"Not life but love," corrected Rebecca. *"Love isn't easy but it sure is hard enough."*

"I stand corrected," replied Gavin. "Anyway, life or love it equates to the same thing."

"Aren't we getting too philosophical for tonight," stated Veronique. After consuming several glasses of wine she only just managed to pronounce the word philosophical. "Let's just empty our minds and enjoy a stress free walk home."

"My legs still ache from walking down here. Whose idea was it to walk?" commented Rebecca.

"Yours," replied Veronique and Gavin simultaneously.

CHAPTER ELEVEN

Sorrow

Even the police were shocked and they had dealt with many a death scene.

The next morning it seemed life had returned to a relaxed and happy mode, but it was just the lull before the storm. During the night hidden forces had set the wheels of murder in motion. Within less than an hour death would return.

A blurry-eyed Rebecca ungracefully descended Gavin's mahogany staircase. Her parents were seated in the living room. They watched their daughter reluctantly embrace the day.

"Looks like you enjoyed yourself on Gavin's yacht last night," remarked Godwin.

"Urr, don't remind me. Just how much wine did I drink!" muttered Rebecca.

"It would seem more than you should have done," commented Ursula. "Did you sail anywhere of interest last night?"

"Just out to sea, drifted awhile before returning to the marina. We watched the sunset as we lay out on deck, and then played a few games of Yatzy down below. Gavin really knows how to sail. He is also very possessive, not allowing either Veronique or myself to help. Oh I tell a lie, he did let Veronique take the helm for five minutes."

"I have never been on a yacht. I suffer with seasickness so it is not advisable," responded Ursula.

"How long have you both been up?" asked Rebecca as she flopped onto the sofa.

"Since 7am," replied Ursula.

"And it is just as well we did because Loretta and Tobias arrive at the jetty in an hour, and they will be wanting a lift home," informed Godwin.

"Haven't Gavin and Veronique gone to meet them?" questioned Rebecca as she lay back on the sofa.

"Not exactly, they are still in bed," responded Ursula. "I have already given Gregori his breakfast, and he is now playing happily in his room with his toys."

"And as it seems a shame to wake Gavin and Veronique, given how hard they work, we thought we would collect Loretta and Tobias from the jetty," mentioned Godwin. "That's if we can borrow your car," he casually stated. During their stay in Martinique, Godwin had failed to persuade Rebecca to let him drive her new Mercedes. This was his last opportunity to do so before returning to Texas tomorrow. Rebecca glanced at her father. Her physiognomy conveyed a cunning demeanour.

"Why is it Ma that grown men still act like a child when it comes to cars?" she stated, still looking at her father.

"It's not just cars Honey," replied Ursula. Godwin smiled at his daughter as he implemented his charm.

"Do you remember Rebecca, when you asked me for a horse. Did I say no; no I did not. If my daughter wants a horse then she will have a horse," recalled Godwin.

"I was five years old and we lived on a ranch with several horses. It wasn't exactly too hard to fulfil my wish," stated Rebecca.

"Nor is it too hard to let me fetch Loretta and Tobias in your new car. Tomorrow we return home to that rusty old tow truck. My heart saddened that I never got to drive a brand new Mercedes," responded Godwin dramatically.

"Talk about emotional blackmail," stated Rebecca. "Anybody would think you've had a hard life."

"Take no notice of him," intervened Ursula. "We better go and wake Gavin and Veronique, else Loretta and Tobias will be left stranded at the jetty."

"It does seem a shame to wake them," reflected Rebecca, looking at her Pa. His smiling face looked back at her, almost like a cheeky but adorable child.

"Is that a yes then?" assumed Godwin. Rebecca paused for a moment to reflect if she should concede. It would not be right to refuse her father's smiling face.

"Given the circumstances and the fact I am too hung over to drive myself, I guess it is a yes," replied Rebecca. Her father let out a joyous cry.

"Fantastic!" he exclaimed.

"I don't know Pa, you are worse than a kid at Christmas," stated Rebecca. "Mind you drive carefully and don't scratch my paintwork."

"Of course I will. I shall drive like a soaring eagle gliding on the breeze," stated Godwin in a poetic fashion.

"I'll go and make you a coffee Rebecca," said Ursula, standing up. Godwin quickly interrupted her.

"Oh there is no time for that my good woman, we best be going," came his deep southern drawl.

"There is plenty of time and it will only take a couple of minutes to do the coffee," responded Ursula as she headed into the kitchen.

"Honestly Pa, it only takes fifteen minutes to get to the jetty. You have heaps of time," remarked Rebecca.

"Well I did not want to rush now did I. You said to drive carefully," returned Godwin in his defence. Of course deep down he could not wait to get behind the steering wheel.

"My car keys are upstairs, I'll just go and fetch them," said Rebecca, getting up from the sofa.

"Now that is a good idea. I certainly can't drive the Mercedes without them." Godwin watched as his daughter went upstairs. How proud he was of her. He would have preferred her to be living at home in Texas and working on the ranch, but he accepted it was not meant to be. Ursula returned with a tray of coffees and a plate of coconut slices.

"We have time for another coffee," she said, placing the tray on a nearby side table. "Where is Rebecca?"

"Gone to fetch the car keys," informed Godwin. "It will be a pleasant change to drive such an elegant vehicle from the rusty old junk of a wagon back home."

"I must admit that I feel like royalty when I am in her car. The Mercedes is so upmarket," remarked Ursula, secretly pleased that Godwin was going to drive the vehicle. Rebecca descended the stairs slightly more vibrant than a moment ago. "I have poured you a coffee," said Ursula, passing Rebecca her mug. "Help yourself to a coconut slice, it will help to soak up some of that wine you had last night."

"Thanks Ma," replied Rebecca as she received the mug of coffee. "Here are the keys Pa. You will be ok driving now, won't you?"

"It may have escaped your memory but we do have cars in Texas, and I have been driving for over forty years," replied Godwin.

"You cannot compare driving your rusty old tow truck to the sophistication of a brand new Mercedes," returned Rebecca.

"The technique is still the same," he responded. Godwin soon drank his coffee and did not hesitate in hurrying up Ursula to finish hers.

"Do you know Ma, I can't remember the last time I saw Pa so excited," stated Rebecca. "Anyone would think he has won the lottery or some such thing."

"Your Pa is like most men Honey, primitive and easily pleased," replied Ursula.

"Excuse me!" exclaimed Godwin. "I am still in the room you know. I know I am often the subject of most people's conversation, being such an interesting person an all, but it is only polite to wait until one has left the room before you should converse. After all, one should respect one's modesty." His comment caused Rebecca to laugh. Ursula gave an astonished glare, the whites of her eyes conveyed surprise and sarcasm.

"And also like other men he suffers with illusions of grandeur," mentioned Ursula, adding to her previous comment.

"I am still in the room," commented Godwin. "And after all that Loretta and Tobias have done for us whilst we have been here, the least I can do is fetch them from the jetty."

"I will wait to see Loretta and Tobias then I must be getting back to Calypso Tavern. Saturdays are always busy," said Rebecca.

"Has Gavin found a buyer for Calypso Tavern?" enquired Ursula.

"No not yet," sighed Rebecca. "I hate the prospect of someone else owning what is rightfully mine. Whether I stay at Calypso Tavern remains to be seen."

"I know you really want to stay in Martinique, but with all that has happened do you really think it is the best option?" questioned Godwin.

"You really must stop trying to persuade me to come home to Texas. If I decide to leave Calypso Tavern it does not mean I shall leave Martinique, so don't get thinking I might be coming home," replied Rebecca.

A Certain Dilemma

"But you said it Rebecca, Texas is home," added Ursula. "Would it be so terrible to try and settle back on the ranch? People always ask after you."

"Well let's see how things pan out after the sale of Calypso Tavern. If I find I hate the new owner and can't settle elsewhere in Martinique then I won't have anything to lose in coming home," reflected Rebecca. "But I really can't see me returning to Texas. I feel at home in the Caribbean. If it wasn't for the slavery trade we would always have lived here."

"I understand your sentiment, you can't blame us for trying. Why not come and stay for Thanksgiving?" suggested Ursula.

"You know what, I may just do that," agreed Rebecca. "I will make more of an effort to come over, especially at holiday times."

"By this time tomorrow we shall be on our way," commented Ursula as she reached for her coffee.

"Have you not finished that coffee my good woman? We really aught to be leaving," remarked Godwin assertively. Ursula took a finale swig, stared at her husband and replied in a genteel voice:

"Oh yes I have oh noble one." She placed the empty mug on the tray.

"You two make me laugh," said Rebecca. "Go and fetch Loretta and Tobias now, before I change my mind in letting you drive my Mercedes." Godwin jumped to his feet.

"The chauffeur is driving the Mercedes now whether you are in it or not," announced Godwin to his spouse. He quickly left the house. Ursula stood up to follow her husband.

"Oh my! I wish you were this eager to take me shopping back home," she said, walking after him. Godwin rushed to the Mercedes and opened the passenger door.

"Your carriage awaits," he said in a posh accent, mildly bowing as Ursula approached.

"Oh la de dah," responded Ursula, getting into the car. Godwin closed the door and did a quick cantor to the driver's side.

"Au revoir," he said, giving a polite wave to Rebecca. She stood on the veranda somewhat dubious at seeing her father getting into the driver's seat.

"Get away with you," she replied. "And don't scratch my paintwork."

"You need not worry," said Godwin. "This is my domain."

"Now pay attention," commented Ursula. Godwin took a momentary pause as he held the steering wheel. He viewed the elegant layout of the control panel. He certainly felt proud and privileged. He familiarised himself with the controls. The first thing he did was to activate the convertible roof. The mechanism softly sounded as the roof concertinaed backwards, allowing the autumn sun to shine in their faces.

"Fasten your seatbelts," he said. Godwin turned the ignition. The impressive dashboard with its various gadgets and controls became illuminated. Godwin was completely enthralled by the vehicle. "It's like a science fiction spaceship. Ready for take off," he said, glancing across at his wife.

"You make sure you know what you are doing," rebuked Ursula, applying a little grey matter to quell Godwin's overexcited imagination.

"I know exactly what I am doing," replied Godwin. "Sit back and enjoy the ride."

He slowly turned the car around. The vehicle seemed to float on a cushion of air. Such was the contrast to his rusty old tow truck. Effortlessly the Mercedes glided down the palm-fringed driveway. Majestically they waved at Rebecca. Even Ursula was enthralled. Godwin was not her husband but the chauffeur and she was a famous film star. Rebecca smiled and waved back to them. She watched until they were out of sight, obscured by the surrounding vegetation. Rebecca turned and entered the house, only to be greeted by Gavin running down the stairs.

"I've overslept. I shall be late collecting Loretta and Tobias from the jetty," he said.

"All taken care of. Ma and Pa have gone to fetch them in my Mercedes," informed Rebecca.

"You finally let your Pa drive your Mercedes!" commented Gavin.

"I hope I don't regret it," stated Rebecca. Veronique appeared at the integral balcony, holding Gregori in her arms.

"I am surprised Gregori did not wake us up sooner. He must be wanting his breakfast," said Veronique as she commenced descending the stairs.

"That's because he has already had his breakfast. Ma fed him earlier," informed Rebecca.

"I will surely miss them when they return to Texas tomorrow," reflected Veronique. "After Gregori's kidnapping, I never expected to leave him in the hands of anyone else. Your folks have reinstated an element of trust in human nature."

"It's as well they were here to fetch your folks from the jetty," added Gavin.

"Have you allowed your Pa to drive your Mercedes?" questioned Veronique, realising they had no other form of transport. She placed Gregori in his playpen. He was clutching Marmajuke.

"Don't sound so surprised," replied Rebecca.

"I thought that was one argument Godwin would not win," added Gavin as he flopped on to the sofa.

"We did not want to wake you so I felt backed into a corner. I feel to hung over to drive myself so it was the easier option, and it really put a smile on Pa's face. That and the prospect of me returning to Texas," informed Rebecca.

"What! You're thinking of leaving?" questioned Veronique as she sat next to Gavin.

"You know I'm not happy with things so it is a possibility," confessed Rebecca. "I am indecisive. I did not tell my folks I may return to Texas because the sheer hint will excite them. I then will disappoint them if I decide otherwise."

"Hey we don't want you to leave. I know things are not ideal but Calypso Tavern needs you," remarked Gavin. They now all sat on the two sofas, Gavin and Veronique on one, Rebecca opposite.

"I know; it is only a possibility. We shall have to see how things transpire," stated Rebecca. "My folks are of the opinion that life only gets worse for me here. To some extent they are right. I do feel torn and don't know how to heal."

"We must discuss this in more detail. I will involve you in the sale of Calypso Tavern to make sure you are happy with the new owner. I am sure any buyer would welcome your invaluable commitment," stipulated Gavin. "We all know recent events have been hell for us all, but we have to make our lives here better."

"I really want to stay so you don't need to persuade me. Yet it seems at too high a price and I am not sure if I can afford it, metaphorically speaking of course. One silly notion that is always in the forefront of my mind is that parents know best, and my parents want me to return home," stated Rebecca.

<>

Godwin drove the Mercedes carefully. He was overjoyed that he had persuaded Rebecca to let him drive her elegant vehicle.

"I feel as though we are floating on air, like astronauts with zero gravity," he remarked as they cruised along, the breeze whirling around their faces.

"Not so much floating on air but being dragged through it," remarked Ursula, not too thrilled about the breeze ravaging her hairstyle. Godwin ignored her request to close the roof.

"This is a once in a lifetime experience my good woman. Sit back and enjoy being ushered in such a fine vehicle," declared Godwin, acting like a teenager who had been given his first sports car.

"Compared to your rusty tow truck that is not difficult to imagine," replied Ursula. "You just ensure you know how to drive it."

"It's an automatic, like most cars they simply drive themselves," stated Godwin. "Let's put some music on." He reached for the radio button but Ursula knocked his hand away.

"You concentrate on the road and stop acting like a teenager," she rebuked.

"My good woman, I think I may buy me a Mercedes when we get home to Texas." Ursula threw one of her typical glances as she replied:

"Did we win the lottery and you forgot to tell me?"

"I could get rid of the truck..." began Godwin but Ursula quickly interrupted.

"You ain't gonna get a dime for that rusty junk of metal. How you gonna afford a Mercedes?"

"I could sell up to Brett, our ranch hand. You know he wanted to buy the business from us. We ain't getting any younger so we need to think about passing on our cattle trade."

"That's as maybe," replied Ursula. She became distracted by the speed they were travelling at. "Mind you concentrate on the road, I think we're going too fast and there's a bend ahead of us."

"I know how to drive," answered Godwin.

"Then stop pressing the accelerator pedal and try using the brake," she hastily said.

"I ain't pressing the accelerator pedal."

"Then how come we're getting faster?" quizzed Ursula.

"Because we're going down hill that's why."

"Then press the brake pedal," urged Ursula. "Else we won't make the bend."

"That's just it, I am pressing the brakes but the car ain't slowing down," panicked Godwin. The Mercedes swerved precariously as he tried to remain in control.

"I thought you knew how to drive the car?" questioned Ursula. "Stop messing about."

"I ain't messing about woman. The brakes ain't working."

"Oh my God!" panicked Ursula. "Oh my God do something… look at the control panel… press a button, maybe you need to flick a switch to get the brakes to work," she uttered in desperation.

"The brakes worked fine before, but they ain't working now," stated Godwin, pressing down firm on the brake pedal. He attempted to slow the car by using the handbrake, but that also failed to work. Ursula snatched her handbag and grabbed her cell phone.

"I'm ringing Rebecca, maybe she can advise what to do." Within seconds Rebecca answered her cell phone. "Rebecca Honey, we can't stop the car, the brakes ain't working. What can we do?"

"Just press the brake pedal that's all you do," remarked Rebecca.

"Try the brakes again," said Ursula to Godwin.

"I am, I am but it ain't making no difference," uttered Godwin.

"The car won't slow down," said Ursula to her daughter. "Watch out for the bend Godwin!" she panicked. "The cars getting faster and faster!" exclaimed a terrified Ursula.

"Turn the engine off, side crash the car to the edge of the road," shouted Rebecca. She heard her mother scream out:

A Certain Dilemma

"We're going over the edge!"

"Ma...Ma..." cried Rebecca.

"No..." came the piercing scream from Ursula. The car left the road. It was travelling too fast to make the bend. The Mercedes plunged over a hundred feet as it dived through the air. Rebecca's new supersonic four wheels burst into flames on impact. Rebecca heard the sound of the crash, followed by the explosion. The noise was horrific. Her parents' screams were piecing but they soon diminished as they became engulfed in flames.

"Ma! Ma!" shouted Rebecca. The signal ended, nothing but silence. Rebecca turned to face Gavin and Veronique. "They've crashed... they've crashed... the lines dead... Ma!" she shouted once more down the phone. "I must go to them." Mixed emotions overwhelmed Rebecca. Her only impulse was to get there. The reasoning of how she would get there seemed unimportant. She had no means of transport but that did not stop her leaving the house as if to jump in her car and drive to them.

"I'll come with you, as a nurse I should be able to help," remarked Veronique. "Gavin you'll have to watch Gregori and call the hospital for an ambulance. I'll ring to give you the precise location." Veronique grabbed her car keys and rushed out of the front door after Rebecca. Veronique saw her wandering around aimlessly, stunned and transfixed. "My car is over here," shouted Veronique as she jumped the veranda steps. Rebecca intuitively followed. Veronique's white Dodge estate was parked at the side of the house.

"They were at the corner bend in the road. I remember Ma saying that. It must have been Viper's Bend," uttered Rebecca as they got in the car.

"We shall be there in no time at all," stated Veronique as she drove away.

"They have to be all right," muttered Rebecca. Her adrenalin was running high. She tried to think rationally.

It all seemed to have happened so quickly, yet at the same time in slow motion. She replayed those last moments in her mind as she tried to telephone her mother, but the reception was unobtainable. "Why is her phone not ringing?" moaned Rebecca.

Veronique was determined to reach the crash site as quickly as possible. At times she even exceeded the speed limit if the road condition allowed her to. Soon they were approaching Viper's Bend. This notorious black spot had contributed to Ursula and Godwin's fate.

"I think this could be it," pondered Rebecca. "Is that smoke I can see?"

"I will pull up over here," replied Veronique as she abruptly swerved on to the grass verge. They left the car and ran to the edge of the road. The gentle autumn breeze blew the smoke towards them. They stood at the edge and looked down into the valley. The Mercedes was unrecognisable. Orange flames and black smoke bellowed upwards from the wreckage like a raging volcano.

"They're dead!" cried out a distressed Rebecca.

"No, not necessarily," comforted Veronique. "They may have gotten out before the car caught fire. Let's follow the road down into the valley," suggested Veronique, attempting to be positive and control the situation. They rushed back to the white Dodge estate. "Ring Gavin and tell him to send an ambulance to Viper's Bend," ordered Veronique.

Veronique continued to drive as Rebecca contacted Gavin. In a sombre voice Rebecca informed him of the location. Gavin held his mobile in one hand, the landline receiver in the other as he relayed the information to the hospital. The paramedics were on their way. Rebecca could not mention that the Mercedes had burst into flames. The realisation was too horrific. The vision of the burning wreckage seemed edged in the forefront of her mind, almost as if she were still looking down into the valley. Rebecca knew her parents were dead.

A Certain Dilemma

From Viper's Bend the road arced to the right before curving to the left as it descended into the valley. The road lived up to its name as it mirrored the shape of a snake. It also had the equivalent of a deadly bite if one drove too fast, unable to complete the bend. The white Dodge estate curved around the final part of the road. The sight of smoke appeared in front of them.

"There they are," said Rebecca.

The stricken Mercedes lay in close proximity to the valley road. Veronique pulled over. Rebecca rushed out of the car, leaving the passenger door open. Even though it was autumn the sun's heat was still strong. One easily felt its vigour. However, the heat from the burning wreckage gave adequate competition.

"Ma! Pa!" shouted Rebecca, hoping they were safe close by. They could have survived the crash and escaped the Mercedes before it exploded. Rebecca was desperate for that to be the case. She turned on the spot, looking at the surrounding landscape. "Where are they?" she screamed out. All that could be seen were rocks, trees and exotic vegetation. The bellowing smoke doused the tropical vicinity. Rebecca stood and stared at her burning Mercedes. "They're still in the car!" she cried out, dropping to her knees. "It's all my fault, it's all my fault. I shouldn't have let them take my car."

"No it is not you fault," responded Veronique. She crouched at Rebecca's side and embraced her. Rebecca was too emotional. Her cries were very chilling. They remained on the ground looking into the flames. Rebecca was dazed and distraught, her mind awash with negative thoughts. She was possessed with self-recriminations. What agony her parents must have endured, and it was all her fault. She should have stuck to her original decision and not allowed her Pa to drive the Mercedes. He would not be familiar with the controls. He obviously had not realised the speed he was travelling, such is the ease of acceleration and smooth driving of a new vehicle.

Especially with him being used to his rusty old tow truck where more pedal pressure was needed on the accelerator.

A few moments later the paramedics arrived, followed by the police. As with all automobile accidents the police are always alerted. Veronique left Rebecca sitting on the loose terrain. She greeted the paramedics, her work colleagues. Veronique briefed them on what had happened, not that much explanation was needed for the scene was self-explanatory. It was clearly visible to anyone that Viper's Bend had taken another life. Overwhelmed by grief Rebecca screamed out. Veronique rushed back to her side. One of the paramedics administered a sedative. Rebecca was out of control, not in an aggressive way, but emotional.

One police officer spoke to Veronique. It was time to document the scene. The conversation was strained because Rebecca was too distraught. Veronique hugged her, unable to do anything else. A further police officer utilised state provisions and applied his fire extinguisher to douse the flames. He emptied the foam filled canister. The contents sprayed over the burning wreckage like a fluffy white blanket. The flames disappeared, quelled by the foam that now outlined the Mercedes. The car was upright as if intentionally parked. However, gravity now played a cruel twist. The foam slid downwards and revealed the charred human remains of Ursula and Godwin. Rebecca screamed hysterically at the sight. Her parents stared back like a haunting scene from a horror movie. Even the police were shocked and they had dealt with many a death scene. Veronique and the police officer managed to assist Rebecca into the police car. Rebecca cried out as if in utter agony.

"Does anyone know exactly what happened?" asked the police officer.

"It's all my fault!" screamed Rebecca.

"No it is not," replied Veronique. "You have no cause to blame yourself." Veronique then continued to answer the police officer's question. "Rebecca's parents were driving to the jetty to meet my folks, who are returning from holiday. I think there was a problem with the brakes or something. Ursula rang Rebecca just before they crashed, saying the brakes were not working."

"There was nothing wrong with the brakes," sobbed Rebecca. "It's a new car, the brakes were fine. Pa just wasn't used to the car. It was his first time in driving it. I should not have let him drive it," she wailed. Her breathing was spasmodic.

"He would have known how to use the brakes," remarked the police officer.

"He was probably pressing the accelerator pedal by mistake. He wasn't familiar with the car," cried Rebecca. "It's all my fault."

"I think we need to get back to the house," suggested Veronique. "You know where we live, at the plantation," she stated to the police officer.

"Of course," agreed the police officer. "I will come over to see you later to take official statements." Still visibly upset, Veronique helped Rebecca out of the police car.

"It's best not to look," stated Veronique as Rebecca attempted to glance over her shoulder. She had to look once more and view her burnt out Mercedes that had trapped her parents in death. Veronique turned Rebecca's head and lightly pressed it towards her shoulder as they walked away from the carnage. They had just returned to the white Dodge estate when Veronique's mobile rang. It was Gavin.

"Hi Gavin, we are coming home now," said Veronique melancholy.

"Is everything ok?" enquired Gavin.

"No," came Veronique's concise response. She could not elaborate any further. It would be too insensitive with Rebecca present. "We will see you in a few minutes," she said and ended the call.

The drive home was silent. Rebecca sat in a trancelike state. Her tears had stopped but her breathing was heavy with intermittent pants. Nature's lavish environment that often lifted one's spirit failed to register the slightest cheerful sigh. Once more death had hijacked the Harrison household. Gavin impatiently waited on the veranda. His mind mulled over the worst scenario. Gregori sat in his playpen in the living room, playing happily with Marmajuke and his toy helicopter, completely oblivious to the sombre mood. Such bliss is early childhood, living in a world of fun, toys and where every fairytale seems a reality.

Gavin watched as Veronique drove her white Dodge estate up the driveway. Once out of the car Veronique looked at her husband. Her facial expression deemed sadness. She gently shook her head from side to side. Gavin interpreted this to mean that the situation was serious. But how serious was it?

Rebecca got out of the car. Veronique walked over to her to give assistance. Rebecca looked up at Gavin and burst into tears. Veronique hugged her and led her into the house.

"The crash was fatal," mouthed Veronique to Gavin as she passed him on the veranda. "The police will be here shortly," she said. Gavin followed them into the house as his mobile rang.

"Yes!" he said abruptly.

"Well that's a fine greeting I must say," said Tobias. "I assume you forgot we were returning home today."

"No not at all, it's good to hear from you. Where are you?" replied Gavin. His mind was not functioning coherently.

"We are at the jetty waiting for you," answered Tobias.

"Oh yes of course. Sorry to keep you waiting. I will come and fetch you now," informed Gavin hesitantly. He felt it would be inappropriate to mention the sudden tragedy, not that he knew the exact details to comment.

"Is everything all right?" enquired Tobias, noticing Gavin's distant manner.

A Certain Dilemma

"No...I mean yes...I'll see you in fifteen minutes," stated Gavin and ended the call. He turned to face Veronique, who was now sitting beside Rebecca on the sofa. "That was Tobias," interrupted Gavin. "They are at the jetty. I need to go and fetch them."

"Take my car save getting yours out of the garage," suggested Veronique. "The keys are on the hall table." Gavin agreed and left the house.

En route to the jetty he drove past the burnt out Mercedes. He noticed three parked police cars, the ambulance and various police officers. Amongst them stood Detective Martinez. The police officer who was first at the scene had taken the account of possible faulty brakes seriously. For two reasons the officer deemed it appropriate to alert his superior. First, it was the officer's duty as the scene was a suspected homicide; and second, the officer was aware of previous criminality aimed at the Harrison household. Detective Martinez would be intrigued by a further crime against the family.

Detective Martinez had rushed to the scene. He ordered crime scene investigators to detail a forensic report of the incident. Gavin looked across as he drove past. What he saw was worse than any horror film. The sight of Ursula and Godwin's charred skeletons stared back at him. The white foam had remained in their eye sockets and mouth. This only heightened the shock.

"What the hell happened?" sighed Gavin, averting his eyes. He continued to the jetty, trying to quell the haunting image of Ursula and Godwin's burnt remains.

Loretta and Tobias anxiously sat on a bench at the quayside.

"I wonder what the problem is?" said Loretta. "Why didn't you ask him?"

"I couldn't, he hung up on me. It's probably nothing," said Tobias.

"Whatever it is it cannot be any worse than what we've already been through," reflected Loretta.

"It'll be the plantation. I bet we've had another takeover bid, or problems with ants," assumed Tobias.

"Yes that'll be it," sighed Loretta. "Oh here comes Gavin driving Veronique's car." They stood up, picked up their suitcases and walked over to him. Gavin parked the white Dodge estate. He descended the vehicle and approached them. His facial expression was gaunt and fearful. Loretta knew something awful had happened.

"Let me take your cases," said Gavin. "They seem heavy." He reached for them. They let him take their luggage and he briskly walked away, back to Veronique's car. Loretta and Tobias noticed the absence of a welcome home hug. This only led to further speculation of what was wrong.

"You seem preoccupied Gavin, is everything ok with the plantation?" asked Tobias as they followed behind him.

"The plantation…yes…everything is fine," responded Gavin in a nondescript tone of voice.

"Then what is wrong? I can tell something has happened," questioned Loretta sympathetically. Gavin stopped and placed their suitcases on the ground. He looked up at his adoptive kinfolk.

"It's Rebecca's parents, they have been killed in a car crash." There was no easy way to break the news.

"Oh my God no!" stated Loretta, shocked by the news.

"When did this happen?" questioned Tobias.

"Just now," replied a sombre Gavin. "They were driving Rebecca's new Mercedes down to meet you when it happened. It would seem they went off the road at Viper's Bend. That's why I wasn't here to meet you."

"This is terrible. How is Rebecca?" asked Loretta.

"She is in a mess. Veronique is with her now at the house. We best be getting back," remarked Gavin, picking up the suitcases. "The police will be coming over any time soon, and

I best warn you we will be passing the crash site on our way home. My advice is not to look." In a melancholy mood they got into the car and Gavin began the journey home.

Often one does not welcome the anticlimax feeling of arriving home after a joyous holiday, that climb down to normal mundane life, but that feeling was by far preferable than grief. Loretta and Tobias were deeply saddened, especially in contrast to a wonderful holiday they had experienced. When they passed the crash site it only augmented their sadness. Gavin had advised them not to look, but human nature demanded otherwise. The vision of horror was too much to bear. Loretta cried. Tobias did not hide his emotions either.

"What exactly happened?" questioned Tobias.

"I don't know all the details myself yet, except they rang Rebecca just before the crash," relayed Gavin.

"I know Godwin was looking forward to driving the Mercedes," remarked Tobias. "What a tragedy to end this way. I shall miss him." They reached home and called in to see Rebecca. Loretta was in floods of tears as she greeted her.

Detective Martinez also visited them. He had taken statements pertaining to the tragic sequence of events. He also informed them that forensic checks would be carried out on the Mercedes, to determine if there was any mechanical fault. In the meantime one was left to cope with their grief and bereavement.

The grieving hours turned into days. Rebecca employed the services of Chester Hargreaves to deal with her parents' estate in Texas. Although she had previously been indecisive about returning to Texas, she did briefly consider the move and to take over the reins of their ranch. But her life had been through enough upheaval over these last few years. Could she tolerate a further move? But what connection did she have in Texas now her parents were dead. Finally, she decided it was best to continue living in Martinique. The ranch she would put up for sale. Rebecca was an only child so in the absence of a will she stood to inherit her parents' estate.

With regard to the funeral, Rebecca knew her parents did not object to cremation. However, given the circumstances of how they died she undertook the traditional burial to be appropriate. Rebecca also decided to have them buried in Martinique. She saw little point in having them taken back to Texas. This meant she could frequently attend their graveside.

A week after the accident Fr Vincent conducted the funeral. Of course it was a sombre affair, as they often are. Amongst the mourners were Sebastian and Dominic. They were reluctant to attend, largely because Sebastian was trying to distance himself from the family. Since the last escapade he had wanted to keep a low profile. Gregori's kidnapping and the fact he had advised Gavin to sell Calypso Tavern were still current issues. Sebastian had not recovered from being thrown into the spotlight. He felt jinxed that the slightest contact with Gavin would result in adverse consequences. He even mentioned to Dominic whether the crash was an accident. Were there sinister connotations at force? To put it mildly, had Susannah tampered with the brakes? Sebastian drew the conclusion that Susannah was not dead. There were just too many coincidences. However, regardless of his trepidations, to not attend the funeral would only result in awkward explanations the next time he met Gavin. Perhaps Sebastian was overreacting. He was certainly grateful for Dominic being level headed.

Within the congregation was Detective Martinez. Earlier in the morning he had received the forensic report from the crime scene investigators. The result was worrying. After the funeral it was imperative to discuss the matter with Rebecca. Detective Martinez seized his opportunity during the wake at Gavin's house. The living room was full of people, including family and friends from Texas. Those that had travelled overseas were staying at the house. It was on occasions like this that Gavin's Hispanic dwelling was used to its full potential. The noise level was high due to copious conversations. All guests were eating from the Caribbean buffet supplied by the caterers that Gavin always employed. Detective Martinez approached Rebecca.

"Hello Rebecca," he began. "I know this must be a difficult day for you, but I need to have a private word with you and Gavin."

"Of course," responded Rebecca. "My head is buzzing anyway. I could do with some peace and quiet. I never could handle people fussing over me. It was horrendous at Greg's funeral, now this."

"I have already spoken to Gavin, he is waiting for us in his study," informed Detective Martinez.

"We had better go then." They left the living room. Once inside the study, silence fell for a brief moment. Gavin and Rebecca casually leaned against the desk. Detective Martinez declined Gavin's offer of a chair and remained standing.

"I will come straight to the point," he began. "I have received the forensic report and must inform you that the car crash was not an accident. The brakes on your Mercedes Rebecca had been tampered with."

"How can you tell that, given the state of the vehicle after the crash?" quizzed Rebecca.

"I can confirm the validity of the report. There is no need to doubt it. I also commissioned a toxicology report, which confirms that an accelerant material had been placed under the bonnet, causing the Mercedes to instantaneously burst into flames on impact. Your parents most likely would have survived the crash, had the Mercedes not ignited. Therefore we are treating your parents' death as murder."

"This is unbelievable!" sighed Gavin. "You know exactly what I am thinking now, don't you!"

"Susannah?" replied Detective Martinez.

"Yes!" confirmed Gavin. "She has got to be alive and she has got to be responsible for this."

"Does Susannah really want to kill me?" questioned Rebecca. "That was my car, she wouldn't have realised my parents would have driven it."

"What's the betting she thought the car was mine. She knew I always fancied a Mercedes," assumed Gavin. "Your car is often parked outside my house."

"Yet all indications are that Susannah is dead," remarked Detective Martinez.

"I won't be told otherwise, but as far as I can see, all indications are that she is alive," repeated Gavin angrily. "Who else would cause us this much grief?"

"Could it be Kirsti Løvik?" said Rebecca.

"Whoever it might be this investigation will take priority," assured Detective Martinez. "In the meantime be extra vigilant. Always check under your bonnet for anything unusual and try your brakes before driving away. Do several emergency stops, and tell the same to Loretta and Tobias. We are now looking for a murderer, be it Susannah, Kirsti Løvik, Gabriella Korakova or someone else."

CHAPTER TWELVE

Disaster

The joyous spirit of a moment ago suddenly turned to panic.

Death is always difficult to deal with. Rebecca's grief was exacerbated by the fact her parents were murdered. She was extremely angry. An accident is always easier to come to terms with but a premeditated murder (even if Gavin was the intended target) was harder to comprehend. To compound matters the perpetrator was still at large. The family now believed that the culprit could only be Susannah. She was the only common denominator with all the tragic events they had suffered. Her relentless attacks were constant and damaging. Legally she may be dead, but one would be a fool to believe that. Even Detective Martinez had accepted that Susannah was alive. He had placed her top of his most wanted list. He had also informed the Norwegian authorities that there was strong evidence to suggest she was alive and possibly living in Norway. The hunt for Susannah was widespread. Her manipulative skills may have achieved success thus far, but her time must surely be running out.

Kirsti Løvik had also been re-questioned but she denied any knowledge of Susannah being alive. To aid her defence she had successfully passed the polygraph test. Naturally, Karl was concerned. He may have loved Kirsti Løvik once, but his loyalties were firmly with Gavin. They were lifelong friends, having grown up together in England. Their bond was invincible. Perturbed by Kirsti Løvik's possible involvement, Karl decided to confront her. He arrived at her office shortly after 10am. Her secretary Lana cordially acknowledged his presence. She attempted to buzz her employer but Karl was too impatient. He briskly walked towards her office. Without even knocking he opened the door and entered. Lana had managed to forewarn Kirsti Løvik. The Norwegian entrepreneur remained seated at her desk as Karl entered. Her appearance conveyed sophistication and beauty. She had retained her youthful demeanour yet her scornful expression temporarily overshadowed her prettiness. Kirsti Løvik was riled by Karl's insolent attitude.

"To what do I owe this pleasure? And thanks for knocking," she sarcastically said.

"I know you have been interviewed by the police," began Karl as he walked towards her.

"What has that got to do with you?"

"Gavin has suffered enough. You may have bluffed your way with the police, but I know the lies you can tell," replied Karl. He stood in front of her. Her desk was between them.

"Don't you give me attitude," rebuked Kirsti Løvik, looking up at him. "Now leave my office before I call the police."

"I will leave when I'm ready. Tell me you are innocent and did not tamper with Rebecca's car, thinking it was Gavin's," said Karl, leaning on her desk. His threatening manner was intentional.

"Don't come the tough guy with me, I don't answer to you. Now leave my office."

A Certain Dilemma

"I'm warning you Kirsti Løvik, leave Gavin alone or you will have me to deal with," threatened Karl.

"You don't scare me, and you do not want me for an enemy. I am powerful and could easily crush you if I choose, so think again macho man," replied a confident Kirsti Løvik. Karl remained persistent as he continued.

"We already know you have been bidding to take over the plantation, just to spite Gavin and ruin his business."

"I am not bothered about Gavin anymore. You are wasting my time. Now leave my office," defended Kirsti Løvik.

"You and me we used to be good together, now all we ever do is argue," reflected Karl, attempting to appease the situation. He sat on the edge of her desk. "Can't you just leave Gavin alone? He does not deserve this."

"I do not do sentiment, you should know that, and my brother did not deserve to die in the cable car crash so don't expect me to feel sorry for Gavin."

"Is that a confession?" assumed Karl.

"You can think what you like I don't care. Now get out of my office."

"Don't treat me like a fool as if I'm some schoolboy to be sent to the headmaster," reacted Karl, his temperament augmenting.

"Get out of my office!" repeated Kirsti Løvik sternly.

"Why are you so bitter and twisted? You are like a stone statue cold and inhumane." That comment caused Kirsti Løvik to act aggressively. She stood up in anger.

"Who the hell do you think you are?" she retorted. "You would be nothing without Gavin. At least I am successful by my own means."

"You are only where you are due to your deceased husband. You had nothing before inheriting his money," stated Karl. Kirsti Løvik slapped Karl across his face. She could not resist her momentary fit of rage.

"How dare you say that!" She intended to hit him again but Karl grabbed her arm and pushed her down into her seat.

"Now I want the truth. Is Susannah alive? And if so where is she?" demanded Karl aggressively. Kirsti Løvik refused to answer. She glared at Karl; the anger in his eyes was unmistakable. "Well is Susannah alive?"

"Like I have already said to the police, Susannah is dead. The last time I saw her was in prison before I was released. What more can I say for you to believe me," responded Kirsti Løvik. "I have already answered to Martinez and the poly test proves I was not lying. Susannah is dead." Karl refrained from questioning her denial. He moved away.

"Just keep away from Gavin else I won't be responsible for my actions," threatened Karl. He went to leave the office.

"Bother me again and I won't be responsible for my actions either," seethed Kirsti Løvik. Karl left her office, slamming the door behind him.

<>

For grief-stricken Rebecca it was like a cruel fate of déjà vu. She had struggled to come to terms with Greg's murder, now she was repeating the same inner turmoil over her parents' death. Despite her grief she exercised her responsibility to sort out her parents' estate. Chester Hargreaves proved a valuable asset as he guided her through the financial and bureaucratic process of probate. Being the only child Rebecca would inherit the Texan ranch and cattle trade. Temporarily, she had to return to Texas. It was inevitable to sort out various matters. At her request Chester Hargreaves travelled with her. He had never been to Texas yet quite fancied himself being a cowboy, wearing leather chaps and riding a horse. Gavin drove them down to the jetty. The seaplane would ferry them to the Dominican Republic where they would catch a flight to Dallas.

"I have been meaning to mention this to you since the funeral," said Gavin to Rebecca. They stood on the jetty waiting for the seaplane to arrive. "I do not know how to say it without sounding insensitive," he hesitantly continued.

"Oh just say it," replied Rebecca. "Life is too short to beat about the bush."

"It is with regard to the sale of Calypso Tavern."

"You have found a buyer," she coldly replied.

"No, not really. I thought maybe you would like to buy it, that's if you decide to sell your parents' ranch," commented Gavin. Rebecca paused. Why was everything like a double-edged sword? She would without any hesitation buy Calypso Tavern, yet did her parents have to die for it to happen.

"Even if I do sell the ranch it is not worth $3million. I still can't afford to buy Calypso Tavern even if I include my parents' life insurance settlement," answered Rebecca.

"How about 50% ownership with me. $1.5million, could you afford that?" suggested Gavin. Rebecca wanted so much to own Calypso Tavern. Gavin's suggestion was a better option than some outsider invading what she felt is rightfully hers. She turned to address Chester Hargreaves.

"Is this a viable option?" she questioned.

"It certainly is, but of course it depends how quickly we sell the ranch," advised Chester Hargreaves. "It could be weeks or months before the sale goes through."

"I owe the bank $2million plus interest, as long as they know there is a buyer they won't mind waiting awhile longer. I can afford to cover the shortfall," responded Gavin. Rebecca spoke freely as she contemplated Gavin's suggestion.

"Up until this moment I had been indecisive about selling the ranch, not knowing if it was the right thing to do. I have even thought about returning to Texas and run the ranch myself. You should have said something sooner Gavin, it would have made my mind up and stopped my mind whirling around in never ending thoughts," explained Rebecca. She did not need any time to think. Too much time had already been wasted. "The answer is yes, I will buy 50% of Calypso Tavern for $1.5million."

"Fantastic," reacted Gavin. "I will inform the bank."

"Here comes the seaplane," commented Chester Hargreaves.

"Thanks Gavin," said Rebecca as she threw her arms around him. "I feel I have a future now. I know I've been curt but I can't help it."

"You don't need to apologise. Hurry back as soon as you can," stated Gavin. He watched as they boarded the seaplane. Rebecca smiled back at him as she looked out of the window. The noise of the engine dispersed a flock of birds from the nearby treetops. Moments later the light aircraft veered away from the jetty. It skimmed across the Caribbean Sea before lifting effortlessly into the pale blue sky above. Gavin returned to his Mustang. His worst nightmare was coming true. Susannah was alive but where was she? She was probably watching him now, hiding behind a tree and pointing a gun at him. Before getting into his car and driving home, Gavin looked around but saw no one.

The hunt for Susannah was arduous. The Martinique police force with Detective Martinez at the helm had joined forces with the Norwegian constabulary. Perhaps it would be easier to find a needle in a haystack. Despite all relentless efforts she eluded captivity. Detective Martinez had a margin of success regarding the kidnapping of Gregori. The woman on the CCTV footage had now been identified as Tanya Quaker. She had been an inmate with Susannah. They had even shared a prison cell. This endorsed the belief that Susannah was not only alive but behind the kidnapping of Gregori. Was Susannah also Gabriella Korakova? Or was the Russian a third party? There was no mention of her in the prison records. The gap was narrowing. Detective Martinez was hopeful of an arrest. Unfortunately, all known friends and family of Tanya had not heard from her in months. It became apparent that Susannah and Tanya, with or without Gabriella Korakova had planned this escapade with meticulous attention. They had covered their tracks well to avoid detection. Passport control records revealed that Tanya had left the country shortly after the kidnapping. Was she in Hong Kong with Gabriella Korakova? That is where the ransom money had been transferred to, but no longer remained. The money had been traced from Hong Kong to an account in South Africa where the trail went cold. Yet the burning question was where is Susannah? If she had tampered with the brakes on Rebecca's Mercedes then she must be in Martinique.

<>

After seven weeks in Texas sorting out her parents' estate, Rebecca returned to Martinique. Chester Hargreaves had returned a couple of weeks earlier having dealt with all the legal ramifications. The ranch was sold not to a single investor or budding entrepreneur but to the seven ranch hands that ran the business. Each managed to raise an equal share of the sale price. The ranch proceeds coupled with her parents' life insurance settlement, enabled Rebecca to buy her 50% share in Calypso Tavern. She had paid Gavin $1.5million. This allowed him to repay the bank the $2million used for the ransom along with a nominal amount of interest. Before returning, Rebecca had looked up old acquaintances, merely to say goodbye and to leave them an open invitation to visit her in Martinique. Now with all her ties to Texas severed, she decided to remain in Martinique for the rest of her life.

Rebecca saw Gavin waiting at the jetty as the seaplane descended onto the Caribbean Sea. She quickly picked up her suitcase to meet him.

"Welcome home partner," stated Gavin as he embraced her.

"It is great to be back," sighed Rebecca.

"I know Marcus will be glad to see you. I think he needs a break from acting manager in your absence," remarked Gavin. He noticed how happy Rebecca seemed from when he last saw her. Gavin took hold of her suitcase as they walked towards the car.

"We kept in close contact. There was scarcely a day going buy without me ringing Marcus or with him contacting me. Such is the wonders of modern technology. Whatever did we do before the days of the internet and e-mails," mentioned Rebecca.

"I wouldn't know how to function," responded Gavin. "The ski resort is at its busiest time now with winter upon us and I'm in daily contact with Karl. At least business is better this year than on the same time last year. There has been an increase in bookings due to the above average snowfall for mid November."

"That's a bit of good news for a change," commented Rebecca.

"And how are you? You look terrific," said Gavin

"I'm doing ok. Keeping busy has always been a good healer for me."

"We have missed you on Friday nights on the yacht so keep this Friday free," mentioned Gavin as they walked towards his Mustang.

"I'm looking forward to it."

Conversation flowed easily during the drive home. Rebecca was glad they had patched up their differences. But then that was only due to her buying 50% of Calypso Tavern. However, a noticeable silence fell as they passed Viper's Bend. The image of the burning Mercedes flashed in their minds. Rebecca still recalled her mother's scream as they went over the edge. Rebecca was first to break the silence.

"Any news where Susannah might be?" she questioned.

"Not yet," replied Gavin. "Incidentally, we still need to check our cars for any booby traps and test the brakes before driving away."

"I will kill her if ever I see her," stated Rebecca coldly. "Even if I am caught I don't think there is a jury in the whole world that would find me guilty. She killed Greg. I buried him on our wedding day, and now my folks' horrific murder. They must have really suffered. No, there isn't a jury that would find me guilty. It is beyond comprehension to let that bitch live."

"I couldn't agree more. This nightmare will never end as long as she is still alive," reflected Gavin. "But let's try and remain positive. We do have stringent security measures in place, along with the entire police force on both sides of the Atlantic. She will be caught soon."

"Now I am back I need to think about buying a new car, so that's my task for tomorrow."

"That reminds me, Veronique said you can borrow her car in the meantime. It's not as if we need two cars now she is on a career break."

"Thanks, that will be a help till I get myself sorted with transport. By the way, how is Gregori?"

"He never stays still. He is running everywhere, talking a lot more and slowly driving us insane. He has this habit of waking up at six in the morning and tries to drag us out of bed so we can make his breakfast. At least we have a break from him on Friday evenings as he sleeps over at the cabana, so Loretta and Tobias have the pleasure of being woken up at 6am on a Saturday morning."

"Gregori has a jovial spirit, which is just as well considering his kidnap ordeal," reflected Rebecca. "Do you think we will ever be free from Susannah?"

"Yes I do. With all the police forces involved from here and in Norway; the security systems at work; the passport control and all the CCTV monitors, she cannot evade justice for ever," replied Gavin. Despite sounding confident, deep down he had reservations, but he did not want Rebecca to see this. Gavin dreaded every day wondering if it would be his last. Susannah had killed so many people. It seemed evident that one day she would succeed in killing him. It was not easy for Gavin living life under threat of assassination.

Rather than return to an empty apartment Rebecca agreed to stay the night at the house. Besides, now she was a business partner Gavin wanted to celebrate her fortune, be it tinged with sadness. Yet this momentous occasion could not pass by unmarked. It was a cause for celebration. Heaven knows the family needed to clutch at any happy event. Back at the house Gavin popped the champagne bottle and officially welcomed Rebecca. Tobias and Loretta were present along with Loretta's culinary expertise. She and Veronique had once again prepared a buffet. Rebecca appreciated the offer and toasted her new business partner.

"My life has centred around Calypso Tavern for many years now. I will endeavour to continue its success. If only other factors in my life had been different. But here is to the future and we will be happy. Thank you Gavin," toasted Rebecca. They all acknowledged and drank their champagne. It was refreshing to see Rebecca smiling once more. Tobias pulled Gavin aside.

"Just after you left we had another email from Scott Myles. He is insisting we by a gun for our own protection. Are you sure you don't know him? He seems to know you," said Tobias.

"He is persistent, I will give him that, but you know my feelings on guns. I don't think they should be in the public domain. This Scott Myles whoever he is must be on a good commission," said Gavin.

"Well I replied back to that effect and to stop pestering us. He is an eager salesperson."

"That is the perils of the internet. Too many junk emails," said Gavin. "Yet the thought of having a gun to kill Susannah with is tempting. No doubt he has read our press reports." Rebecca came over.

"Well partner, do we need to have a board meeting?"

"Yes," replied Gavin. "There is no time like the present. I declare the meeting open. You can make all of the decisions. Meeting closed." They laughed.

<>

It was midday at Snøby and late November. The twilight sky stood in contrast to the snow covered mountains. Adrenalin was running high. The pre-Christmas ski chase was ready to commence. The season was turning out to be one of the busiest for the ski resort. Snøby was well attended with scores of people taking a pre-Christmas holiday. Others would be arriving over the next few weeks to celebrate Christmas in a traditional picturesque setting. From the upper mountain range the resort could be seen below. The chalets appeared like currents in a coconut cake. Snow covered spruce trees were lit up with decorative lighting. The twelve-minute ski run was a route many skiers took to return to their chalet. However, today the route would be used for the ski chase.

Karl and five other ski instructors will have a ten second head start as they begin the chase. The crowd of spectators would then count down from ten as the competing tourists prepared for push off. This sporting game was for experienced skiers only. The tourists would need a lot of skill to vigorously chase after the instructors. To aid distinction from each other the instructors wore orange florescent jackets. There is not a championship trophy or accolade for anyone who happened to finish the course ahead of an instructor, but any fortunate person who did was allowed free drinks all night in the bar. This was enough of an incentive for the guests to partake in the chase. If they were not enticed by the spirit of the occasion then it was the alcoholic spirit that generated the enthusiasm.

All resumed their starting positions. Karl and the five other instructors stood in line. Their ski sticks were held in front ready for the push off. The tourists raised humorous banter as they gathered behind them, eager to make chase. Per Jørstad, a staff member stood to one side. He was ready to give the signal to commence the race. He stood with his one arm raised, holding the Norwegian flag. Its red background with a blue cross that was edged with white was clearly visible as it blew in the wind. Per Jørstad swiped the flag downwards. The race had begun. A cheer went up from the spectators as they watched from the side of the ski track. To keep with tradition the crowd shouted out the countdown as the ski instructors raced ahead.

"10, 9, 8, 7, 6..." The twenty participating tourists acquired their position to give chase. "...5, 4, 3..." shouted the crowd. The flag was raised again to give the signal for the others to chase after the ski instructors. "...2, 1," continued the crowd. The signal given, the spectators cheered once more as the twenty experienced skiers set off in pursuit of the instructors.

Dark shadows loomed across the piste, caused by the moonlight not the sun. The winter sun remained hidden. The celestial fire failed to rise above the horizon. November always said goodbye to the sun until February. The drawback of having twenty-four hours of sunlight during the summer equated to twenty-four hours of darkness during the winter. But the snow dispelled the total depths of darkness.

The race was the highlight of the day's skiing activities. Karl with his Olympic level ability was leading the way. He took the race quite seriously, judging himself as if it were an Olympic event. To finish first was a must, hypothetically

A Certain Dilemma

winning the gold medal. The cable car travelled above them. The people inside watched the race unfold beneath.

Approximately thirty seconds after the chase had begun, a huge firework display emanated from the mountain peaks. The spectators' attention was divided between the race and the magical picturesque display above them. Fortunately for those at the foot of the mountain, they caught sight of both acts of entertainment as they looked up at the ski chase. The skiers dropped down the mountainside to a blaze of fireworks beyond them.

The firework extravaganza with its shimmering sparkles of colour, coupled with extremely loud bangs, lasted for several minutes. The loud bangs sent shudders through the spectators. Gasps of fright were audible by all, including the skiers. After the last firework had fizzled out, the crowd remained looking into the twilight sky, hoping for an encore. Seconds later a gentle rumbling sound became the unexpected encore. Visually there was nothing to see at first, but as the sound increased to a thunderous roar, the crowd witnessed the descent of snow from the upper mountain peaks.

"It's an avalanche!" shouted someone. The joyous spirit of a moment ago suddenly turned to panic. In disbelief the spectators watched as the heavy-laden snow on the mountain peak shuddered. Within seconds it became dislodged. The vast ice packed snow crashed from the mountaintop. This in turn triggered further sheets of snow to dislodge, increasing the velocity and strength of the avalanche. It was like a giant tsunami. The wall of snow plunged downwards, heading for the tourists and skiers.

"It is coming straight for us!" came a voice. People rushed to the cable car station, hoping to escape, but this would prove to be futile. There just was not enough time to reach safety. The passengers in the travelling cable car saw the travesty unfold, but were powerless to do anything. They were compelled to witness this life-shattering event. The avalanche gained momentum and its roar increased. People fled in all directions trying to escape its path. No one could run due to all the snow. It was worse than trying to run in water.

The thunderous roar of the avalanche distracted the skiers. They momentarily stopped. Karl turned and faced the approaching wall of snow. He had sensed danger at the unexpected firework display. He knew the vibration caused by the loud bangs would be powerful enough to trigger an avalanche. The impending wall of snow was gaining speed. It was time for emergency measures.

"Quick, loosen your foot bindings on the skis and loosen your ski stick straps!" shouted Karl to his fellow skiers. "And don't forget to spit!" The instructors and skiers grouped together and implemented the safety procedures. To avoid broken limbs it was essential to loosen their foot bindings and ski stick straps. Should the unthinkable happen and they are caught in the avalanche then the force of the travelling snow would whip their skis and ski sticks around like helicopter blades. This would result in their arms and legs being broken if the bindings were still tight.

In the event of being buried in the snow, then the survival technique is to spit. The feeble human body would lay entombed in the snow. One would be confused and disoriented, and unable to fathom which way is up. Gravity remains constant so by spitting, whichever way the spit falls then the task is to dig in the opposite direction until one has reached the surface.

The avalanche was invincible and roared like a fierce lion devouring its prey.

"Follow me!" shouted Karl as he resumed skiing. No one could afford to waste any time. The advancing avalanche would not relent. Their chance of survival was slim. They were high up on the mountain range with no place to hide, but had the geographical landscape thrown them a lifeline? Halfway down the mountain was the intersection to the adjoining mountain. If they could manage to descend to the intersection and cross over to the neighbouring mountain, then they could escape the avalanche. Karl was no fool; he knew the mountain range like the back of his hand. He was also accustomed to the characteristics of an avalanche. Its speed, power and force were fuelled solely by gravity. It seemed illogical that zillions of dainty fluffy white snowflakes could club together and create such havoc. Individually, each snowflake was fearless, powerless and void of any strength. Yet united together with gravity for fuel, they mounted terrific strength, and became a force completely invincible by mankind. Whatever stood in its path would be obliterated. Trees pulled up by their roots, cabins crushed, the snow crashing through the wooden structure like someone blowing down a pyramid of cards. Even huge heavy rocks were hijacked along the way. These great boulders that were adopted by the avalanche added to the mighty force of destruction.

The spectators that had been in joyous spirits as the ski chase began were now terrified. They were confused at what to do. Intuitively they headed back to the cable car station. Yet did anyone really believe they would be safe there? Their presumed sanctuary was in the path of the avalanche.

Periodically Karl looked over his shoulder, to judge if they were retaining an adequate distance from the avalanche. Yet each time he looked the impending wall of snow had considerably closed the gap between them. This was a race he knew he would not win. He caught sight of the indiscriminate avalanche engulfing the spectators who had not managed to reach the cable car station. Seconds later the presumed sanctuary fell victim as the snow bulldozed its way and annihilated the wooden structure. The tourists on the cable car watched in horror. Their fears were soon realised. They became the next target. The force of the avalanche was twisting the pylons that supported the cables. The cable car jerked precariously, throwing its passengers about. The equipment could not sustain the powerful might of the ferocious wintry weapon. The pylons collapsed and the cables snapped like a feeble piece of string. The cable car dropped into the mouth of the avalanche. Karl and the other skiers paused as they witnessed the demise of their fellow friends and families.

The roaring wall of snow continued relentlessly, becoming more dangerous as it picked up rocks and debris along the way. The cable car was propelled in the midst of the rushing avalanche like a giant snowball. The passengers were now dead, their broken bodies tossed about like clothes in a washing machine. There was no time for sentiment. Karl and the other skiers raced ahead, anxious to reach the intersection. The intersection was in view, but could they travel the distance? The encroaching avalanche was closer to them than they were to the intersection.

The skiers were breathless and felt the physical pain of pushing their bodies to the limit. But this did not deter their efforts. They skied with all their might, keeping the intersection in sight. They had to make it. The skiers felt the gush of wind as the wall of snow pushed them. The avalanche had caught up. Snow and debris flew past them. Stronger than any blizzard, the tempestuous snowstorm overwhelmed the skiers. Karl felt the mighty weight bear down on him as he became sucked into the grip of the roaring wall of snow. No one could escape. Their bodies rotated within the whirling snow like a ceremonial dance with death.

The avalanche ploughed down the mountainside leaving behind a trail of death and destruction. It finally came to rest in a valley edged out in the lower mountain range. Nature's rugged terrain had acted like a damn, preventing the avalanche from engulfing the village that nestled at the foot of the mountain. However, Snøby, Gavin's ski resort was decimated.

CHAPTER THIRTEEN

Merry Christmas Gavin

Yet that which dealt such beauty and pleasure could also deal death and destruction.

The last six months could scarcely have been worse for the Harrison household. The ant infestation in the sugar despatches had resulted in the temporary closure of the plantation. The many ruthless takeover bids from Global Incorporations Ltd, headed by Kirsti Løvik. She had also orchestrated the drugs raid on Calypso Tavern, which had brought unwanted publicity. The kidnapping of Gregori leading to a $2million ransom demand, thankfully those agonising forty-eight hours led to his safe return. However, Calypso Tavern had to be put up for sale in order to secure the ransom. There was wild speculation as to whether Susannah was alive, especially as the woman identified with kidnapping Gregori was Tanya Quaker, a former cellmate with Susannah. Neither of them had been captured. The ransom also had not been returned and was last traced to South Africa. Who was Gabriella Korakova? And why was she involved? Or perhaps the Russian identity was yet another disguise for Susannah? The unanswered questions just seem to multiply.

The murder of Ursula and Godwin had caused untold grief, particularly for Rebecca. In a mild upturn of fortune, Rebecca had managed to buy a 50% share in Calypso Tavern out of her inheritance. Everyone now lived in constant fear, having to carry out safety checks on their car and testing the brakes. All of these problems seemed to revolve around Susannah. No one believed she was dead. But where was she? And now finally the avalanche disaster that had destroyed Snøby.

Reports of the devastation reached Gavin intermittently. All communication with Snøby had been temporarily lost. His first knowledge of the incident was a brief bulletin on the evening news. It was reported that a tributary factor to the avalanche was the higher than average snowfall. A rescue mission began almost immediately. Survivors spoke how they were buried alive in the snow for several hours. They were eternally grateful when rescued. Yet their story was few and far between. Many bodies had been recovered. Although official numbers had yet to be declared, it was clear from the outset that the fatality count would be high.

Gavin tried ringing Karl, but no answer or any reply to his e-mails. It was several days later when Gavin received an e-mail from Per Jørstad, who had survived the ordeal. It was early evening and Gavin was sitting at his desk in the study, using his laptop when the e-mail arrived. The subject heading read: 'Bad News.'

Hi, Gavin, it is hard to write this e-mail but even harder to say. It is like living in a war zone, devastation everywhere, so many dead, so many missing. Everyone is upset. We have lost over 50 guests, all killed in the avalanche. I was buried in the snow but managed to claw my way out. Worse still Karl did not make it. The rescue team recovered his body earlier today. It seems he broke his neck...

A Certain Dilemma

Gavin paused from reading any further. That was the news he dreaded. His lifelong friend killed at his ski resort. How many more deaths will weigh on his conscience? Gavin was overwhelmed with guilt. His wealth had delivered yet another bitter blow. He knew if Karl had to die young then he would have chosen exactly this way. Karl loved the snow, and loved skiing. It is what made him feel happiest. Gavin continued to read the e-mail.

...The cable car station and all the chalets have been destroyed. The upper mountain peaks and pistes are inaccessible at this moment in time. Karl's ski lodge has also been destroyed. The guest lodge has survived but with a few broken windows. It was fortunate that the guest lodge is situated at the foot of the mountain. The lower ridge acted like a damn and stopped most of the avalanche. All remaining staff and guests are in shock. Many people sit in the lounge crying silently. Some have left and gone home. No one knows what to do. All that remains of Snøby is the guest lodge and nursery slopes.
The police have taken many statements from everyone. They seem to be treating this as a criminal act. Why would they think that? It was just an avalanche. I have been questioned over a firework display but we did not organise one. It must have been someone else further up the mountain range. I am meeting with the insurers tomorrow. I will keep you informed.

Farvel for nå.

Per Jørstad.

Briefly Gavin formulated a reply:

Hi Per, thank goodness you have survived. I am very upset with the news, especially regarding Karl as I have known him all my life. I am glad you have contacted me as I have been trying for days to get through to you. I guess the avalanche has caused a loss of communication. I will be travelling to Norway the day after tomorrow. Can you meet me at Røros airport at 10pm Saturday evening? You must be going through hell but I thank you for keeping control of the situation.

Hilsen fra meg.

Gavin.

Gavin logged off his laptop and left the study. He felt emotionally drained. He entered the living room. Veronique was relaxing on the sofa watching TV. She noticed her husband seemed solemn.

"Don't tell me more bad news?" she said.

"I have just had an e-mail from Per. Karl is dead. They found his body earlier today. He had a broken neck," replied Gavin. Veronique stood up and hugged him. "How much more grief do we have to suffer?"

"I know, it is very sad but we manage to carry on as time passes. Most of our grief is down to Susannah."

"Well at least she can't be blamed for this. An avalanche is an act of God," remarked Gavin. "What God would do this?"

"I think I should come with you to Norway, you can't do this alone." Veronique clenched her husband as if her life depended on it. Her love for him was solid. No power on earth or within the universe could weaken her devotion.

"No, you need to stay here with Gregori," said Gavin. "I know your folks would look after him but he will miss you too much, and I don't want him upset after what he has been through."

"He could come with us. We could spend Christmas in Norway," suggested Veronique, trying to make light of the situation. Gavin sighed as he broke from the embrace. He moved over to the sofa and fell onto the padded cushions.

"I need to sit down. I haven't the energy to stand," he uttered. Veronique sat beside him. "In all honesty, a depressing scene of people crying is not good company for a two-year-old." Gavin looked at Veronique as he put his arm around her. "I will call you each day and speak to Gregori before his bedtime. It won't be a pleasant trip but I will manage, one has to."

"I am worried about you Gavin. You need me with you. Gregori is resilient. He will be fine with Mama and Pa. He even seemed to have a great time with his kidnapper, so he won't feel bad."

"I take it the little fellow is asleep upstairs."

"Yes, I checked in on him whilst you were in the study."

"We must decide what to do for his third birthday," said Gavin.

"Let's get Christmas over with first before we contemplate what to do for January sixteenth."

"He is growing up fast. We shall have to sort out his schooling."

"I have already got him enlisted at our local school, just to be safe. But if we decide otherwise there is time to change," commented Veronique. Gavin's mind refocused on Per's e-mail.

"There are over fifty people dead," he stated, staring into the yucca plant in front of him. His sombre mood became interrupted by the sound of a car pulling up outside. "Who can this be?" Gavin got up and looked out of the front window. He saw Detective Martinez approaching the house. From his hastily gait Gavin knew it was not a sociable visit. Veronique remained on the sofa whilst Gavin let him into the house.

"I know it is getting late, but I have received information which I need to make you aware of," began Detective Martinez as Gavin greeted him on the veranda.

"Come inside," responded Gavin. "Have you arrested Gregori's kidnapper? Is it Susannah?" Detective Martinez passed through the doorway.

"Hello," said Veronique as he entered the living room. "Please sit down." Detective Martinez sat in the armchair. Gavin resumed his seat on the sofa next to his wife.

"No," answered Detective Martinez. "We are still looking for Tanya. And still no evidence to confirm if Susannah is alive. I am here in connection with the avalanche."

"The avalanche!" remarked Gavin. "You know about the avalanche, but why is that of interest to you?"

"As you know I have been in communication with the Norwegian police regarding the death of Tor Hegland, or should I say his murder, and the situation regarding Kirsti Løvik trying to sabotage your plantation. Truls Haugvik, my counterpart in Norway, rang me earlier regarding the avalanche. Due to your high profile and notoriety he took an immediate interest in the avalanche, which has destroyed your ski resort. The result being that the authorities have proved the avalanche was not accidental."

"Not accidental," repeated Veronique.

"You have lost me now. Who can create an avalanche?" questioned Gavin.

"Person or persons unknown organised a firework display, using extremely loud bangers with the deliberate intent of causing an avalanche. The sound vibration was all that was needed to trigger the deadly chain of events. The Norwegian police have arrested Kirsti Løvik. Due to her location and prior attacks against you she is the likeliest culprit. They have also checked her computer records and they came across the name Gabriella Korakova."

"She has the ransom," stated Gavin.

"It would seem so. She denies any involvement of course, but further interrogations are taking place," added Detective Martinez.

"But you have already questioned her before and she denies it all," mentioned Veronique.

"I know, but perhaps we have been too complacent. She has always been questioned then released, thanks to her experienced and effective lawyer," replied Detective Martinez.

"So perhaps she is carrying on from where Susannah left off," commented Gavin angrily. "Kirsti Løvik was in prison with Tanya Quaker, and it was her brother, Susannah's husband, who died on the cable car accident nine years ago. Perhaps Gabriella Korakova is an accomplice, possibly an employee. To what extent do we know of her connection with this Russian?" questioned Gavin.

"That is what we aim to find out," said Detective Martinez.

"Kirsti Løvik would no doubt want revenge on Karl for killing Susannah. She hates Karl so that would make sense if Kirsti Løvik caused the avalanche. You can't let her get away with this. Karl was my best friend she had no right to kill him, let alone all the others that died in the avalanche." Gavin was clearly riled that his lifelong friend had actually been murdered.

"Can they prove it was Kirsti Løvik?" asked Veronique.

"Mostly the evidence is circumstantial," replied Detective Martinez. "But forensics are investigating and compiling evidence which will hopefully incriminate her, such as any traces of firework residue in her office or home or on her clothes. She certainly has the motive and the pieces do fit together confirming her guilt. I knew I could not trust her to keep a distance from you. There is no way she will escape incarceration. Did she kill Tor Hegland? Was she involved in kidnapping Gregori? The polygraph test confirmed she did not. Yet her link to Gabriella Korakova proves otherwise. Perhaps the polygraph test was not as accurate as we would have liked. But regardless of this she has incriminated herself beyond suspicion. We will find the evidence to prove her guilt," stated Detective Martinez. "Anyway, I am flying over to Norway day after tomorrow to question her further."

"Would that be flight SAS 142?" questioned Gavin.

"It is with Scandinavian Airlines but I don't know the flight number," replied Detective Martinez.

"There is only one flight due so it must be the same. I am also booked on that flight," informed Gavin. "You see Veronique, you don't need to worry, I shall be fine. I will be with Detective Martinez. We can keep each other company during the ten-hour flight. If you haven't got accommodation sorted you can stay with me at the guest lodge."

"That would be appreciated, and it would save the department some funds," replied Detective Martinez. He then gave a philosophical statement. "Never in all my years on the force have I been involved in such a convoluted criminal case as yours Gavin. I hardly know which matter to deal with first. The sabotage attacks on your plantation; drugs at Calypso Tavern; Gregori's kidnapping; Ursula and Godwin's murder, and now the avalanche. They all centre on Susannah and Kirsti Løvik. I shall need to retire after this case."

"But it does all make sense if it is Kirsti Løvik. She was in prison with Tanya so they are obviously working together. Plus the link to Gabriella Korakova," said Gavin.

"That is the assumption," replied Detective Martinez.

"I am glad you came over tonight," remarked Veronique. "You have given me some relief. I can finally accept that Susannah is dead. We were just being paranoid, and who could blame us for thinking she was still alive. It is now obvious that Kirsti Løvik is the culprit. All we need to do is find Tanya and get her to confess against her."

A Certain Dilemma

"Trust me, I have officers on duty round-the-clock until Tanya is apprehended, and we still hope to retrieve your $2million ransom," said Detective Martinez.

"If we can end this agonising nightmare once and for all, it will be well worth losing the two million dollars," concluded Gavin. He stood up and walked over to his drinks cabinet. He made himself a whisky and soda. Detective Martinez declined Gavin's offer of an alcoholic beverage for he was on duty. Instead, Veronique made him a cappuccino. Despite feeling sad and bereaved, Gavin felt a glimmer of hope. After the tribulations of the last six months there was an end in sight. He drank his whisky and soda in one gulp. He welcomed the solution that would bring justice and eradicate all his problems. The culprit was Kirsti Løvik. The evidence was stacked against her. Detective Martinez was determined to get her convicted. All those niggling doubts wondering if Susannah was alive could be laid to rest. Kirsti Løvik had already admitted sabotaging the plantation and the takeover bid. That was just out of spite to ruin him. She has access to illegal substances in the guise of her perfumery empire. She has confessed to planting the drugs at Calypso Tavern or arranged for Tanya, her prison associate to have done the deed. The CCTV footage confirms Tanya with Gregori, no doubt under Kirsti Løvik's instructions to kidnap him. The killing of Ursula and Godwin were unintentional. It was likely that she or Tanya mistook the Mercedes to be Gavin's car. Kirsti Løvik had failed to ruin Gavin's plantation business so she arranged to ruin his ski resort instead. She certainly had motive and methodology. Had she intended to kill Karl? They were no longer the impetuous lovers anymore. She held him responsible for killing Susannah, so it would be fitting if he were killed in the avalanche. Yet who killed Tor Hegland? Kirsti Løvik had no cause to kill him. Perhaps his murderer was an unknown assailant, someone with a grudge? Maybe the person the police first arrested but subsequently released due to forensic evidence was the true murderer. It is within the realms of probability that the forensic evidence could have been flawed.

<>

The flight to Norway was laborious. Detective Martinez read through his notes to question Kirsti Løvik. He knew how elusive she could be. He had to secure a positive result. Either her confession or gather enough evidence to take her to trial. He was banking on the forensic team finding traces of gunpowder residue to connect her to the firework display. That would incriminate her for certain.

Gavin sat next to him, trying to concentrate on the in-flight film. His mind drifted to the chaos that would confront him in Norway, meeting grieved relatives; attending the memorial service that had already been arranged. How to rebuild Snøby? But the hardest of all would be attending Karl's funeral. Karl was like a second brother to him. He had easily fitted into the role of best man at his wedding, especially in the wake of Greg's death. Karl had even taken the bullet that Susannah had meant for Gavin. Now Karl too had become a victim in Susannah's quest for revenge, courtesy of Kirsti Løvik.

Detective Martinez and Gavin arrived at Røros airport shortly after 10pm. Per Jørstad greeted them. It was a sad reunion. There was a lot to discuss about the ski resort but Per Jørstad refrained. The business could wait till tomorrow. Per Jørstad drove them to the guest lodge. The broken windows had been repaired. Most of the guests had vacated and as all new arrivals had been cancelled, there was plenty of room for Gavin and Detective Martinez to stay.

The log fire in the lounge burnt ferociously. This made the guest lodge very cosy and comforting. Outside the temperature was −15 degrees Celsius. The surrounding

A Certain Dilemma

landscape was buried under several feet of snow. It was three weeks before Christmas, but the festive season was far from their minds. Although Gavin and Martinez had managed a nap during the flight they soon retired to bed. Tomorrow would be a difficult day.

<>

Kirsti Løvik sat impatiently in the interview room at the local police station. Her lawyer sat with her. The two were alone and were waiting for Detective Martinez to enter. She listened to her legal representative, who endorsed their pre-arranged responses to the questions they assumed Detective Martinez would ask. Similar to the time she had been interrogated at Oslo police station, Kirsti Løvik would voice her objection to him now as she did then. The interview room resembled similar furnishings. An oak table with two chairs either side, positioned in the centre of the room. On the table stood the electronic equipment to record the interview. Detective Martinez entered the room, followed by his Norwegian counterpart Truls Haugvik. Kirsti Løvik gave a contemptible glare at Detective Martinez as he sat opposite her. There were no pleasant introductions. The proceedings would be strictly formal. Truls Haugvik activated the recording. He then stated the date and named the occupants who were in the room. To conclude the formalities Detective Martinez read Kirsti Løvik her rights.

"You do not have to say anything but it may harm your defence if you do not mention when questioned something which you later rely on in court. Anything you do say may be given in evidence," he stated. To begin with he addressed the issues he had already raised during the polygraph test, to see if her answers would be any different. "You have admitted attempting to sabotage Gavin's sugarcane plantation by planting ants in the sugar despatches, and trying to buy his business at a reduced price, just out of spite. Do you still hold a grudge against Gavin?"

"My client has already answered that question to which you hold documentation," replied her lawyer. Kirsti Løvik remained silent. Her glare was fixed straight ahead.

"It is in your own interest Kirsti Løvik to answer my questions for there is strong evidence connecting you to these crimes," stated Detective Martinez.

"Circumstantial evidence which will not hold up in court," affirmed her lawyer. Detective Martinez maintained his direct approach as he posed his next question, hoping to initiate dialogue with Kirsti Løvik.

"We have now identified Gregori's kidnapper as Tanya Quaker. You were both imprisoned together. Did you conspire with her to kidnap Gregori?"

"I do not know this Tanya woman," responded Kirsti Løvik defiantly.

"You were both imprisoned at the same time," reiterated Detective Martinez.

"So were hundreds of other women. I was only in prison for a few weeks. I did not speak to most of them," she replied dismissively. Detective Martinez sensed she would refute all of his questions, but he would still ask them. The more he could get her to speak the more chance she would contradict herself. He had to flush out the truth for he was now convinced she was the conspirator and using Tanya like a puppet to act out her deeds.

"What is your connection with Gabriella Korakova?"

"Excuse me?" questioned Kirsti Løvik.

"Gabriella Korakova received the $2million ransom in Hong Kong. Who is she?"

"I do not know anything about the ransom," replied Kirsti Løvik.

"My client has already answered these questions so please do not ask them again," remarked the lawyer.

"I have not asked about Gabriella Korakova so please confirm your knowledge and whereabouts of this person," reiterated Detective Martinez.

"There is no such person, not that I am aware of," replied Kirsti Løvik.

"Her details were on your computer," continued Detective Martinez.

"Yes but, I am confused. She does not exist. She is a name I have in reference to my business. I have plans to export my perfume to Russia. I wanted a Russian name to authenticate the brand of cosmetics," informed Kirsti Løvik.

"So you are Gabriella Korakova," assumed the detective.

"Yes in a sense, but I did not go to Hong Kong or have anything to do with the kidnapping or ransom," stated Kirsti Løvik. "You must believe me."

"The coincidence is too great. You must be involved," accused Detective Martinez.

"You can think what you like. Poly test me again if you want to," voiced Kirsti Løvik.

"So Gabriella Korakova is a name you have made up!" stated Detective Martinez.

"Yes."

"And you really expect me to believe this?"

"My client can prove this business arrangement I am sure. It is up to you to prove otherwise," remarked the lawyer. Detective Martinez was losing his patience. Yet he had to persevere and prove Kirsti Løvik was guilty.

"In the line of your perfumery business you have access to illegal drugs such as heroin from the plant extracts that you use as ingredients to your perfume. You have already confessed to planting a stash of heroin in Rebecca's office at Calypso Tavern in a further attempt to ruin Gavin. Are you still trying to ruin Gavin?" asked Detective Martinez. Kirsti Løvik looked away, refusing to answer the question. "Why won't you answer?" he added.

"How many times do you ask me the same question," she said angrily. "My boredom limit is low. You are determined to make me guilty, no matter what I say." Detective Martinez continued to ask his questions despite her lack of cooperation.

"Did you or Tanya interfere with the brakes on Rebecca's Mercedes, causing the death of her parents?"

"No," replied Kirsti Løvik.

"I do not believe you."

"You do not have to believe my client, just provide the proof," intervened the lawyer.

"What can you tell me about the recent avalanche that killed over fifty people, including Karl, and caused major damage to Gavin's ski resort?" stated Detective Martinez.

"I jumped for joy that Gavin's ski resort has suffered a setback," remarked Kirsti Løvik sarcastically. "Am I to be arrested for that?"

"What about the mysterious firework display that caused the avalanche. Did you have any involvement with that?" asked Detective Martinez.

"I do not like fireworks," she flippantly replied.

"Karl, your former boyfriend was killed in the avalanche. How do you feel about that?" questioned Detective Martinez. Again Kirsti Løvik replied mockingly.

"I have cried every day since, so many tears," she dramatically said, placing a hand on her heart.

"I believe you did orchestrate the firework display. The avalanche was just another attempt to ruin Gavin. Maybe you did not expect so many people to be killed," surmised Detective Martinez.

"You can think what you like," remarked Kirsti Løvik flippantly.

"You should take the matter more seriously," scolded Detective Martinez.

A Certain Dilemma

"You want to waste my time then I shall waste yours," she said, giving him a forced smile.

"Are you still intending to take over Gavin's plantation business?"

"Oh not that again," she swiftly replied. Her lawyer intervened the conversation.

"I see little point in asking my client repeated questions on matters she has already answered. This is tantamount to police harassment, which will leave us no alternative but to file a lawsuit against you if it continues," stated the young and conceited lawyer.

Detective Martinez persevered with his interrogation but to little effect. Any questions referring to matters already covered by the polygraph test were thwarted by the threat of legal action against him. Subsequent questions received either an answer of 'No comment', or a complete denial by Kirsti Løvik.

"You have already admitted being Gabriella Korakova so you must have the ransom. There is too much evidence to let you walk free," stated Detective Martinez. The interview concluded with her lawyer welcoming their day in court. Yet Detective Martinez knew there was not enough evidence to get a conviction. But the search would continue. Kirsti Løvik's bank accounts would be scrutinised to see if any connection to Hong Kong, South Africa or Gabriella Korakova.

The forensic team failed to find any evidence linking Kirsti Løvik to fireworks. Her lawyer gave a smug expression knowing his client was a free woman. A negative result left Detective Martinez frustrated, and at a loss with how to proceed with the case. He had hoped the detailed forensic search of her house and business would have yielded results. His only hope now was to find Tanya Quaker and get her to confess.

The white wooden church, which peacefully stood, was a focal point in the small town of Oppdal. The snow-covered mountain range provided a wintry backdrop as mourners entered the religious dwelling. A brief flurry of snow fell as if paying its respect. Gavin along with friends and colleagues from the ski resort entered the church for Karl's funeral. His relatives from England were present and staying at the resort. Yesterday the same church had been host to the memorial service for all those killed in the avalanche. Survivors had attended the service, some telling their story, others too upset to speak, but all praised the rescue team that had saved them. The priest had read out all the deceased names during prayers. The service had been televised across the nation for the whole country to pay its respect. In Norway snow was a large part of everyone's life, mostly enjoyed by skiing and other winter sports. Rarely did snow play an adverse card. Yet that which dealt such beauty and pleasure could also deal death and destruction. It had been a difficult day to deal with, but for Gavin, attending Karl's funeral was harder.

Karl's body was laid to rest in a private cemetery. The ski resort stood beyond, overshadowing the mourners. The sun was unable to rise above the mountainous horizon due to the time of year. The night-time sky embraced the scene. It was midday and the snowy surroundings gave adequate light for all to see. Karl's coffin was lowered into the ground. A semi-circular wall of snow and earth grouped the mourners as they stood at his graveside. The priest recited the usual responses as the coffin was laid to rest. Gavin was still and silent, his mind filled with memories of Karl.

The following day was Thursday, a week before Christmas. Gavin and Detective Martinez returned to Martinique somewhat depleted and less spirited than their arrival in Norway. Neither felt the pre-Christmas spirit. Detective Martinez had failed to secure a trial or confession from Kirsti Løvik. His Norwegian counterpart Truls Haugvik would continue to investigate those responsible for causing the avalanche, and not forgetting the unsolved murder

A Certain Dilemma

of Tor Hegland. Gavin felt drained both emotionally and physically. The rebuilding of Snøby would be a mammoth task. Chester Hargreaves as Gavin's solicitor will have his work cut out dealing with the insurance claim, which one could best describe as an administrative nightmare, especially with the many counterclaims from bereaved relatives. The compensation package will be great. Nevertheless, the material element would be replaced, but sadly the human loss cannot be restored.

It was late afternoon and Veronique stood at the jetty. She held Gregori in her arms as they watched the seaplane return. The little infant was so excited that his Daddy was coming home. The still waters of the Caribbean Sea were ripped apart as the seaplane touched down, leaving a tempestuous wake as it pulled alongside the jetty. Gregori waved as he spotted his dad through the small rounded window. Gavin waved back and smiled. The sight of his son and wife lifted his sombre mood. Veronique lowered Gregori to the ground. In his typical boisterous mien he ran down the boardwalk to meet his father. Gavin descended the seaplane and smiled as his son ran towards him. Gregori's happy face could have outshone any clown. His chubby legs propelled him into his dad's arms. Gavin lifted Gregori up into the air, turning around on the spot.

"How is my big boy?" he stated.

"I've been playing with my toys," responded a giggly Gregori.

"Have you been a good boy for Mummy?"

"Yes," he replied. "And I have been painting pictures."

"Pictures," remarked Gavin. "You must show me when we get home."

"Yes," agreed Gregori. "Me and Mummy have also put the Christmas tree up."

"I bet it looks fantastic."

"Yes, and the lights are so pretty. They are all different colours."

"Do you have a favourite colour?"

"Yes. I like the yellow ones and the big star," said Gregori excitedly. Gavin walked towards Veronique. Detective Martinez followed behind, carrying their suitcases. Veronique greeted her husband with a kiss.

"Glad you are back," she stated. "Hello Detective Martinez, shall I drop you off at the police station or your home?"

"Definitely my home," he replied. "I can catch up with the paperwork tomorrow. I will keep you informed of any progress."

Although happy to oblige, Veronique was pleased when she had dropped Martinez at his home. She wanted her husband all to herself. She drove Gavin's Mustang as Rebecca was still driving her white Dodge estate. Gregori was singing *The Mango Tree* nursery rhyme as he sat in his child seat. In a relaxed demeanour Veronique drove homeward bound.

"I have arranged with Rebecca for us to have a nice relaxing evening on the yacht," informed Veronique.

"But it is Thursday, we normally do that on Fridays," replied Gavin.

"I know but I thought it would be good to catch up and enjoy some quality time," stated Veronique.

"Can I come?" called out Gregori.

"No sweetheart because it will be dark and you can't swim," replied Veronique.

"But I want to," insisted Gregori.

"When you are older," remarked Gavin. "Besides, Grandma and Granddad will be looking after you. You can sleep in your bed at the cabana."

"But I want to sleep on the yacht," replied Gregori. "I will be a good boy."

"You are always a good boy, but the police won't let you stay on the yacht because you can't swim. Daddy will be in

A Certain Dilemma

trouble if he let you stay on the yacht, and you don't want that do you," explained Gavin.

"No. But when will you teach me to swim? Then I can come on the yacht," suggested Gregori.

"When you are older," replied Veronique. "Until then you have to stay with Grandma and Granddad. Why don't you take Marmajuke with you tonight?"

"Ok," sighed Gregori reluctantly. "But can I have ice cream as well?" he added pleadingly.

"Of course you can," confirmed Veronique. She turned matters to a more serious note. "Any joy in Norway?"

"No on all accounts," replied Gavin. "It's almost four weeks since the avalanche. If Kirsti Løvik is the culprit the proof has not been found. She is still a free woman."

"I fail to accept the proof is not there. The police must be incompetent. They know she is Gabriella Korakova, what more proof do they need?" aired Veronique. She could see her husband was tired and not very talkative. In any case she did not want to pursue the issue. It would only upset them further. An evening on the yacht was the right remedy.

Later that evening Gavin and Veronique strolled down to the yacht. Rebecca had already driven down to the marina to arrange a light buffet and a few bottles of wine. The evening unravelled with much needed merriment. Rebecca was the proud owner of Calypso Tavern, well 50% owner but as she ran the business it felt all hers. She received great comfort in knowing that Greg's pride and joy now belonged to her. Her late parents' estate had all been finalised. She still missed them, especially at this time of year. Their killer still had to be sought. Was it Kirsti Løvik? She hoped the police investigation would soon result in a conviction.

Gavin felt at ease on the yacht and enjoyed the evening. He managed to push the overhanging worries to the back of his mind. Veronique had the right idea to take the yacht out. It was a welcome respite. Did they truly believe Susannah was dead? The answer was yes. But after all the havoc she had caused, how could they be so complacent?

Gavin steered the yacht away from the marina. He heard the distant sounds of classical music coming from the cabin. Beethoven's moonlit serenade played as the full moon appeared from behind a cloud. Its beam shone on the black sea like a torch that was lighting the way. Gavin eased his yacht, eventually allowing her to drift. He joined Veronique and Rebecca below deck.

"How is that for a coincidence. The moon came from behind a cloud as you played Beethoven's moonlit serenade," said Gavin.

"How poetic," remarked Veronique. "It's the classical CD you bought me for my birthday."

"Sounds very relaxing," added Rebecca as she sipped her glass of white wine.

"Are we ready to play Yatzy?" asked Veronique.

"If we must," replied Gavin, sitting beside his wife. "What is there to eat? I am famished."

"Grab a plate and help yourself. There are loads of nibbles," said Rebecca. Gavin dashed across the cabin.

"I shall be thinking it is Saturday tomorrow," stated Veronique.

"Well I'm glad it is not. I think I may start looking for a new car. Treat myself for Christmas," mentioned Rebecca.

"These flapjacks taste great," remarked Gavin, returning to his seat.

"It's my Ma's recipe so they will taste wonderful," said Rebecca. "We always had some at Christmas."

"The first year without them is always the worst," stated Gavin.

"Are we all ready for Yatzy?" chimed Veronique, steering the conversation away from a sombre mood.

"If we must," muttered Gavin.

A Certain Dilemma

After a few hours the frivolous evening drew to a close. Gavin steered the yacht back to the marina. Rebecca returned to her apartment, leaving Gavin and Veronique to spend a passionate night on the yacht. They welcomed the privacy.

At dawn Gavin and Veronique walked back to the house. Before leaving the yacht they ate breakfast. This was a mixture of leftover nibbles from last night. They viewed the sunrise as they meandered home and admired nature's true beauty. Veronique enjoyed this romantic start to the day. Even after four years of marriage and all the heartache she was still a romantic. She expressed how the tropical vegetation never dies during winter, just like her love for Gavin. Slowly they approached their Hispanic dwelling. Veronique checked the mailbox as they passed by.

"The postman has been," she stated. "There's one for you Gavin without a postmark. It must have been hand delivered. It looks like a Christmas card."

Gavin received the white plain envelope. His name and address neatly written. They entered the house as he opened the envelope. The Christmas card pictured a wintry landscape that was full of silver glittered mountain peaks. He opened the card and read the greeting inside. He remained silent for a moment, stunned by what he had read. Veronique noticed his frozen façade.

"Is there a problem?" she hesitantly remarked. Gavin looked up at her but failed to speak. He passed the Christmas card to Veronique. She quickly read its contents. "Oh my God, no! This can't be true!" she muttered. "We must call Detective Martinez immediately." She gave the card back to Gavin as she dashed to the telephone. Gavin opened the card and re-read the inscription.

To my dearest Gavin.

You will die before midnight tonight. There is no need to inform the police as they cannot save you.

Merry Christmas

Susannah.

CHAPTER FOURTEEN

A Raging Furnace

Incidentally, did you like my Christmas card?

Operation 'House Arrest' was a day like no other. Gavin and Veronique remained in the house with four armed police officers, including Detective Martinez. Loretta and Tobias stayed in the cabana with Gregori. An armed officer accompanied them. Gavin had alerted Detsen to the imminent danger and had ordered all staff to remain in their homes. For security reasons the plantation would remain closed for today. Several armed police officers took refuge in Gavin's office, where they had a clear view of the house and surrounding area. Detective Martinez was determined to capture Susannah. He took her death threat very seriously.

Rebecca had been informed of the sinister development and was instructed to remain at Calypso Tavern. Her own security guards were put on high alert. Rebecca was angered by Susannah's death threat. Nothing would please her more than to kill her. It was obviously Susannah who had tampered with her Mercedes, therefore responsible for her parents' death. Rebecca spent the day seething with anger. Her mind driven with nothing else except how she wanted to kill the bitch.

From within the house Detective Martinez kept in constant contact with his officers deployed on site. Susannah, an accomplished master of disguise, induced Detective Martinez to authorise his colleagues to apprehend anyone approaching. He did not want the elusive Susannah escaping yet again. He was wise to her deceptive nature. She may have fooled him before but not this time. Applying foresight, he had plain-clothes officers casually walking around Gavin's estate and neighbouring vicinity. Their casual attire hid their bulletproof vests. He did not want any visible police presence deterring Susannah from stepping out into the public domain.

The morning passed slowly. Every minute seemed like an hour. Susannah did not make idle threats. Her Christmas card firmly stated that Gavin would be dead before midnight. She had also stated that the police could do nothing to stop her. So what has she planned? Did that woman have any conscience? Yet everyone had to admit that Susannah never accepted defeat. In which case death loomed nearer for Gavin. Tension was high. Hardly anyone spoke. Silence was everywhere and all were wondering how this day would transpire. For the police officers the day seemed extremely boring. Just lying in wait. Yet their boredom was soon lifted when a parcel arrived at the house. The courier service delivered the package. Detective Martinez suspected it was a bomb. Was this how Susannah was intending to kill Gavin?

The small ten-inch box was left outside. The bomb squad had been alerted and were on their way. Detective Martinez questioned the courier, who became quite nervous at the thought he had carried a bomb. Gavin came to his defence. He was their regular courier so they already knew him. It was clear for all to see that the courier was innocent. Gavin fetched him a glass of whisky to steady his nerves. The courier was ordered to stay until officers at HQ could check his background.

The bomb squad soon arrived. They were dressed in protective clothing. This would only shield them from flying debris. A direct blast would kill them. The team of professionals were eager to deal with the package. Nerves were running high. Everyone moved to the rear of the house in case the bomb exploded. They were griped in fear. Just how much more anguish must they suffer. Yet with human nature being inquisitive, everyone wanted to watch the proceedings, but of course this was too dangerous. The success rate of defusing a bomb was low. A controlled explosion was often the only outcome.

The bomb squad hid behind their vehicle. They operated the robot by remote control. Probably a mundane exercise for them, but it was nail biting for the Harrison family. The mechanical device looked cute. Its feeble construction was a lifesaver. Gregori would love to play with the robot. The excited child wanted to watch from the cabana window but of course this was too dangerous. Loretta had to keep hold of him as they hid behind the sofa. If the bomb exploded it could so easily shatter the windows. The robot began to unwrap the parcel. The bomb squad could follow the proceedings by a web cam attached to the robot. The receiver was in their armoured van.

The remote controlled robot had successfully removed the outer packaging. Its metal claw clipped the lid and opened the box. It could be at this point that the bomb would explode. The robot paused. The web cam focused on the box. The squad officer could not see any trailing wires attached to the inside of the lid. This was encouraging but not conclusive. He adjusted the device to view inside the box. There seemed to be a letter resting on a gun. The robot clenched the letter in its claw. Once the letter was removed the squad officer could see the gun lying in the box. He controlled the robot to return to the van. The squad officer retrieved the letter but the task was not over yet. The robot returned to the package and lifted it up. There could still be a hidden device. The gun dropped out as the package was turned upside down. The box was now empty. The robot dropped it to the floor. Instead of that dreaded explosion, silence followed. It transpired that the package was not a bomb. Everyone's safety was now assured. The squad officer used a megaphone and alerted everyone to the false alarm. He also passed the letter to Detective Martinez, who read out the contents to Gavin and Veronique.

"Dear Gavin, Please be warned that Susannah is alive and is going to kill you. I have tried my best to stop her but I did not succeed. I have sent you this gun to protect yourself. I have to remain anonymous.

From someone who cares."

Gavin was not allowed to keep the gun. It was vital evidence. All wondered as to whom the donor was. Perhaps Tanya had seen the error of her ways and wanted to make amends. Detective Martinez would be investigating further. At least the courier was allowed to leave.

In contrast to the nerve-racking morning, the afternoon transpired uneventful. Hours passed slowly, and everyone's boredom increased. Veronique tried to be as hospitable as she could by providing light refreshments, but she was far from hungry. She was sick with worry. To ease her anxiety she would ring Loretta and have a chat with Gregori. Gavin too felt angered and inactive to solve his situation, but enjoyed chatting to his son over the telephone. The innocence of a child's view of the world gave respite to the tension the whole family were under. Yet the moment the conversation with Gregori was over, Gavin experienced a surge of uncertainty.

A Certain Dilemma

Would he survive this night? Would he see his son again? Susannah did not make threats lightly and had always succeeded before. Why would tonight be any different?

Every minute seemed an eternity. However, one would be forgiven for wondering if Susannah's threat was a joke. There seemed little sign of her, and in what way would she actually kill Gavin? Why forewarn someone that you are going to kill them? It did not make sense. Yet this merely suited Susannah's twisted mind. Perhaps she had no intention of showing herself, just secretly revelled in causing such mayhem. She had always enjoyed keeping Gavin and Veronique dangling emotionally, as if puppets on a string.

The day lingered, exacerbating one's frustration. Detective Martinez constantly checked and counterchecked with his colleagues, but no sign of Susannah. Feeling restless, Gavin walked around the living room. He was too irritable to remain sitting on the sofa. Conversation was spasmodic but helped to lesson the boredom. Yet in the absence of light-hearted banter, prolonged moments of quietness shrouded the household.

Night-time approached adding to the deathly silence. Gavin became more agitated, wondering what Susannah was planning. He did not like being imprisoned in his house, although he realised it was for his safety. Gavin and Veronique now sat on the sofa. They embraced each other. The telephone rang, breaking the initial silence. Veronique got up to answer it.

"Hello," she said.

"Hi Veronique, it's Rebecca. How are things going?"

"We haven't heard anything all day from Susannah. This morning an unexpected parcel arrived. We all thought it was a bomb," replied Veronique.

"No kidding," remarked Rebecca.

"The bomb squad arrived but thankfully it was not a bomb. Someone had sent Gavin a gun with a letter saying Susannah is alive."

"Who was it from?"

"We don't know, perhaps Tanya with a guilty conscience."

"You both must be going through hell, just as well we had our evening on the yacht last night because it couldn't happen tonight," stated Rebecca.

"Too right," responded Veronique. "We are clutching at straws trying to think what Susannah can possibly do. I hope this mess is sorted soon. We can't go on like this. Police are everywhere, but I don't see what they can do. Susannah is not gonna show her face here. She must know the police will be waiting for her."

"Listen I won't keep you, but I think I left my cell phone on the yacht last night. I've been looking for it all day. The last time I used it was when I rang Marcus from the yacht. Any chance I can go and have a look?"

"Sure no problem. You know where to find the spare key, just help yourself," agreed Veronique.

"Thanks. I'll speak to you later," said Rebecca and ended the call. Veronique returned to the sofa and resumed her seat next to Gavin. Detective Martinez was sitting in the armchair. "It was only Rebecca," said Veronique to him. Gavin picked up on their conversation.

"Rebecca wants to go to the yacht?" he questioned.

"Yes, she seems to think she left her mobile there last night." Gavin paused for thought. Had he realised where Susannah could be? It is Friday, where would he normally be on a Friday night, the yacht. Is it conceivable that Susannah could be hiding on the yacht waiting for him to show up? But Susannah would not expect him to be there tonight, after receiving her death threat as if nothing had happened. It seemed too improbable. Yet Gavin could not sit at home

A Certain Dilemma

wondering. He needed to find out for certain. It was worth pursuing and if nothing else would ease the boredom. If Susannah was hiding on the yacht then Rebecca was walking into a trap. Gavin abruptly got up and headed for the kitchen. Veronique noticed his perplexed demeanour. Being the dutiful wife she followed him.

"What's wrong?" she questioned. Gavin leaned against the kitchen unit. He looked across to ensure the police officers were not too close. He did not want them to overhear.

"Keep your voice down," he whispered. "I think I know where Susannah might be."

"What! Where?" replied Veronique.

"Where we would normally be on a Friday night, the yacht."

"We must tell Martinez. He can go..."

"No!" interrupted Gavin. "What good will that do? She seems very capable of avoiding justice and imprisonment. If we are to have any quality of life then I have to kill her. I have to check the yacht. If she is there then Rebecca is in danger."

"But how can you do that when we are surrounded by police? Martinez is not gonna let you leave the house," whispered Veronique.

"I know that," replied Gavin. After a brief pause he continued. "My mind is racing with all kinds of thoughts, ideas of what to do." He reached for a glass out of the cupboard and poured himself some water. He drank the refreshing liquid then turned to face Veronique. "What if I sneak out of the upstairs back window, on to the veranda roof, then I can climb down and make my way through the plantation fields around the back of the house. If I turn the upstairs lights off I should not be spotted."

"You can't do this it is too dangerous. You must let the police handle this. We only ever make matters worse, and Susannah always gets away," pleaded Veronique, trying not to raise her voice. She was deeply concerned with any notion of Gavin leaving the house.

"Not this time she won't. I will approach the yacht with caution, and I know exactly what to do. Don't you see, I have to kill her, else we might as well let her kill me because I can't carry on like this," urged Gavin. His mind raced ahead. He needed an excuse. "You must cover for me. I will make out that I'm having a shower. Give me half an hour and then raise the alarm that I have sneaked out of the house. You can say that I mentioned earlier about leaving my mobile on the yacht so you assume I have gone to fetch it. Better still, I will leave you a note upstairs saying that I needed to get out of the house so I have gone to the yacht."

"I don't like this," stressed Veronique, almost pleading with him not to leave the house. "Let me come with you. Two heads are better than one."

"Now that would be silly. I can't risk you getting hurt. I need you to cover for me here, ok."

"Is everything all right?" asked Detective Martinez as he entered the kitchen.

"Yes, everything is fine," replied Gavin quickly. "Except for the obvious," he added, hoping the detective had not overheard their conversation. If he had, surely he would mention it.

"Did you want something, a coffee perhaps?" asked Veronique. She desperately wanted to divulge the possibility that Susannah could be on the yacht. She felt pressured by her husband's suggestion.

"No, no, I'm not thirsty," replied Detective Martinez.

"I was just saying to Veronique that I shall go and have a shower. It will help me to relieve the boredom," remarked Gavin.

"What a difficult day this has been. Perhaps it is just a hoax. Maybe Susannah is playing games with us," responded Detective Martinez. "A shower seems like a good idea."

A Certain Dilemma

"I'll be down in a few minutes then," stated Gavin. He looked at Veronique as he left the kitchen. It was a meaningful look. Veronique wanted to grab hold of him and persuade him to remain in the house, but how could she do that with Martinez present. Reluctantly she had to agree with Gavin's plan. She saw him disappear into the living room. Veronique followed behind and linked her arm with Martinez. She felt she needed the added support. Panic embraced her tightly. She wanted to scream out but curtailed her emotion. Instead, she stated:

"Let's return to the living room." They entered in time to see Gavin ascend the mahogany staircase. Her watery eyes gazed up at the only man she had ever loved. Her beating heart thumped louder. She knew Gavin was running into danger. He soon disappeared from view. She loosened her grip, allowing Detective Martinez to return to the armchair. Veronique composed herself and sat on the sofa. All was silent except for the sound of running water. Veronique noticed that the time was 7.45pm. She had to wait thirty minutes before raising the alarm. Detective Martinez looked at her. Why could he not see the anguish in her face? Was it not part of his job to be perceptive? Surely he understood physiognomy. Veronique wanted to blurt out the truth and tell the detective that Gavin was not taking a shower, but had sneaked out of the house to kill Susannah. Yet her dilemma was torn between disobeying her husband, but then run the risk of Susannah killing him at a later date; or to keep quiet as her husband wished, but then would Susannah succeed in killing him on the yacht tonight? Either scenario resulted in Gavin being killed. This was more than Veronique could bear. What was she to do?

Rebecca drove Veronique's white Dodge estate to the marina. She had viewed various cars today but had not made a decision. Except her replacement car will not be a Mercedes. She wanted a completely different make, model and colour. To drive another Mercedes would cause unwanted reminders of her parents' final moments. She will probably never forget the tragic event as it unfolded. Nor the horrific sight of their burnt remains. Any new car will have to be completely different to stop the haunting memories. This situation was similar to the time when Rebecca had rearranged her apartment after Susannah had killed Jeswana. The change then had helped to heal the wounds.

Rebecca pulled up at the marina and got out of the car. She walked across the boardwalk to Gavin's yacht. She climbed aboard and moved towards the life jacket box. It was a fibreglass container attached to the port side of the deck. She opened the lid and rummaged for the spare key. Her attempts were in vain. She proceeded to search each life jacket in case the key was hidden amongst them, but it was not there. Rebecca sighed impatiently.

"Looks like a wasted journey," she muttered. She closed the lid and began to leave the yacht. However, as she passed the cabin door she tried the handle. To her relief the door opened. She descended below deck. All was dark. She fumbled for a light switch. She knew there was one by the entrance. After a few failed seconds Rebecca banged her leg on a side cupboard. She let out an expletive.

"Where is the damn light switch," she said. The neon lights of the marina harbour shone through the nearby porthole. Its beam rested on one of the wall lights. Rebecca noticed this and stretched across to flick the switch. Before she had managed to activate the light fitment the main cabin lights came on.

"Hello Rebecca," said Susannah, standing proudly. Rebecca turned to see the woman she hated the most standing three yards away from her. "Are you not pleased to see me?" she added in a smug voice.

"How come you're not dead?" replied Rebecca, having gathered her senses. Susannah laughed, her vibrant auburn hair bobbed gently above her shoulders. This wig hid the blonde fashion hairstyle of Chantelle Duveton.

"Thanks to a bulletproof vest my life was spared when Karl tried to stab me to death with a ski stick. As if that would finish me off," declared Susannah.

"Then maybe I will finish you off," threatened Rebecca.

"You did not succeed before and you won't now Rebecca, or should I say Cassandra," replied Susannah, exhuming her posh accent in a condescending manner.

"Are you and Kirsti Løvik in this together?"

"Up until a couple of weeks ago Kirsti Løvik did not know I was alive. I knew the police would question her so I maintained a distance. It was better for her that she believed I was dead. That way she could not be caught out by police questions, like she was caught out during my trial," informed Susannah. "Yet what joy I received when reading about the ant infestation of Gavin's plantation and then the closure, not to mention the takeover bids. I thought good on you Kirsti Løvik, bankrupt him."

"You think you're so smart," sneered Rebecca.

"But I am smart. That's why I had plastic pockets of raspberry sauce attached to my bulletproof vest to simulate blood, should I be shot, courtesy of theatrical cosmetics. There was Gavin shooting at me from the cable car as I tried to axe through the cables. I was being perspicacious and thinking ahead. If I ended up in a no win situation then I would bide my time and pretend to be dead. Many soldiers in past wars have done the same behind enemy lines, so I was more than prepared to follow suit. Only it was not as a result of Gavin or anyone else shooting me, it was down to Karl and a ski stick. Yet the end result was the same. When Tor Hegland appeared on the scene, all he saw was a defenceless woman being brutally attacked. In his quest to save me, assuming I was an innocent victim, he declared I was dead. It was his way of being cautious and to appease Karl's vicious onslaught.

Can you imagine how I felt, lying there and hearing him say I was dead? Either I was a good actress or he had no medical abilities. What else could I do but let him carry my body away."

Rebecca knew this was her chance to kill the pompous English wretch. Susannah may delight in revealing the truth but her sick denouement will be short-lived. Susannah continued her statement. She was proud of her conquest.

"Tor Hegland looked after me for a while. He nursed my fractured skull, thanks to Karl bashing me over the head with the fire extinguisher. I was semiconscious as Karl stabbed me, so I could scarcely fight back. Thankfully Tor Hegland rescued me. To be honest he fancied me. Of course I led him on, but then as time went by he realised his mistake. He was going to report me to the police. He even tried persuading me to hand myself in and for me to relent from seeking to kill Gavin. He appealed to my better nature." Susannah laughed at the apparent hypocrisy. "Of course as you may know he died. In hindsight I guess there was no other option. He had a weak heart you know, so he could have died at any time. I really can't take all the credit," she flippantly remarked.

"Do you have a conscience or were you born evil?" commented Rebecca in disgust.

"That is a harsh thing to say. I never did any wrong before Gavin killed my husband. Incidentally Rebecca, what is it like to be an orphan?"

"You killed my parents!" shouted Rebecca and launched herself at Susannah. Rebecca applied a tennis motion and used a backhander to wallop Susannah across the face. Susannah was ready for the fight. The punch hurt but it did not stop her retaliation.

"What a pity it wasn't you who died in the car crash," said Susannah, defending herself. She grabbed Rebecca's hair and smacked her in the face. Rebecca returned the assault and kneed Susannah in the groin. Rebecca then used her

A Certain Dilemma

bodyweight and knocked Susannah to the floor. Within the confines of the cabin the two females wrestled. Aggression was high; hatred was higher. Punches and kicks were numerous. To inflict pain was paramount.

Susannah was pleased with this little diversion. She assumed Gavin would realise that she was on the yacht and could not resist the impulse to come after her. It was just perfect to hide in the dark and surprise him. Third time lucky. This time she will shoot him. However, Rebecca had turned up unexpectedly. Never mind, this is just the warm up act.

The fight continued. Rebecca banged Susannah's head against the wooden floor, dislodging the auburn wig that emulated Susannah's previous hairstyle. The short blonde hairstyle of Chantelle Duveton was revealed.

"You are gonna die for killing Greg and my folks. Even if I die in the process, so be it. You will not live past this moment!" screamed Rebecca, her heightened temperament in full force. Susannah lifted her legs up as if to perform a backward roll. This enabled her to push Rebecca away.

"If your folks hadn't died then you would not have been able to buy Calypso Tavern," panted Susannah. "It was a happy day for me when Gavin put Calypso Tavern up for sale." Rebecca regained her balance and stood up. Like a bull charging towards its matador she ran into Susannah, knocking her backwards against the cabin wall. In defence Susannah head-butted Rebecca and threw her to the floor. Rebecca used the cabin seats for leverage and pulled herself up. Both females felt breathless and refrained for a few seconds from their physical attack.

"You can kick and punch me all you like," gasped Rebecca. "But I am gonna kill you." Rebecca quickly employed a karate kick at Susannah, hitting her in the face. She then followed it with another kick to the stomach. Years of dance training were most useful. Susannah stumbled backwards, but managed to use the cabin wall to retain an upright position.

"Nice try cowgirl but not good enough," panted Susannah, attempting to conceal the pain. "I must admit I am completely baffled as to why you're so hung up on Greg. He did not love you."

"What rubbish! It won't work Susannah. Your words don't hurt me," reacted Rebecca angrily.

"Oh how gallant," mocked Susannah, accentuating her English accent. "Do we still feel lonely at night? No Greg to snuggle up to. Mind you I must confess that Greg was good in bed," said Susannah, deliberately provoking Rebecca.

"How pathetic you are. You really are clutching at loose straws, desperate to have the upper hand," replied Rebecca in a contemptible voice. "Greg would never come anywhere near you."

"Believe what you like cowgirl, but I actually liked the butterfly tattoo on his buttocks, did you?" came Susannah's antagonised reply. Rebecca screamed out in anger as she attacked Susannah, bashing her face with her arm. How did she know about Greg's tattoo? He would not have slept with her. Rebecca's temper was unstoppable. She dragged Susannah to the floor and punched her several times. Rebecca used her bodyweight to keep her down. In spite of this Susannah reached inside her trouser pocket and withdrew her pistol. The fun of fighting was now over. It was time to exact her revenge.

Rebecca reacted on seeing the firearm, and managed to knock the gun out of Susannah's hand. She punched Susannah in the face yet again. They wrestled ferociously, each attempting to grab the gun. Rebecca was evil as she fought Susannah. The gun lay a few feet away. Susannah managed to break free and reached out for it.

"Oh no you don't, bitch!" shouted Rebecca. She threw her body on top of Susannah. The gun was inches away. Susannah screamed out in pain but this only fuelled her anger. Susannah was determined to get the gun. She acted like a wild lion

A Certain Dilemma

and pushed her body upwards, causing Rebecca to fall away. Again Susannah reached for the gun, her hand grasped the weapon. Rebecca gripped Susannah's arm with both hands. She pulled Susannah towards her. She had to get the gun from her. Susannah tried to aim the gun at Rebecca. They struggled on the floor. The only thing Rebecca could do was bite into Susannah's arm until she dropped the weapon.

"Stop fighting now!" shouted Gavin as he stood at the cabin entrance. He was holding a ten-litre can of petrol that he had taken from the storage cupboard on deck. Rebecca quickly grabbed the gun and crawled away from Susannah. Both females were breathless and looked dishevelled. Susannah slowly rose to her feet. She was obviously annoyed at losing possession of the gun. She saw her auburn wig lying on the floor. Rebecca also stood up and aimed the gun at Susannah.

"How nice of you to join us," stated Susannah, panting for breath. She continued to speak. "I knew you would think I was here and could not resist coming to see me. Incidentally, did you like my Christmas card? I have lost count how many times I have tried to kill you by surprise. Yet it always ended up with someone else being killed, like Rebecca's folks. I mistakenly thought the Mercedes was yours. So I thought this time I would try a different approach, and let you know I was going to kill you, to see if that brought better results," said Susannah between gasps of breath.

"The only person doing any killing is me," retorted Rebecca, holding the gun. Her aim poised with her finger on the trigger.

"No Rebecca," intervened Gavin. "Don't incriminate yourself. I am gonna kill her and make it look like an accident." Gavin removed the cap from the petrol canister.

"You can't kill me Gavin," said Susannah in a mellow voice. "You still love me."

"You make me sick!" shouted Gavin. "Did you kidnap Gregori?" he angrily questioned.

"Now Gavin, you must know that was Tanya, but I did organise it, and thanks for the $2million. And just to put your mind at rest I am Gabriella Korakova. I pinched the name from Kirsti Løvik. She told me in prison that she was going to use the name for her Russian business identity," confessed Susannah.

"Let me shoot the bitch," stated Rebecca.

"No," reiterated Gavin, but Rebecca defied him. She pulled the trigger, but the safety mechanism jammed. Rebecca quickly dislodged the barrel. The gun was fully loaded. She successfully re-primed the weapon and resumed her aim. Susannah took advantage of the opportunity to escape. She ran at Gavin, eager to get past him, but Gavin was not going to let her escape. They struggled briefly. Susannah kicked him and bit his cheek, but Gavin's strength prevailed. He trapped Susannah in a deadlock around her throat and doused her in petrol. The inflammable liquid splashed everywhere, including over Gavin. He frantically shook the canister. Some of the liquid even went down her throat. Susannah coughed and spluttered as Gavin threw her back into the cabin. Rebecca seized her moment and aimed the pistol. Without any hesitation she pulled the trigger. The bullet hit Susannah in the shoulder, causing her to fall backwards. Rebecca pulled the trigger again, but once more the mechanism jammed.

"What is wrong with this gun?" she cursed. Susannah sat helpless on the floor in the far corner. Her shoulder bleeding, but it did not stop her vicious tongue.

"How to sabotage your empire was such a delight to work out," shouted Susannah with much hatred in her voice. "Who likes sugar the most? Ants. I remember saying to Kirsti Løvik, how I wished ants would ruin your plantation business. I was proud that she had followed up on my plan to destroy you." Despite her verbal attack, Susannah recognised her

A Certain Dilemma

vulnerability. Her mind searched for a method of killing Gavin and saving herself.

"Did you also cause the avalanche?" questioned Gavin, as he approached the wretch that had blighted his life for the past nine years. He still carried the half emptied canister of petrol.

"Of course I did," Susannah vehemently replied.

"She also killed Tor Hegland," added Rebecca. "Let me shoot her head off."

"No, Rebecca, put the gun down and leave the yacht. I shall burn her to death and send her to hell," stated Gavin. Rebecca screamed in defiance and frustration. She wanted to kill Susannah. In a fit of rage she aimed the pistol and pulled the trigger. Susannah was defenceless and screamed out in fear. There was nowhere to hide. As fate would have it, the mechanism jammed yet again.

"Oh this blasted gun!" shouted Rebecca, throwing the weapon across the cabin.

"Forget the gun, there are some matches in the drawer by the sink. Fetch them for me," ordered Gavin.

"With pleasure," responded Rebecca. She rushed over to the drawer at the far side of the cabin. Susannah once again seized her opportunity to escape. Despite her wounds, she stood up and ran at Gavin, hoping to knock him out of the way. She had to try but once again she failed to overpower him. Gavin bashed the petrol canister into her face. He then dropped the petrol canister and began to strangle her. He clenched his hands so tight till she could scarcely breathe, but that was not tortuous enough. He threw her back down to the floor and picked up the petrol canister. Some of the liquid had spilled over the cabin floor. What remained, Gavin poured over Susannah's bedraggled body as she lay panting for breath. Rebecca handed the matches to Gavin.

"Leave the yacht now and unleash the ropes from the moorings," commanded Gavin to Rebecca.

"You must come as well," stated Rebecca, concerned for Gavin.

"I will be fine, just untie the ropes."

"Make sure you kill her," seethed Rebecca. She stared down at Susannah before leaving the cabin. Gavin struck the match. The flinthead flickered into a bright flame. Susannah lay on the floor. Her terrified eyes looked up at the burning match.

"Please Gavin, don't do this, don't set me on fire," begged Susannah. Gavin stood over her.

"You can burn in hell," he said, and dropped the match. Susannah attempted to catch it in her hands, hoping to douse the little flame, but she did not succeed. The moment it landed in her lap she became engulfed in fire. Gavin quickly stepped back and stood at the cabin entrance. Susannah screamed like a burning witch. Gavin did not feel guilty. He watched her suffer. She tried rolling on the floor to quell the flames but to no avail. The petrol drenched flooring soon ignited. Susannah stood up, encircled by flames. Her clothes, hair and body were burning ferociously. Susannah screamed in agony as she staggered towards the cabin entrance. The pain was horrific. All Susannah could think of was to jump overboard. Let the sea quench her burning body. Gavin was not going to kill her, she was so adamant of that.

Gavin ran to the helm and started the motor. He drove the yacht away from the shore. Rebecca stood on the boardwalk, having untied the moorings. She saw flames and smoke bellowing up from the cabin. Gavin swiftly manoeuvred the vessel away. Rebecca watched, expecting the yacht to fully explode with Gavin on board. Like a scene from a horror movie, Rebecca saw the burning Susannah stagger out of the cabin. Rebecca shouted out:

"Gavin...Susannah!" She pointed towards the cabin. Rebecca watched. Her conscience neither troubled at the sight of the burning Susannah, nor at her screams. "How fitting for you to experience your previous faked death. On behalf of my folks and Greg, along with all those you killed, burn in hell," muttered Rebecca, not that Susannah could hear her.

Gavin jumped down from the helm and ran to the cabin entrance. He saw Susannah standing like a burning effigy. She stood in the doorway holding on to the rail. Her pain must have been immense, but she was not getting away. Susannah reached out to Gavin as he stood in front of her. Surely he will help her? Susannah looked into his eyes. Her body was completely engulfed in flames, the cabin a blazing inferno behind her. Gavin felt no remorse. He kicked Susannah back down the steps into the raging furnace that was once his cabin. Her agonised screams pierced the roaring flames. Tragically for Gavin, his petrol splashed trousers caught fire. This in turn ignited his arms and body. They too were soaked with petrol. Rebecca screamed out as she saw Gavin on fire, but he was not going to burn alive. He ran to the side and dived overboard into the cool Caribbean Sea. For several moments he swam under the water to quench the flames. Rebecca anxiously watched.

Gavin emerged from the water and swam ashore. He lay on the pebbled harbour and turned to look at his yacht. Moments later the yacht exploded. What a suitable demise for Susannah. The scene was like a re-enactment of when Susannah had first faked her death seven years ago. This time she will not be returning. Her plan of revenge was now destroyed in the flames that had consumed her body. Completely ablaze, the burning vessel slowly diminished into the sea, taking Susannah's charred corpse with it. Rebecca ran over to Gavin.

"Are you badly hurt?" she said, helping him to stand up. She noticed the burnt scold marks on his clothes.

"No, I am fine now that bitch is dead," panted Gavin. "It is all over, finally over." He felt immense relief having killed Susannah. She could no longer terrorise his family.

Stillness returned to the marina. The sea had swallowed the burning yacht. Several pieces of debris floated amidst the ripples that drifted ashore. The screech of car brakes soon dispersed the tranquillity. Gavin and Rebecca turned to see three police cars driving down to the marina, braking suddenly. Detective Martinez and his colleagues had arrived to apprehend Susannah. Veronique had raised the alarm that Gavin had left the house. For once Gavin's plan had been successful. Veronique had insisted on travelling with Detective Martinez down to the marina. She could not bear the suspense any further. She ran towards Gavin, the constabulary followed behind.

"Are you all right?" she shouted to him. Gavin nodded his head. He embraced his wife. "You're all wet. Where is the yacht?"

"She is dead, burnt alive on the yacht," he stated.

"What happened?" urged Detective Martinez. Gavin broke from his embrace with Veronique. He began to state the edited version of events. Veronique stood by his side, Rebecca a few paces away.

"I needed to get out of the house. I couldn't stand being cooped up all day," began Gavin. "There was a file on my yacht that I needed so I thought I would come and get it. I did not want to bother you about it. When I got here Susannah was on my yacht. She threw petrol all over me. We fought as she tried to set me on fire. The result was that she also ignited herself. Petrol had spilled everywhere so the cabin was soon ablaze. I was set on fire but managed to dive overboard. Susannah fell into the flames. It was self-defence," informed Gavin. Did the detective believe him?

"And you Rebecca, what brings you here?" questioned Detective Martinez.

"I was on my way down to the yacht. I had left my cell phone here last night. When I got here I saw the yacht on fire.

I then noticed Gavin coming out of the water," she responded innocently.

"Then how did you bruise your face and cut your lip," mentioned Detective Martinez. He had noticed Rebecca's dishevelled appearance.

"Like a fool, I slipped and fell on my way down here," she replied unconvincingly.

"Also Susannah admitted to everything," intervened Gavin. "Killing Tor Hegland, Rebecca's parents, Gregori's kidnapping and starting the avalanche."

"I see," remarked Detective Martinez. "Well that will tidy up the paperwork. I can close this case at last. I will need statements from you but maybe that can wait until tomorrow. You are sure Susannah is dead?"

"Yes," replied Gavin. "There is no way she can be alive. She was completely on fire."

"I will arrange for divers to recover her body," said Detective Martinez.

"Thank God it is all over," sighed Veronique.

They slowly walked away from the shore. Detective Martinez glanced at Gavin. They briefly made eye contact. Martinez was no fool, he knew there was more to the sequence of events than what Gavin and Rebecca had said, but he would not pursue the matter any further.

"It might be advisable for you to go to hospital Gavin and get checked over, make sure those burns are correctly treated," remarked Detective Martinez. "The same goes for you Rebecca. There's no telling what injuries a fall can cause. It's almost as if you had been in a fight." Neither Gavin nor Rebecca made any further comment. They knew he suspected foul play but so what! Susannah was dead.

Detective Martinez gave them a lift back to the house. Veronique applied her nursing skills to address Gavin's superficial burns. Loretta and Tobias were informed of the dramatic events. They too were relieved Susannah was finally dead. Gregori was fast asleep so remained at the cabana. Rebecca stayed over at the house and recounted the fight she had suffered with Susannah. The punches were still hurting her. Rebecca managed to dismiss the thought that Greg had slept with the wretch. Just because Susannah knew of his butterfly tattoo, that did not prove anything. Susannah was merely applying her usual truculent behaviour. Nevertheless, one can give an element of credit to Susannah, for she certainly went down fighting.

<>

Christmas day brought the usual ritual. It was now traditional for Gavin to visit Greg's grave as well as his parents. He squatted down and placed a festive wreath by Greg's headstone.

"Merry Christmas brother," said Gavin. "At least Susannah is now dead. She can't hurt us anymore. That is the best Christmas present ever." He paused for a brief reflection. "Actually that's not true. The best Christmas present would be to have you back."

"Daddy, Daddy," called out Gregori as he ran from the house towards his father.

"And here comes your nephew," mentioned Gavin. Gregori ran to the graveside.

"Did you just put the circle of leaves there?" asked Gregori, indicating to the wreath.

"Yes I did put them there for your uncle Greg as it is Christmas," replied Gavin.

"Was uncle Greg a nice person?"

"Yes he was. You would have liked him and he would have liked you."

"Is that why you named me after him?"

"Yes son."

"If I have a brother will he die young too?" Gavin hugged him.

"No, but that is why we all should be good and nice to each other to make the world a better place to live in, because we don't know when we will die," reflected Gavin.

"Oh I nearly forgot, Mummy said dinner is ready."

"Uncle Greg liked his food. If he were here today he would eat up all your dinner," teased Gavin.

"No he wouldn't," laughed Gregori.

"Yes he would," said Gavin. "Come on we must not keep Mummy waiting." Gavin picked his son up and began walking back to the house. He gently lifted Gregori up and down in his arms, causing the infant to laugh.

"Daddy, you know all this sugar you make?" questioned Gregori in between fits of laughter.

"Yes," replied Gavin. He lifted Gregori up onto his shoulders.

"Well where are all the sweets?" asked Gregori, his little legs dangling down Gavin's chest.

"Sweets?"

"Yes Daddy, sugar makes sweets so it would be a good idea if you make sweets with the sugar you make," stated Gregori, applying childhood logic.

"Maybe that is a good idea," responded Gavin, completely amused by his son's imagination.

"How many sweets would all our sugar make?"

"An awful lot."

"Then why don't we make sweets and sell them to all the girls and boys," suggested Gregori excitedly.

"What! There wouldn't be any sweets to sell because you would eat them all," joked Gavin.

"No I wouldn't," laughed Gregori.

"Yes you would," replied Gavin, tickling his son's legs.

"Well maybe a few," admitted Gregori in fits of laughter.

"And when you are all grown up you can be a director on the board of sweets."

"Don't be silly Daddy. I could never be bored of sweets," replied Gregori. Gavin laughed at his son's inadvertent misunderstanding. On approaching the house, Veronique stepped out on to the veranda.

"Gavin, there is a Scott Myles on the telephone for you, he sounds American," informed Veronique. She assumed Scott Myles was a business associate. Gavin entered the house still carrying Gregori on his shoulders. He put his son down and went to the study. Gavin did not know Scott Myles. He was not a current business associate as Veronique had assumed. Yet the name seemed familiar. Of course, Scott Myles is the pertinacious salesperson that keeps bombarding him with emails to buy a firearm. However, little did Gavin realise the consequences of this telephone call. Scott Myles had a secret. It was a secret that would simply change everything.

Scott Myles knew that Gavin would not be pleased. But the time had finally come to speak out. Scott Myles had no other option. Despite the repercussions, the truth had to be told. Gavin might believe his nightmare was over following Susannah's death, but the murderous aftermath was about to begin. Scott Myles had meant to contact Gavin sooner, but as time elapsed it seemed harder to do. But then again Susannah had controlled him. How she had enjoyed applying her fiendish and manipulative streak, such was her blackmail. How could he have been so stupid? Would Gavin ever forgive him? Under the weight of his troubled conscience Scott Myles sighed heavily. Why had he allowed Susannah's twisted judgement to influence him?

"Hello and Merry Christmas," said Gavin. "And I do not want to buy a gun or anything else."

"Hello Gavin and I am so sorry but I hope you will let me explain," replied Scott Myles nervously. There was a time when Gavin would instantly have recognised the voice, but it had been many years and Scott Myles had acquired an American twang. He had purposely cultivated a profound New York dialect. It was an essential requirement for Scott Myles to blend in with the Yanks. But now at last he could speak more freely.

"Who is this?" questioned Gavin.

The story continues in:

*Truth, Lies
And
Revelations.*